"You want to talk?" murmured
Robyn.

"I have lots of wants," he said. "Talking is only one of them." He ran his forefinger over the fullness of her lips.

"I think we'd better stick to talking," she cautioned, but she could feel her resistance fading. "The others are waiting for us."

She lifted her chin until her lips met his. He kissed her eagerly and the loneliness of the past two weeks faded with his touch. But no matter how many nights she had lain awake longing for him, Robyn couldn't allow that to happen again. The more she made love to him, the more painful the parting would be when the time came for her to leave.

"I can't stay away from you, either," he murmured. "It's stupid to even try."

ABOUT THE AUTHOR

Nancy Landon's *Sound Waves* had its beginnings when, as a public-relations consultant, Nancy helped stage a dance for students at the North Carolina School for the Deaf. Her interest in the hearing impaired was further sparked when she heard about a kennel in Oklahoma City that trained hearing dogs, so she decided to make this the focus of a book. The final impetus for *Sound Waves* came when Nancy, along with her husband and three children, took in the Labor Day Raft Race down the Arkansas River. Seeing the race as a perfect vehicle for pitting her hero and heroine against each other, she wove her story around the festive event, and used her native state of Oklahoma as the setting.

In the past, Nancy has pursued newspaper and magazine writing, as well as public relations, but she now works full-time—eight to ten hours a day—writing romance novels. *Sound Waves* is her second Harlequin Superromance.

Books by Nancy Landon

HARLEQUIN SUPERROMANCE

358—MIDNIGHT BLUE

Sound Waves

NANCY LANDON

Harlequin Books

TORONTO • NEW YORK • LONDON
AMSTERDAM • PARIS • SYDNEY • HAMBURG
STOCKHOLM • ATHENS • TOKYO • MILAN

Published October 1990

ISBN 0-373-70424-0

To my older son, Robert Baker, and his love, Nancy, for embracing each other with such warmth and gentleness;

To my daughter, Lisa Kleymeyer, and her own dear Alan, for treasuring their love above all else;

To Barbara and Hal Pickens for the sizzle in their marriage;

To Carol and Carl Smith for the fun in theirs;

To Jan and Art Berland, for their creative teamwork and sensuous natures;

And finally to Annelle and Nick Nichols, dear friends, who, devoted to each other, faced life alone and lived to relish it together.

CHAPTER ONE

THE SQUEAL of fast tires on hot pavement ricocheted up the street, scattering goose bumps over Robyn Woodson's arms.

Through the smoke from her charcoal grill in the curve of the tree-shaded cul-de-sac, Robyn fixed her gaze on the distance and steeled herself for what was to come. At any moment the vacation-crazed teenagers who had terrorized the quiet Bethany neighborhood with drag races down Lancer Lane would whip by in motorized blurs, and the road that sliced three streets into six cul-de-sacs would once again become a raceway.

A raceway, she reminded herself, that was too near the house she shared with her deaf father.

"Relax, Robyn. Once those kids see the sawhorses we stuck in the middle of the street, they'll leave."

Robyn turned to Joe, a veterinarian and her father's long-time poker buddy. Today Joe was manning the grill beside hers at the neighborhood's annual June picnic. "I hope so. I worry about the children," she said. She diverted her gaze to the boys and girls. At the moment they were parading in a circle on their gaily decorated bicycles.

"And you're worried what might happen to your dad when he walks up here—right?"

"I'm not even sure he'll come, Joe. I begged him. I badgered him. I even tried to reason with him, but he wouldn't promise me he'd come. Every time I talked about it, he got that faraway look in his eyes, and I felt guilty for even suggesting it.''

"Does he know about your phone call?"

Robyn poked disconsolately at one of the plump chicken breasts sizzling on her grill. Her old boss in Washington, D.C., had phoned last week to persuade her to return to her job. Since then all she'd been able to think about was how much she had missed the challenge, her friends and her life there during the past eighteen months. Her boss had begged her to bring the "old Robyn sparkle" to the office. The old Robyn sparkle. Did she still have it, she wondered?

"I haven't told him. I don't want him to feel guilty about keeping me here. Besides, I can't think about leaving until I'm sure he'd be safe by himself. Until I'm sure he's over losing Mom."

"Did you visit that kennel I told you about?"

"Yes, and I met Kendra. We really hit it off."

"But?"

"But no luck. She said there's a three-year waiting list for a hearing dog."

"What are you going to do then? Give up?"

"No."

He chuckled. "Atta girl. You deserve to go back to D.C., if that's what you want."

"But Dad seems so helpless without Mom."

"You might have to give him a gentle shove, Robyn."

"I just wish he'd leave that house because he wants to, because he's ready to begin a new life. Not because I want him to."

"Well, it looks like you're getting your wish, sweetheart. Look." With an infectious smile creasing his face, Joe directed Robyn's attention down the hill before them. His voice cracked with husky sentiment. "Now there's a sight for sore eyes."

In the distance, Robyn saw the distinctive, burly figure of her father, lumbering toward the picnic from their house at the end of the cul-de-sac. She wanted to dash down the street, fling her arms around his neck and tell him how much she loved him for coming. Her heart suddenly ached. How hard it must be for him to come to the picnic for the first time in twenty-five years without her mother at his side.

"Eight months is a long time to stay cooped up in a house," Joe said, refilling his grill. "I was beginning to wonder if Jonathan would ever come out again."

"So was I. I guess he needed time." And a nagging daughter.

Watching the children, who now were playing capture the flag on a nearby lawn, Robyn couldn't help reminiscing about earlier neighborhood picnics. Then she had been a carefree child without family responsibilities weighing heavily on her shoulders. She had looked forward to the day's festivities with as much excitement as she had anticipated her birthday.

In those days Bethany had been a small town outside the far northwest fringe of Oklahoma City. As Robyn had grown, so had the big prairie city, spreading its arms until Bethany lay like a child cuddled in its parent's embrace.

A third of this year's one hundred picnickers were children. They cavorted around the cul-de-sac, seemingly unaffected by the ninety-degree heat that had wilted their elders. The youngsters had always liked her father, and the feeling had been mutual. Robyn was counting on the affectionate boys and girls to help fill the void left by her mother.

Robyn considered the picnic from the perspective of a deaf person. "Today's going to be hard for Dad. So many people talking at the same time. He'll be confused for sure.''

"He'll manage. If you like, I'll remind folks to speak slowly and look Jonathan square in the face when they talk.''

"That would help.'' Robyn knew she couldn't expect even her father's best friend to understand the challenges such a crowd presented to a profoundly deaf person. Still, if she hoped to return to her job in Washington in three months, she had to help her father learn to do for himself. Getting him to leave the house and mix with old friends was the first step.

She hooked her tongs on the grill's side handle and yanked off her chef's apron. "Watch this for a minute, will you? I promised Dad I'd help him when he got here.''

Joe winked his approval. "Sure. Take your time.''

Warmed by Joe's understanding nature, Robyn started jogging down the hill.

Almost to the intersection, her father, wearing khaki-colored carpenter's overalls, spotted her. He smiled and waved. Robyn smiled back. She wouldn't chide him for not changing into the clothes she'd laid out for him. She wanted today to be fun for him. Maybe, after a good time with friends and neighbors, he would end this period of depression and solitude that had stretched into eight months. She desperately wanted the day to be a new beginning—for both of them.

The familiar screech of cars racing in the distance drove a shaft of fear through Robyn's heart. Remembering what Joe had said about the roadblock around the corner, she tried to ignore the queasiness in her stomach.

When she neared the intersection, she glanced to the right, down Lancer Lane, in search of the sawhorses to re-assure herself that the road was safe. Like a child's forgotten toys, the black-and-white striped wooden barriers had been tossed onto lawns adjacent to the street. She shuddered. Lancer Lane was wide open to traffic again.

The screech of tires sounded closer now. A fierce protectiveness rose within her. She had to warn her father about those kids and their lightning-quick cars.

Before she could communicate the danger to him with hand gestures, the squeal of a car rounding the near corner reverberated in her ears. She froze as she spotted a metallic-blue sports car speeding their way. A steady honk rent the air with its warning.

Frantically she waved her hands at her father.

Mistaking her message, he stepped from the curb into the street, his adoring eyes fixed on his only child's face. As he neared the center of the street, he opened his arms wide for the bear hug she loved.

The sports car whipped in front of him, startling him. His arms flailed, and he rocked back on his heels. Terror and confusion contorted his face in an open-mouthed frown.

A second sports car, this one red, followed in hot pursuit. The driver leaned on his horn while his car skidded out of control on the street, grazing Jonathan's backside and knocking him to the pavement in a heap.

Robyn's heart pounded as she sprinted to her father and sank to her knees beside his motionless form. Blood trickled down his face from a gash in an angry-looking lump already swelling on his forehead. His mouth was slack, his face ashen, and his lips had taken on that sickening blue color she had seen on her mother's face when she died.

Dear God, if her father died, it was her fault. Her own selfish fault, because she had practically forced him to come to the picnic.

In seconds neighbors crowded around her and her father, offering assistance, giving advice. A man Robyn had known since childhood ran to the red sports car, which had stopped just beyond Jonathan, and yanked open the driver's door. He jerked the youthful driver to his feet. The boy was about sixteen, his bronzed face pale for someone of his obvious Spanish-American heritage. Perspiration beaded his forehead. His wide brown eyes were fixed on her dad.

Joe pulled a second youth from the car, a blond, broad-shouldered boy. His clothes, unlike his friend's, spoke of affluence. Rich or poor, Robyn didn't care. The thought of what their careless, inconsiderate joyriding had done to her father repulsed her.

Jonathan lay sprawled on his side in the middle of the street, his knees drawn up to his chest. His eyes were closed. He clutched one thigh with hands striated by concrete burns.

Robyn's hands trembled as she reached out to touch his face. She willed him to open his eyes. His eyelids fluttered, then opened halfway. Pain showed on his knitted forehead and in his eyes.

"Dad, are you okay?" The exaggerated movements of her signing hands conveyed her anguish. As her hands came to rest on her father's chest, a tall man with sun-streaked blond hair pushed through the crowd and knelt opposite her at Jonathan's side.

His concerned blue eyes sought Robyn's approval. Nodding, she gave it to him. He pressed the tips of his fingers to the pulse point on Jonathan's neck.

"This is my father," she said, a quiver in her voice. "His name is Jonathan. It's my fault. I never should have—"

The man shot her a stern look. "You can help your father by calming down. The name's Greg. Greg Michaels."

She silenced her babbling and waited while he examined her father with fluid, caring movements. He drew Jonathan's eyelids up and frowned as he looked into his eyes. "How does it feel, sir? Your head, I mean."

Jonathan, his eyes glazed and dilated, tried to force himself up with his free arm. The moment he pressed his weight onto his hand, he moaned and fell back with a grimace. Pain and fear flashed in his eyes. He looked to Robyn to speak for him.

Before she could help him, a shuffle by the sports car distracted her. The blond teen, struggling against the firm hold Joe had on his muscular arms, spat out, "You'd better let me go, man."

"If you think I'm letting you go before the police come, you're nuts, young fellow," Joe told the red-faced youth. "You and your friends have been asking for trouble, using our neighborhood for a racetrack. Now you've got what you've been asking for. Look at that man down there. You almost killed him!"

The surly blond gave a shrug of indifference. "Killed him? Get serious. The old man has a minuscule scratch on his head." He lifted his chin defiantly. "Manuel here honked his horn. Anyone with a brain would've known not to step into the street in front of us."

He glanced at his dark-haired buddy. "Don't worry. You didn't do anything wrong. If there's any trouble, Dad will take care of it." He glared at Robyn's father. "What's the matter, old man? You blind or something?"

Robyn gritted her teeth and resisted the urge to plow her fist into the young man's face. "Blind? No, my father isn't blind. His eyes work perfectly well. It's his ears that don't work. You see, Mr. Smart Mouth, my father is deaf!"

"Deaf?" The youth blanched and turned to his friend. "Manuel, he—he can't hear."

The dark-haired boy shut his eyes and hung his head.

"No wonder your father didn't break his stride when that kid honked his horn," the man caring for Jonathan said. "I wondered, but then I thought maybe he was tied up in his thoughts."

"He couldn't hear the horn or the tires." She shivered at the memory of the shrill sound. "I never should have talked him into coming to the picnic. He didn't want to come. He wanted to stay right where he was, in his workshop. He would have been safe there."

"Guilt's a dangerous sentiment," Greg warned her, as if he knew from experience. "And it won't help your father."

Someone thrust a first aid kit into Greg's hands. He ripped open a package of sterile gauze, applied pressure to Jonathan's head wound, then doused the gash with hydrogen peroxide.

Jonathan squeezed his eyes shut and bore the pain in silence. The tears that spilled over his lids expressed feelings his lips couldn't. Robyn wished she could trade places with him. She was the one who deserved to suffer.

"Can I do anything to help?" she asked, needing to feel useful.

"Here, hold this fresh pad on that wound while I check your father's thigh. I'm worried about a concussion, too. We need to get him to the hospital."

While he ministered to her father's leg, Robyn followed Greg's directions, thankful for the calming effect he had on her jangled nerves. She noticed her father's eyes reflected embarrassment as well as pain and fear. She knew he felt humiliated when his actions made him appear as if he couldn't function as well as a hearing person.

"Tell your father I'll try to move his leg to see if it's broken. Tell him my name is Greg, and tell him I just finished an emergency first aid course at my plant."

While repeating the messages to her father verbally, Robyn signed them, as well. She finger spelled the name Greg. Jonathan acknowledged the messages with a nod, his jaw clenched at the pain.

After a few manipulations, Greg gave Jonathan a reassuring smile, then turned to Robyn. "Looks like we can move him. No need for an ambulance. I'll go with you to the emergency room. We can take my van."

"Thanks," Robyn said, desperately needing the strength he offered. "I sure appreciate your help."

"Can I go along?"

Two hands lightly squeezed Robyn's shoulders. Looking back, she found Lillian Chatwell, the woman who lived across the street from her and her father. Lillian had been her mother's best friend, but Robyn wasn't sure her father would appreciate her company. Ever since Robyn had made the mistake of telling Lillian about her opportunity to return to her job in Washington, Lillian had irritated the heck out of Jonathan. "I don't know, Lillian. Maybe you should stay here."

"Your father might need both of you on the way to the hospital. Then who'll drive? I'll tell you who. Me!" She glanced at Jonathan, and her features softened. "No lectures today," she signed. "Promise."

She turned to Greg and smiled brightly. "Lillian's the name. And this pretty young lady's Robyn."

Greg acknowledged Lillian with a polite handshake, but his eyes warmed when he turned to Robyn. "I'll be right back with the van," he said, patting her hand. "Don't you worry. We'll get your dad fixed up in no time."

Robyn was puzzling over the sudden appearance of the helpful stranger when Joe, still wearing his apron smeared with orange-red barbecue sauce, showed his concern for her by putting in his two cents' worth.

"You don't know that man. You'd better let me go with you to the hospital."

The thought that this Greg person was anyone to fear hadn't crossed Robyn's mind. He knew first aid. He'd helped her dad. She wanted him to go to the hospital with her—in case her father needed him. "I'd rather you stay here," she told Joe, "so you can keep an eye on those boys until the police come."

Joe set out to do just that, gripping the boys' arms as if they were belligerent cattle resisting inoculations. Figuring they deserved Joe's roughshod treatment, Robyn concentrated on comforting her father, occasionally glancing around anxiously for Greg's van. Suddenly she felt a warm hand on her elbow. Looking up, she found Greg smiling a welcome mixture of strength and reassurance. He winked at her, and in spite of her distress over her father, she found herself smiling.

"I'm ready if you are," he said, indicating with a nod a maroon van parked at the curb.

Together they helped Jonathan to his feet. Robyn hopped into the van first, through the side door. She spun around to help Greg position her father so that he lay on a gray velour bench seat with his head in her lap. Greg took a captain's chair and swiveled to face her, while Lillian climbed into the driver's seat and started the engine.

"You live around here?" Robyn asked.

"As of today, I do." He hunched and pointed out the window toward the end of the cul-de-sac where Robyn lived with her father. "That stone house is mine—the one with the moving truck parked out front. Next to the one-story brick.''

"Well, I'll be darned. So you're the one who bought the Attallas' old place. We live next door."

Lillian whipped around a corner with squealing tires. Greg glanced over his shoulder in disbelief. "Does your neighbor always drive like this?"

"Afraid so. Sorry. I should have warned you, I guess. But I'm sure glad you came along when you did. We heard someone was moving in, but we didn't expect anyone until next week." She whispered behind her hand. "There isn't much in the neighborhood that gets by Lillian."

He raised his brows in amused acknowledgment. "My lease was up on my apartment. I did some fast talking, and the realtor let me move in early. I was unloading my truck when I heard that godawful screeching sound. The next thing I knew your father was lying in the street. Seeing him like that gave me quite a fright."

"Lucky for us, you kept your cool. I sure didn't."

Jonathan moaned, and Greg moved to his side. Robyn stroked her father's steel-gray hair from his forehead, and Greg checked his pulse.

While he tended to her father, Robyn decided Greg was probably a few years older than her thirty-one. She marveled at the ironic timing of their meeting. Many times since she'd returned from Washington and found her mother dying of leukemia, she had wished for someone her age in the neighborhood to talk to. There, where she had grown up, most of the neighbors were retirees or young couples with children. Now that someone her age had moved in, she'd be leaving soon. That is, if her father could learn to live by himself.

She glanced out the window and sighed, admitting that was a might big if. After today's accident she had doubts her father would be safe living by himself, without someone to alert him to the sounds of danger. If only she could find a way to get him one of those hearing dogs....

Kendra Lewis, the owner of a kennel in northeast Oklahoma City, recently had begun to train hearing dogs. In a demonstration, Robyn had seen how Kendra's dogs could spring into action. If a hearing dog had heard that kid honk his horn, he would have recognized the danger and tugged her father onto the curb.

Robyn wanted her old job more than anything, but she wasn't willing to pay the price of her father's safety. No matter how much she longed to resume the career she loved, she couldn't leave her father unless he had one of those dogs. And if she couldn't get one for him soon, she'd have to figure out a way to persuade him to go to Washington with her—no small feat. She glanced into his face and gauged her chances.

She might as well try to persuade a mule to win the Kentucky Derby.

THE RIDE to Baptist Medical Center of Oklahoma took only ten minutes. Robyn's father saw a doctor without waiting. The antiseptic smell and glistening walls in the sprawling rose brick complex conjured up memories of Robyn's mother's endless, painful tests in her battle with leukemia and the never-ending litany of bad news.

Robyn detested this place almost as much as her father did. Hospitals were for the sick, the injured and the dying, and her selfish motives had put her father there.

When the orderly took her father off in a wheelchair for X rays, she joined Greg and Lillian in the waiting room. Maybe there she'd be able to relax. She paused in the doorway and spotted them sitting side by side in the upholstered armchairs that lined the mauve and gray room. Their heads were bent in conversation.

Robyn smiled. Lillian could grate on a person, but she had the ability to draw even the most reticent into a conversation. And, from all appearances, her new neighbor didn't need too much encouragement to talk.

Robyn let her gaze linger on him, noticing the healthy sheen of his thick hair. He smiled at something Lillian said, his lips full and generous. The outer edges of his blue eyes fanned into tiny lines.

He glanced up and caught her staring at him. He met her studied gaze with a dazzling smile. Under normal circumstances, such a smile might make her heart do back flips. Today that smile did stir a flutter in her stomach, but that flutter drowned in the heavy dose of guilt she had heaped there.

Greg rose to greet her. Robyn looked up to meet his gaze. Accustomed to her father's shorter, stockier build, she was acutely aware that Greg was eight inches or so taller than she was, probably an inch or two over six feet.

"What's the word?" he asked. "Any broken bones?"

"They don't know yet. They've taken Dad for X rays." She sank into a chair opposite Greg and Lillian, leaned back and tried to rub the tension from her aching eyes. "He's frightened and frustrated. His hands are a mess, and he can't sign very well. They sent for a social worker to interpret for him."

Greg returned to his seat, his concern evident in the way he perched on the edge of his chair. "How about his head?"

"You were right. The doctor warned me to watch for a concussion. They took a few stitches in that nasty cut. I'm afraid he could use some first aid for his ego, as well."

"Seems to me the man's ego's the healthiest part of him." Lillian gave her head an imperious shake, loosening the giant ladybug comb from the front of her auburn, six-ties-style beehive. "I'm hoping that blow to his head knocked some sense into the stubborn old coot."

"Lillian, please, not today. Dad's just been through a terrible ordeal. He needs sympathy, not sharp words."

"Robyn, dear, I don't mean to kick the man when he's down, but I'm afraid I'm losing my patience with your fa-ther. Hiding away in his house as if he could shut the world away forever. And he hasn't been fair to you. I hardly ever see the devil in your eyes anymore. You aren't the same person."

Robyn tried to protest, but Lillian shushed her. "Don't say you don't agree with me. If he doesn't try harder to do for himself, you'll wind up living with him the rest of your life—a lonesome old maid."

Robyn opened her mouth to object to discussing her fa-ther's mourning and her marriageability in the presence of a stranger. But good old Lillian narrowed her gaze and shook a ring-clustered finger in Robyn's face. "I told you. It's no way to live, and I, of all people, ought to know. Fifteen years it's been that I'm alone."

Greg's eyebrow arched in response to Lillian's outspo-ken manner.

"Dad's trying," Robyn persisted, "but you know how close he and Mom were. He needs time to get used to being without her."

"Humph! The man's taken long enough!"

Robyn rolled her eyes. She was too tired to argue with Lillian, and she did agree with her neighbor in principle. By way of changing the topic, she turned to Greg and asked, "Do you have any family?"

From the unsettled look on his face, she realized she'd touched on a sensitive subject. Maybe he thought she was inquiring about his marital status for personal reasons. There was a time when she would have been that bold, but today she was embarrassed at the thought.

If Greg had read something more into her question than she had intended, he gave no clue. He answered her with a cool, clipped, "No. No family here." Without another word, he stood, thrust his hands into his shorts pockets and strode across the room to a rack holding magazines.

Robyn couldn't be sure, but she thought she detected defiance in his behavior. She was reminded of the way her father acted when he didn't want to listen to what she had to say. He simply turned his back on her so he couldn't read her signing or her lips. Wondering if she was the only one who'd picked up on Greg's change in moods, she looked at Lillian.

Lillian hitched her shoulders with a wide-eyed what-do-you-make-of-that look. Robyn was frowning when Greg returned with a magazine in his hand. Unsmiling, he flipped through a few pages, then tossed it onto the table beside him.

"I live by myself," he said, delivering his words with measured care while he stared at his folded hands. "My parents are the only family I have...now." He looked up, and Robyn saw a momentary flicker of pain in his expression.

"Now?" Lillian said, not missing the telling pause in Greg's answer.

Robyn didn't much care for the smile lighting Lillian's face. She didn't know who she felt more uncomfortable for—herself or Greg.

"That's right," Greg went on. "I was married...a long time ago."

Lillian arched a brow. "'Was' married, you say?"

"Lillian—"

"No, it's okay, Robyn. I don't mind talking about it," Greg said. "My wife, Chelsea, died when our son was born."

"I'm sorry." Robyn wished she could stuff rags into Lillian's mouth. Already she could sense the question about Greg's son springing to her interfering lips.

Greg evidently decided to answer the question before it was asked. "My son was premature. He didn't make it, either."

"I truly am sorry," Robyn said to her new neighbor.

"It was for the best, I guess." He clasped and unclasped his hands, and one corner of his mouth dipped. "The doctor said there were...problems."

Lillian cleared her throat. "So, where do your parents live?"

Robyn flashed Lillian a look of gratitude for her wisdom at changing the subject. But even that subject appeared to bother her new neighbor. He answered Lillian's question, but he obviously didn't relish the topic of conversation.

"They moved from Tulsa to California several months ago," he said. He picked up a hospital brochure and pretended to study it. "That's when I moved. I've been living in an apartment near my plant for six months."

"You'll like Bethany," Lillian said cheerfully. "Everybody knows everybody. We take care of each other, too. Kind of like a small town."

"You'll have to join us for dinner," Robyn said, picking up on the new direction in the conversation. "We can welcome you and thank you at the same time."

"Nothing against Robyn here," Lillian interjected, "but if you want a good meal, come to my house. Those two Woodsons don't eat anything that tastes worth a darn."

Robyn smothered a grin, thankful for Lillian's light touch. "We eat what I sell in the family business— Meals for the Heart."

"What kind of business is that?" he asked.

"We cook and deliver meals to people who've survived heart attacks."

"Sounds like a good idea."

"Our customers think so. We give them the food they should be eating at a fair price."

"But you leave out all the good stuff, my dear," Lillian said patronizingly. "I, on the other hand, cook a sinfully delightful meal." She winked at Greg. "I'm famous for my cakes. You're invited for dinner at my house, anytime."

"Thank you, Lillian," Greg said, showing amusement at the older woman's invitation. "I'll sure take you up on your offer, as soon as I get settled."

He shifted his gaze to Robyn. She was glad to see the warmth returning to his eyes. "I'd also like to have dinner with you, Robyn—and with your father, of course," he hastily added.

Lillian clucked her tongue and settled in her chair. Robyn shot her a withering glance.

"So, tell me more about your business," Greg said. "Is it going well?"

Robyn tried to ignore the smug look on Lillian's face so she could concentrate on what Greg was staying. "Yes, but it's not actually my business. It was my mother's. She died eight months ago, and I've stayed on to run the business until—"

"Until she can get Jonathan off his rear end to learn to do for himself," Lillian finished for her.

Greg looked at Robyn as if he hadn't heard Lillian's caustic comment. "Eight months ago? That's when your mother died?"

"Yes, in October. On October 31, to be exact. Here, in this hospital."

Greg rested his forearms on his knees and studied his hands. He mumbled, as if speaking to himself, "October 31. Must have been some day."

"Greg, are you okay?"

When he didn't respond, Robyn studied his face and found that his eyes had misted over. What had she said to cause him to slip abruptly into a blue mood?

Lillian interrupted the awkward silence. "Think I'll go downstairs to the snack bar for a cup of coffee. You two want to go? Or could I bring you something?"

At Lillian's words, Greg snapped out of his peculiar mood. "Why don't you stay here with Robyn? I'll get the coffee." He ran his hand over the back of his neck. "How do you take it?"

"Black," Robyn and Lillian answered in unison.

"Two black coffees. I'll be back in a few minutes."

Greg had no sooner disappeared around the corner than Lillian's curiosity tumbled out in a rush of words. "What do you make of that? When you mentioned October 31, he acted like you'd poured a bucketful of ice water down his shorts."

"Lillian, you really must allow him his privacy."

"Could be he needs a bit of drawing out."

"That isn't our place. We aren't his friends yet."

"Give us some time, dear. A week should do."

"You're right about that date, though," Robyn said, remembering his solemn expression. "It did seem to trouble him. Still, I don't think we should pry." She shook her head. "To tell you the truth, I have too much on my mind to go poking my nose into someone else's affairs."

"Affairs. Hmm. Maybe that's it!" Lillian's eyes lighted up. "Maybe he had an affair, and the woman broke up with him on trick-or-treat night. Some treat!"

"Lillian!"

"Okay, okay. I'll leave it alone—for now. Anyway, I think that nurse is looking for you."

Robyn saw the emergency room's head nurse wearing a frown and heading their way. "How's my father?" Robyn asked anxiously.

"He's back from his X rays, Miss Woodson. The doctor would like to see you now. There's . . . a new development he needs to discuss with you. . . ."

CHAPTER TWO

DOWNSTAIRS IN THE SNACK BAR, Greg crammed two quarters into a vending machine, jabbed the black coffee button and braced his forearm against the glass. While the steaming liquid trickled into the foam cup, he pressed his hand against his abdomen, closed his eyes and took two deep cleansing breaths.

Calm down. You've come too far the past eight months to slip into a shell. Don't let questions about your family get you down.

Trouble was, the word *family* still triggered visions of his distraught parents. Visions of his thirteen-year-old brother, Brad, slumped over the steering wheel of the red '65 Corvette Greg was storing in the family garage until his brother turned sixteen. Brad had stuffed rags up the tail pipe and sat with the engine running until he'd snuffed out his problems and with them his young, gifted life.

Greg cursed himself for reacting to Robyn's question about his family in such an ill-tempered manner. She had no way of knowing about Brad's suicide. All she had probably wanted to know was what he'd wound up telling her, with a little prodding from Lillian. That he did not have a wife and children she could befriend. He had to learn to control his emotions better, or he would never make new friends.

He wondered if Brad had any idea how much those he'd left behind hurt in his absence. How his suicide had dulled the glimmer in their mother's eyes over the son she had joyfully conceived when Greg was a college sophomore. After years of trying and several miscarriages, she and his dad had finally produced the second child they had always wanted.

Brad, old buddy, why did you do it? Why didn't you wait for my call?

From some point in his subconscious leaped a voice he had struggled to silence. *Why weren't you there when he needed you?*

Greg slammed his fist against the vending machine. *Stop it! You promised no more recriminations. Think of something pleasant, something to make you smile.*

A vision of Robyn leaped to his mind, a wholesome vision of a lush body, graceful limbs and a vibrant, youthful glow. As she'd jogged down the street to meet her father, there had been a joyful spring to her step. Her silky brunette hair, worn in a smooth, shoulder-length bob, had danced with golden highlights in the midday sun.

Letting his mind replay the vision, he felt a lightness return to his body. That was more like it. After all those months, he was experiencing the emotions of a healthy man, and he relished the feeling.

He felt a smile form on his lips. He liked the way Robyn's cute nose turned up at the end, the way her lovely brown eyes expressed emotions so vividly.

But as delightful as those superficial qualities were, he also admired her for her fierce devotion to her father. That wasn't a quality he often found in women these days. Many of them were so wrapped up in their careers that they paid only lip service to their families.

He directed an accusing finger at himself. Maybe if he had continued to put his family first, as Robyn obviously did, Brad would be alive today.

Damn! Would the guilt never end? He thought about Robyn's outpouring of guilt while he'd examined Jonathan in the street. She certainly didn't seem to have any reason to feel guilty about her father. From Lillian's comments in the waiting room and from his observations, Robyn appeared to be the epitome of the devoted daughter.

The laughter of a child drew his attention from his thoughts. Not ten feet away from the vending machine stood a rosy-cheeked toddler. The girl was yanking a bright red helium-filled balloon by the string tied to her pudgy wrist. Her angelic face, framed by a cloud of blond curls, shone with delight.

Greg smiled at the vision of innocence and felt the old longing. He'd like to have a daughter. But he had to have another son. Not for the age-old reasons some men wanted a son—to make them feel virile, to assure their immortality. He wanted—no, he needed—to have a son he'd name Brad, after his brother. That decision had been part of his healing process after Brad's suicide.

He hoped his son would be able to live the life full of promise that Brad, a gifted child, had denied himself by his suicide. In his dreams Greg pictured his son with Brad's brilliance, his almost adult sense of humor and marvelous creativity. He had fantasized that, as a blood relative, his son might look something like Brad. But he'd raise his son to be better equipped than Brad had been to cope with the pressures of adolescence and the demands of being gifted.

Until he fell in love and married again, his dream of having a son would have to wait. In the meantime, he'd continue to help kids like Brad—gifted, creative youths not in sync with the world.

And today, he reminded himself, *you're going to lighten up, make new friends, put the past behind you.*

"Feel better now?"

He turned to find Lillian standing beside him, a flashing
beacon in her chartreuse-and-white polka-dot sundress.
Her hazel-eyed gaze was fixed on his face with a strong
measure of curiosity. "I'm okay."

"You don't look okay."

Score one for Lillian. "How's Robyn's father?" he asked
evasively.

"We don't know yet, but it's a sure thing he's got himself into quite a pickle. He probably won't be able to use his
scraped-up hands to sign for a while. So now Robyn, in
addition to all her other duties, will likely have to read the
man's mind, as well."

Greg handed her a cup of coffee. "You aren't very sym-
pathetic about Jonathan's problem, are you? About his
deafness and all."

"Not anymore. I suppose that sounds callous to you. But
Robyn's mother was my best friend, you see. For years I
watched Jonathan lean on her. Now he's leaning on Robyn."

"I'd think a man with his handicap would need to lean
on someone."

"Lots of deaf people live independent, productive lives.
Jonathan could improve his lot, but he's too stubborn to
try. He says he's too old to learn."

"It could be he's too frightened to try something new.
Maybe he's afraid of failing."

"So what if he is? He needs to think of his daughter for
a change! Robyn's thirty-one years old, and she isn't getting any younger. She's been here eighteen months, taking
care of her mother before she died and now looking after
Jonathan. She'll never have a chance to meet her special
young man, get married, have her own family if Jonathan
refuses to try. Why, you'd think the man was a hundred

years old instead of fifty-five! Too old to learn new tricks. Humph! He isn't a dog!''

''Maybe Robyn's right. Maybe he needs more time to get over losing his wife.'' He knew how hard that was. Jonathan might need years, not months.

''No! Someone needs to shake up Jonathan Woodson.'' She drained her coffee cup and waggled it in Greg's face. ''I don't see people standing in line for the job. I just might have to do it myself.''

He didn't attempt to interrupt Lillian's emotional tirade. He waited, hoping she had unloaded her frustrations about Jonathan. He was wrong.

''I'd say it's about time Robyn Woodson got back to the business of living her own life.'' She crumpled her coffee cup and tossed it into the waste basket with a flourish.

''What business is that?''

Lillian's gaze suddenly narrowed, and her eyes gleamed. ''Why, young man, do I detect a spark of interest in our Robyn?'' She tapped a finger to her lips and smiled at him, as if she were sizing up a side of beef.

He grinned. Lillian was beginning to grow on him. ''She's easy on the eye, all right. And her devotion to her father's refreshing.''

''So, you're family-minded. I like that.''

Greg held out his hands, open palmed. ''Lillian, please. No matchmaking—okay?''

''Well . . . okay. But, if you ask me, you seem like a man who could use some female companionship.''

He had to hand it to her. She was good at reading emotions. He'd have to be especially careful around her if he didn't want the entire neighborhood gossiping about his family's tragedy. ''I'm a busy man. Besides being in the midst of a move, I own a business. I also do a lot of volunteer work in schools.''

"We'll talk about all that later. What I want to know is, do you object for now—or for always—to my womanly manipulation of your affections?"

He grinned so hard he thought his face would split. Maybe he'd have to fight fire with fire. "Object for always, Lillian? Of course not. I won't object. That is, if you won't object to a bit of matchmaking on my part."

Lillian frowned. "What, exactly, do you mean by that?"

"I mean, Miss Lillian, I saw the concern on your face when I examined Jonathan. You care more for him than you let on, don't you?"

Her eyes grew as round as the polka dots on her sundress. "Me and Jonathan Woodson? You must be crazy! Sounds like you were the one who got bonked on the bean."

Chuckling, he picked up the other two cups of coffee. "You know what Shakespeare said about protesting too much."

"You," Lillian sputtered, "don't know Jonathan Woodson very well, or you wouldn't suggest such a thing. Me and Jonathan Woodson. Humph!"

"Perhaps I was mistaken. Anyway, I think we'd better get back upstairs. Robyn and Jonathan may need us. And, as I recall, I promised Robyn this coffee."

"You go ahead," Lillian said, her red cheeks a clue she was still flustered by his words. "I think I'll have a bite to eat after all." With a dismissive wave of her hand, she spun around and headed for the cafeteria.

Chuckling, Greg angled across the room and rounded a corner to the elevator. He had no sooner punched the up button with his elbow than the door slid open. Two women in hospital greens and a man shepherding three young children got off. That left one passenger. She stood at the back of the elevator and sagged against the padded walls, her eyes closed.

Robyn. Greg's heart lurched at the disconsolate look on her face. He stepped inside the elevator, wishing he could do something to comfort her. "Robyn," he said, feeling her distress when she looked at him with red-rimmed eyes, "what's the matter? Is your father worse?"

At that moment, an orderly pushed an elderly patient in a wheelchair onto the elevator. Robyn accepted the coffee from Greg, her expression grim. "Can we go someplace and talk?" she whispered. "Someplace private, maybe?"

"Sure. Lillian's in the cafeteria. I'm sure she'll find us when she's ready."

"Good. I don't feel like putting up with her probing questions right now."

The elevator door opened at the ground floor, revealing a crowded corridor. "Must be visiting hours," Greg said. "Hmm. Sunday. We probably won't find much privacy around here. Do you want to go outside for a walk? It's a beautiful day."

"A beautiful day." She shook her head and sighed. "At least it was when I got up this morning."

He wondered what news the doctor had given her about her father. Respecting her wish for a private talk, he said nothing. He stepped aside so she could precede him through the automatic doors at the hospital's entrance.

Outside, the sun warmed his face and lifted his spirits. He hoped it would work its healing magic on Robyn, as well.

"There's a lake a couple of blocks down the street," Robyn said. "It's a pond, actually. I used to go there when Mom was in the hospital. I like the ducks."

"Sounds good to me," he said, falling into step beside her.

She took a sip of her coffee and grimaced.

"Sorry it's cold. Lillian cornered me downstairs, and I had trouble getting away."

"She's good at that. Since Mom died, she's been after my father. She has it in her head that Dad could learn to speak if he tried. Unfortunately, she knows a good bit of sign language, so Dad can't pretend he doesn't understand her."

"Could he learn to speak?"

Robyn stared into the distance. "It would be incredibly difficult, but some say it's possible."

"In the waiting room I saw a brochure about implants they do there at Baptist for deaf people. Would one of those help your father?"

"Probably. If he had one, he could hear some sounds. That would make it easier for him to learn to modulate his voice."

"Then why doesn't he have the operation?"

"He's scared to death of doctors. He refuses to consider an operation of any kind."

"Why is he so afraid?"

"When he was young, he lived in the backwoods of northeastern Oklahoma, near the Illinois River. There was one doctor—at least he called himself a doctor—who was convinced he could make Dad hear. He did some pretty terrible things to him in the name of medicine, painful things Dad'll never forget."

"Childhood trauma, huh?"

"Right. Of course, that was back in the Dark Ages, medically speaking. Doctors have learned a lot since then. Still, there's no perfect solution, no medical break-through. Dad isn't willing to take any more chances with doctors, especially with an operation."

"Was you father born deaf?"

"Yes."

"That makes it harder, doesn't it?"

"It means he doesn't have a grasp of the language—"
She sighed. "I explained all this to Lillian, but when she
gets an idea in her head, you can't sway her with facts and
logic."

"I'll bet she frustrates the heck out of your father."

"Boy, does she! But he knows how to get her goat."

"How's that?"

"He turns his back on her when she speaks."

"I did that to you in the hospital, didn't I? I'm sorry,
Robyn. I didn't mean to be rude."

She lowered her lashes—thick lashes that brushed her
cheeks like silk. "I'm sure you had your reasons."

He couldn't tell her about his reasons. The depressing
stories about his brother might taint the friendship growing between them.

"I had my reasons. But none of them justified being rude
to you." He paused, slipping his palm under her elbow. He
liked the feel of her skin in his hand. "How about it? Am I
forgiven? I'd like to be your friend."

She made no effort to brush away his fingers. That
pleased him. When she looked at him, a soft smile had
chased the sadness from her eyes. "I'd like to be your
friend, too. Of course, I forgive you."

"Good." At least he'd made her smile in spite of the obviously sad news regarding her father. He wondered, as
they continued away from the hospital and the noisy traffic
on Northwest Expressway, when she planned to tell him
about her father's condition.

In a few moments they arrived at the picturesque pond
that glittered like a gem in the late June sun. Robyn climbed
the earthen hill that served as the dam. He followed her,
wondering if she had any idea how good her hips and legs
looked as they flexed beneath that red thing she was wearing.

Once she reached the water's edge, she dropped to her knees on the freshly mowed grass that edged the pond like a plush carpet. Squinting against the sun, she waved him over. He chose a spot beside her with a clear view of the pond.

As if the ducks had built-in radar, they skimmed through the water toward Greg and Robyn. She leaned forward and showed her palms to them. "Sorry, guys. No food today." Still they swam closer, as if to see if she was telling the truth. She laughed at their antics, and Greg laughed with her. Their laughter echoed in the canyon created by the surrounding three-story garden apartments.

Across the water, a boy of about five was playing with his Labrador retriever puppy. At their laughter, he snapped his head around, a bright red ball in his hand. He raised his hand and waved wildly. Robyn smiled and waved back. Greg said nothing but observed the joy in her expression as she watched the child. He wondered what thoughts were running through her mind.

He recalled Lillian's comments about Robyn and the sacrifices she was making for her father. Lillian was right. This lovely woman deserved to live her own life—marry, have a child like that cute little fellow across the lake. But she had made the right choice, staying with her father. He admired her devotion.

He decided she was probably avoiding thinking about her father's new problems. If they were going to talk about his condition, however, they needed to start soon. Before long they would have to get back to him, and to Lillian. He decided to help the conversation along by asking questions about Jonathan.

"What does your father do with his time? You mentioned his workshop, and I noticed his overalls."

"He's a carpenter. He built our house after he and Mom were married."

Greg whistled. "He must be some carpenter!"

"Did you notice that building at the end of our drive-way?"

"Yes."

"That's Dad's workshop. He makes hope chests and grandfather clocks. His craftsmanship is superb. The local furniture stores keep him busy."

"Sounds like a good job for someone who's deaf."

"Dad's father and grandfather were carpenters, too. Of course, they weren't deaf, but they taught Dad the trade."

"Did your mother grow up in the backwoods, too?"

"Hardly. She's the one who rescued him from the back-woods."

"He needed rescuing?"

"In a way, yes. Before he met Mother, he didn't have any formal education in sign language or lip reading. She took him to Tulsa. That's where he had his first lessons. He's an intelligent man," she said proudly. "A fast learner. But he would have been much better off if he'd learned when he was a child."

"Sounds like your Mom and Dad were extremely close."

"She was more than a wife. She was his link with the hearing world. Now that she's gone, he just wants to with-draw. Just live with memories and silence."

"And where does that leave you, Robyn?"

Her lower lip trembled, and instantly he wished he'd kept his big mouth shut. "You don't have to answer that," he said, the anguish in her eyes tearing at him. "I had no right to—"

"It's okay," she said, cutting off his apology. "The truth is, Dad needs help, for his own safety, but he doesn't want it. I really don't know what to do with him, and—" she sighed deeply, loudly, as if from the heart "—I do have a couple of things I'd like to do myself."

Now seemed as good a time as any to get her to open up about her father's condition. "Do you want to tell me what's wrong with your father? I get the feeling it's serious."

Her face clouded over again. "Yes. No. Maybe. I don't know. I'm sorry. Now I'm the one who's being rude." She plucked a blade of grass and stared at it as she twisted it between two fingers. "I guess I need time to sort out a few things in my mind."

He gave her hand a reassuring squeeze. "If you want to be alone for a while, I'll wait for you at the hospital." Reluctantly he released her hand, but the moment he did she curled her fingers around his with a surprising desperation.

"Please don't leave. I'd like you to stay."

He wanted to stay, and providing a comforting ear was only one reason. "I'll stay if you like."

"You've been nice today. Most people wouldn't have gone out of their way to help strangers the way you did."

If he hadn't gone out of his way, he wouldn't have met Robyn. He thought she'd almost regained her composure when she blurted out, "Oh, Greg, my dad's broken his arm!"

"That's all?" He moved to sit in front of her, crosslegged. With gentle pressure under her chin, he forced her to look at him. "From the look on your face when I found you in that elevator, I was afraid it was something serious, like brain damage."

"It's not brain damage. But a broken arm isn't minor, not for Dad. With that cast on his right arm, he won't be able to sign worth a darn. His cast will run from his forearm to the middle of his hand, just above his knuckles.

Watch when I sign. See how much I flex and twist my wrist?"

He watched her quick, fluid movements. "Can't he sign with his other hand?"

"Not well. One day when he was a boy, he was in the woods by himself and didn't realize he'd walked straight into the path of a falling tree. It smashed his left wrist so bad he almost lost the use of his hand. In time some of the nerves mended, enough so he could use his hand in his work. But he never regained full use."

"How long will your father have to be in a cast?"

"All in all, three months."

"Hmm. That's rough. Could he finger spell?"

"In a couple of weeks. After the concrete burns heal on his left hand. But long conversations will tax him, and his dexterity isn't the best. Besides the old injury, he's got carpenter's hands. He doesn't exactly move his fingers like a piano player."

"Couldn't he use some kind of a computer?"

Robyn let her hands fall slack in her lap. "'Computer' is a bad word at our house."

"Why?"

"Mom bought Dad a computer for deaf people—a TDD. If he'd use it, he could talk on the phone by typing."

"But?"

"But he won't use it."

"Why not?"

"Computers frustrate him. Mom tried to get him to use his for months. She finally gave up and went back to making all his calls for him. Now he expects the same from me."

Greg furrowed his hair with the fingers of one hand, trying to think of a tactful way to put his observations into words. "Robyn, look, I just met you today. I don't have any right to stick my nose in your business, but—"

"But you're going to do it anyway, aren't you?" she said caustically, a spark of fire in her eyes.

Her problems with her father reminded him of those he had had with Brad. His way of dealing with Brad's problems had been to ignore them. To put up with his younger brother's mood swings, thinking it was just puberty talking, expecting the next day to be better. But Brad's moods had become increasingly blacker until... No! Robyn had to do something to help her father before it was too late.

He made a decision and plunged ahead. "From what you tell me, your dad's not anxious to become independent, is he?"

"That, my new friend, is a gross understatement."

"Which means you can't be independent, either. You can't move out. You can't have much of a social life. You can't get married and have children until you convince him he needs to change his attitude about learning new ways."

Robyn stared at him coldly, saying nothing. He sat there, watching the resentment build in her expression and in the muscles tensing in her jaw.

She rose to her feet, folded her arms over her chest and stared across the water. Suddenly she turned on him, her eyes ablaze with the fury of a mother whose child has been threatened by a bully.

"I've about had my fill of people like you and Lillian. You have no idea what it's like to be in my place. Or to be deaf like my father."

He leaped to his feet, realizing he'd pushed her too far. "I didn't mean to imply—"

"You didn't imply anything. You came right out and said I'm letting my father get away with behaving like a spoiled, insolent child. If he could talk, he'd tell you I badgered him like a fishwife to get him to go to that picnic. It wasn't a particularly enjoyable thing to do when I knew he was still suffering.''

"Listen, I didn't mean—"

"Do you have any idea what it's like to lie there at night and hear him, through the bedroom walls, sobbing because he misses my mother?''

She turned on her heel and stalked off in the direction of the hospital, mumbling something about ill-mannered neighbors.

"Robyn, wait.''

She wheeled around so quickly that he almost ran into her. She jammed her fists on her hips and glared at him, her cheeks blotchy red. "Why? So I can listen to you lecture me again?''

"No, so I can apologize again.'' Lord, this was becoming a habit with him. "I'd also like to offer my help. Maybe there's something I can do to help you and your father in this standoff.''

"There's nothing you can do unless you've got a spare half a million bucks.''

"What does money have to do with this?''

"Simple. Money could get him what he needs to live alone, and he wouldn't have the kind of accident he had today.''

"Robyn, please, can you be more specific?''

The little boy and his Labrador pup bounded over the rise of the hill, followed closely by a young woman. The pup tried to run between the boy's legs. The boy tripped, falling to the ground with a shriek of laughter. The puppy stood over him, licking his face and wagging his tail while his young master giggled with youthful exuberance.

"There's your answer,'' Robyn said with a flick of her wrist.

"That little boy and his dog?''

"Just the dog."

Greg bit his lip, refusing to let his impatience show again. "What about the dog, Robyn?"

"My dad needs a hearing dog."

"A hearing dog," he repeated. "I think I read about them in a magazine recently. They're kinda like guard dogs for deaf people, aren't they?"

"That's right."

He snapped his fingers. "That's the perfect solution for your father!"

"Unfortunately," Robyn said dryly, "it's also the perfect solution for the thirty other people who got their applications in before Dad's."

"There's a waiting list?"

"A three-year waiting list."

"Three years? Why so long?"

"There's only one kennel in Oklahoma that trains them—Kendra's in northeast Oklahoma City. She and her assistant do it in their spare time, and she dumps her own money into it. She simply doesn't have the resources to expand her operation to meet the tremendous demand."

"How long does it take to train a hearing dog?"

"Five or six months. But there's a lot that has to be done before a dog can start the program."

"Like what?"

"Dogs have to be screened and checked for good health. Only one in fifty passes the disposition tests. And of every four dogs in the program, only one makes it all the way through."

Greg whistled. "One dog in two hundred. Not very good odds."

"And it takes lots of time and money to weed out the other 199."

"I suppose they've tried to get grants."

"Yes, without much luck. One civic club adopted the program. That means three or four thousand dollars a year—a drop in the bucket compared to what they need."

She ticked off the needs on her fingers. "A separate building for sound training. Another building to house the dogs with their masters during the bonding process. Extra help. Vet bills. Dog food."

"I suppose we're talking several hundred thousand dollars here."

"As I said, at least half a million."

"I know from personal experience that kind of money is hard to come by these days."

"It's so frustrating to know what my father needs and not be able to get it for him, all because of money, or the lack of it."

Greg's own pet project was on hold for the same reason. "I know how you feel."

"Dad wouldn't have had that accident today if he'd had a hearing dog. They're trained to walk with their masters and pull them off the street when they hear sirens or car horns."

He detected the telltale signs of guilt in her voice. "You blame yourself for what happened to your father today, don't you?"

"Of course I do! If I hadn't talked him into going to that picnic, he wouldn't have been hit. Now he's even worse off. With his arm in that cast for three months, he'll probably lose his contracts with the furniture stores. And his carpentry work is what he does to fill his days. He's going to go nuts with nothing to do."

Poor Robyn. So stressed out with concern for her father. Obviously what she needed was a hug and some gentle comforting. *Whoa, boy!* he cautioned himself. *You only met her a couple hours ago.*

Restraining himself, he brushed her cheek with the backs of his fingers, guiding her to look into his eyes. "I was out of line when I lectured you about finding a way to help your father. I can see you're trying. It's obvious he's more important to you than anything in the world."

"Thanks. I needed to hear that."

"He's a lucky man. I hope someday I have a son or daughter who's as unselfish and caring as you are. I'm sure you feel the same."

Robyn's eyes registered a brief flash of emotion. Hurt, maybe, or some other pain deeply buried that he'd conjured up with his comment.

While he tried to figure out what he'd said wrong, she forced a nervous smile and backed away from him, wiping her palms on the sides of her jumpsuit. "I—I've gotta go. Gotta get to the hospital. Dad's probably waiting for me."

CHAPTER THREE

JONATHAN SAT in a wheelchair, staring at the treatment room walls. He wondered how much longer he'd have to wait for Robyn. An hour ago she kissed his forehead and snuck out to get the medicine for his pain.

Jonathan was no fool. He knew there was a pharmacy in the hospital basement. The errand should have taken her twenty minutes—no more. She was probably off somewhere trying to adjust to the problems his broken arm and scraped-up hands would cause them. That was Robyn's way. She wouldn't want to upset him by letting him see how troubled she was over his accident.

But he could see, all right. Just as he could measure the toll the past eighteen months had taken on her. She wasn't the same Robyn—ever ready with a laugh or a teasing comment. And who could blame her? So much responsibility for one young woman. He hated being a burden to her, and now he would be a bigger one than ever. That's what he got for trying to go to that picnic. If he had stayed home as he told her he wanted to do, he never would have been hit by that car.

The picture of the accident formed in his head. He thought mostly in pictures. He and Robyn had talked about that recently. She told him her thoughts came mostly in words. He wondered how it would feel to have a stream of words running through his mind instead of the beautiful pictures.

Some of the pictures weren't so beautiful. He shuddered at the memory of that red sports car racing down the street at him. The young driver with the dark hair had been gripping the steering wheel with stiff arms and a look of horror on his face. Jonathan would never forget his feeling of helplessness—or that face.

He wiped the vision from his mind. Pictures, words. It didn't matter. If he had stayed home, he wouldn't have made himself more of a burden to his daughter.

His arm throbbed. He didn't know which hurt the most—his arm, his hands or his pride.

He glanced at the sheet of paper in his lap and frowned at the different groups of dots and dashes. The woman in the green jacket had finger spelled Morse code. Then she had signed that he could learn to get his thoughts across by tapping the little machine she gave him. She had put the tips of his fingers on the machine so he could feel the vibrations when he tapped on it. She gave him a choice of that or of a new kind of computer that would make letters appear on the screen when he stared at the keys. A computer? No, thanks!

Instead of poking dots and dashes and trying to remember what combinations made what letters, he'd just as soon finger spell. Then, when his right arm healed, he could sign again. That way neither he nor Robyn would have to learn Morse code.

He tried to move the fingers of his left hand beneath the wads of gauze and creamy white salve the nurse had put on him. His fingers stung as they had the time he burned his hands picking up the tea kettle that had boiled dry because he hadn't heard the whistle. Frustration swept through him like a prairie fire.

Maybe the woman in the green jacket was right. Maybe he should try to learn Morse code. Otherwise, Robyn might insist he try the computer again. When Carol Ann hadn't been looking, he had tried to learn how to work that machine. He'd been so frustrated he'd felt like dumping the fool thing out the window. Being bested by a stupid machine made him feel more helpless than ever.

His mind leaped to visions of the unfinished furniture in his workshop. To the contracts and down payments he'd already accepted from the furniture companies for chests and clocks he had promised to complete by August.

His work gave him a feeling of dignity. He knew Meals for the Heart paid for most of the bills. Still, he prided himself that he provided some income with his own hands.

What would he do with his days and his evenings while he couldn't work? Sit around and watch television? He frowned at the prospect of doing practically nothing. Even though Robyn had bought him a decoder for the television so he could watch shows closed-captioned for the hearing impaired, he didn't care for it much. He didn't like sitting still that long.

Reading was out. His head ached when he read. He had to puzzle over the words to figure out how they fit together, and there were so many he didn't understand. Especially when people wrote in long sentences.

Three months could be an eternity.

One thing for sure, he didn't want to pass his days with Lillian. He didn't want that woman in his house. Lately he had convinced her he shouldn't be disturbed when he was busy in his workshop. He'd told her it wasn't safe to take his eyes off his electric saws and drills to watch her sign.

Now the pest would probably take it upon herself to keep him company. Maybe he'd unscrew the light bulb that flashed when his doorbell rang. Then he wouldn't know when she was there for a visit, and she'd think he was asleep or not at home. Maybe, if he was lucky, she'd get the idea he plain didn't want to see her. The old bag irritated him as much as the poison ivy he used to get as a boy when he lived in the cabin near the river.

He shifted in the wheelchair and let his thoughts drift to his childhood, and his struggle to make others understand him. Until he was six, all he had known was his mother's crude system of gestures. Then a nice Sunday school teacher had taught him to finger spell. Even then he had been frustrated. The few children who lived close by had avoided him. The memory of his childhood was a lonely one.

But the picture that dominated his thoughts was the river. Back then the Illinois had been so clean he could drink from it. How he used to love to swim in that river. He wished he could raft on the water again and lie on the bank to watch the fish swim in the shadows of the trees. He and Carol Ann hadn't gone in years.

Carol Ann. At the thought of her, his chest ached with longing. His thoughts moved to the lucky day he had met the pretty blond woman. Those college friends she'd been with might have been able to hear and learn more than he could, but they hadn't been smart that day. They should have known it wasn't a good idea for beginners to canoe on the river after the spring rains. Not when the rapids were churning like a giant pot of boiling water. When her canoe had overturned, she had almost drowned.

Lucky for Carol Ann he'd been there to pull her out of the water. And lucky for him that angel had come into his life. She had made it rich and full of things he never would have known without her. He figured God had been on the river that day, guiding him to her, guiding her to him.

The days were empty without her. Lately he'd had to work extra hard so he would be too tired to lie awake in their bed and remember how she had felt in his arms. If not for Robyn, he wasn't sure he would want to go on living. But he had promised Carol Ann before she died that he would be brave for their daughter.

The memory of that promise made him sit straighter in his chair. He had to start thinking of Robyn. He had to find a way to convince her that he could live by himself. Then she could get her old sparkle back. Meet a young man. Fall in love. Have children. His grandchildren.

The old fears and frustrations clouded his thinking, weakened his resolve. Maybe that lady in the green jacket had the answers. Before she'd left, she had signed that she would be happy to explain things he could do to help himself. He slumped at the memory of past efforts, of embarrassing failures. He didn't know what she could do to help him that Carol Ann hadn't done. But didn't he owe Robyn one more try?

"ARE YOU AND YOUR DAD going to be okay?"

Standing beside Greg in her driveway, Robyn crunched a magnolia leaf with the toe of her red tennis shoe and thought about his question. Her father was in the house, lying on the couch, his arm throbbing with pain. He couldn't talk, he couldn't sign, and her dreams for the future were as broken as his arm.

If by okay Greg meant would they survive, yes, of course they would. But, she wondered with a stab of remorse, at what price? "We'll be okay," she said, staring at the ground, but she knew she didn't sound convincing. "Thanks for your help."

Suddenly Greg's hand, with gentle urging, was tilting her chin up until she looked into his eyes. Above him the thick, waxy magnolia leaves clattered in the light summer breeze. The sweet aroma of fuchsia petunias flowering in a circle beneath the tree filled her with memories of other nights.

Carefree summer nights when she had stood in the yard with boyfriends.

"If you need anything, I'll be right next door," he assured her. "I should have my phone in by tomorrow. I'll give you the number. Tell your father to call if he needs me. If I pick up the phone and no one says anything, I'll know it's him, and I'll come right over."

"Thanks. I'll give him your message."

As irritated as she had been at Greg for his pompous lecture at the pond, she felt a tingling awareness at his touch. She liked the way his fingers felt on the sensitive skin under her chin. She'd been ticklish there as a child, but he wasn't tickling her now. He was making her feel like a woman, a feeling she hadn't experienced for months.

Even though she was sure Lillian had her eyes trained on them from her front window across the street, Robyn made no attempt to brush Greg's hand away. So what if Lillian knew she was attracted to him?

His eyes, crystal blue, sparkled as he winked at her. Then came that grin, so wide she felt a smile light up her face.

"It's good to see you smile," he said. "When you do, your eyes sparkle."

"Uh-oh, then. Watch out. Lillian used to say I was hell on wheels when my eyes sparkled."

"Well, personally, I'm a sucker for a smile." He spread his arms wide and cocked his head. "I'm yours," he teased her. "Do with me what you want."

What an invitation! She had the impulse to kiss him. She could feel his breath, warm, still smelling faintly of coffee, feather over her face. Would he taste like coffee? Smiling at the thought, she took a lingering look at his lips and stepped back to remove herself from temptation.

"Give me a day or two, and you'll see the real me," she said. "I'm really a very happy person."

"Now how did I guess that already?"

Robyn felt Greg's hand on her arm, urging her closer to him. Was she going to get her kiss wish, after all? She was certainly tempted . . . but reason struck. She had only met him a few hours ago.

"You look like you're doing battle with yourself," Greg said with a light chuckle.

Was she so transparent? "I was thinking I just met you. I don't know what you do for a living. I don't know anything about you except that you're from Tulsa."

"Well, let's see. What should I tell you, and what should I leave out?"

While Robyn rolled her eyes, he pretended to think for a moment.

"Okay, here's the bio. My full name is Gregory Robert Michaels. I own the new aluminum recycling plant downtown. I'm a fair cook. I like the outdoors, especially the water. I like to fish, I like to water-ski and—" he flashed her an outrageous grin "—I think I'm going to especially like living next door to you."

"And you're incredibly shy." Playfully she poked him in the midsection with a stiff forefinger and met firm resistance.

"How about you? Lillian said you left some job to stay here and care for your mother. What kind of job?"

"I planned conventions for a trade association in Washington."

"Washington, as in D.C.?"

"Yes."

"What kind of trade association?"

"Perfume manufacturers."

"Sounds like a woman's dream job."

"It was," she said. "These companies do lots of business in Latin America. So I got to travel to places I never would have seen, otherwise."

"Do you speak Spanish?"

"Luckily, yes. I learned it when I learned English."

"How?"

"With Dad's language problem, he and Mom identified with people who couldn't speak English. When I was about six months old they sponsored a refugee family from Central America through their church. The Mendosas lived in an apartment over our garage for ten years. I grew up playing with their two kids as if they were my cousins. I spent as much time in their home, where they spoke Spanish, as I did in mine."

She paused, relishing the memories. "I liked their home. There was so much lively chatter all the time. In ours, it was much quieter because we signed so much."

"Sounds like a painless way to learn a language—no books! Your friends must have envied you."

"Only when I was chosen as my high school's foreign exchange student. I spent one summer in a village in Mexico."

"Lucky you."

"I guess so," she said, but she still had mixed emotions about the experience.

"But?" he prodded her.

"My stay there was an eye-opener. I learned firsthand how hard it is for deaf children to learn to communicate. The family I stayed with had six kids. Two of them were deaf. The exchange service matched us up because of my experience with Dad."

She banished the memories of the struggling children from her mind. "Anyway, the experience helped me land that job in Washington." She paused, thinking how much she wanted her job back. "It was a good job."

"Hmm. How would you like to come to a party at my house Saturday night?"

"I should ask you what my job has to do with going to your party, but, as Lillian would say, I'm not going to look a gift horse in the mouth. I'd love to go to your party." She couldn't remember the last time she'd been to a party, other than today's ill-fated picnic. "What kind of party is it?"

"I hope you're not disappointed. It's more a meeting than a party."

She snapped her fingers. "Then you'll need food. Enter me. I can pay you back for today by bringing the refreshments."

"I didn't help you because I expected to be paid back."

"Of course you didn't. But are you going to turn down my offer?"

"I'd be nuts if I did."

She laughed. "Anything special you'd like me to bring?"

"Yeah. You."

She smiled, already looking forward to spending an evening in his company. "How many people do you expect?"

"Including you?" he asked.

"Including me."

He knitted his forehead into a frown, as if he were counting in his head. "Is thirty too many?"

"Not unless they're football players or growing boys."

Greg laughed. "No football players or growing boys."

"What time?"

"Seven-thirty."

"And the dress is . . . ?"

"Whatever you want to wear. I volunteered to coordinate a mentorship program for the older gifted kids in the

Bethany schools. I'm giving the party for the people I've recruited as mentors."

Greg's program sounded fascinating. "What will your mentors do with the kids?"

"Work with them on a one-to-one basis. The idea is for the kids to try on professions before they commit years and big bucks to courses of study they might not be suited for."

"What a great idea!"

"I thought Saturday night would be a good time to get everybody together and have a short meeting."

"What kind of jobs do these mentors have?"

"A couple are doctors. Several are lawyers. A few are engineers. Let's see, we also have an architect, a farmer, a television newsman, a novelist, a geneticist and a research scientist, and I'm not through recruiting."

He sidled up to her and talked in an Edward G. Robinson voice. "How about you, lady? Could I interest you in a special deal?"

She backed up a couple of steps to the porch. "Uh-oh. Something tells me I'm going to regret going to this party."

"Now, Robyn. I know you're busy with your business and your father, but think about giving me a couple of hours a week, will you?"

To work with a student, or with Greg? Smiling at the prospect of the second alternative, she weakened in her resolve to say no to volunteer work. When she'd moved to Washington she had overdosed on volunteer work and promised herself she would think carefully about making commitments in the future. This commitment, however, promised proximity to her appealing new neighbor—not an altogether unpleasant prospect. "What do I have to offer?"

"I saw the list of the kids' interests," he said, smiling at something he obviously thought funny. "Restaurant management and international business are on the list. Right up your alley.''

"After all you've done to help Dad and me, I'd feel like an ingrate if I said no.''

"Then don't say it.'' He moved to the steps and, gripping the wrought iron railing on either side of her, demanded her full attention. "I'd really like you to become a mentor. It would mean a lot to me.''

Something in his eyes told Robyn this was, indeed, an important request. "Okay,'' she said, feeling somewhat trapped. "Count me in.''

"Great! I'll have some forms for you to fill out Saturday night.''

"I'm curious,'' she said, sitting on one of the porch steps. "Why did you decide to help gifted kids? There are any number of causes you could have picked.''

He took a long time answering her question, a tip that he might not be telling her everything. "My brother was gifted,'' he said in a soft voice.

Was gifted. Uh-oh. That probably meant Greg's brother was dead. She should have kept her question to herself. From the look on Greg's face, she sensed the loss was a recent and painful one for him.

"Brad died last year,'' Greg said, confirming her suspicions.

"On October 31, by any chance?''

"Right. Strange coincidence about your mother.''

Feeling a rush of compassion, she reached for his hand. "I'm sorry. It's hard to lose someone you love, isn't it?''

"Yeah, it is,'' he said, showing appreciation for her gesture with a gentle smile. I really miss him, especially on the weekends. I used to take him camping then. It must have been a big shock for you, coming home and finding your mother so sick. Lillian told me about it while you were with your father in the hospital.''

"I miss her," Robyn said, letting her gaze drift to the love seat under the magnolia tree. Her father had made it for her mother as a present for her last birthday. "She was bright. She was cheerful. The house isn't the same without her. I keep expecting her to flit through the house in one of her cleaning fits. But . . . she doesn't, of course.''

Greg sat beside her on the steps. She found herself wishing she knew him well enough to bury her head in his chest while she let go of the tears she'd been fighting. But she was the woman of the house now, and women of the house did not dissolve into fits of tears, especially in the arms of near strangers.

But this near stranger made it so easy to feel the emotions she'd bottled up for too many months.

"I'll bet you miss your friends in Washington, too, don't you—and that job?" he said.

"I sure do," she admitted without a moment's hesitation. She wished she could tell him that she missed her job more than she could say, that it had been her life, her fulfillment. Just beneath the surface, however, was a layer of guilt eating away at her, because she planned, come hell or high water, to return to her job in late September. She had to achieve the impossible and persuade her father to go with her—or she had to leave him. But she did not want to talk about either possibility with Greg.

"Ever think you'll go back?"

Could he read her mind? "I—well—maybe."

"Forgive me. That was a stupid question. If you went back, you'd probably have to leave your father, and I'm sure, after what he's been through, you'd never consider leaving him to fend for himself, would you?"

His question totally unnerved her. Before she could think of an answer, he added, "Sure you wouldn't. You're obviously not the kind of woman who'd put her career before her father's welfare."

In her peripheral vision she saw her father at the living room picture window. Seizing the opportunity to end the conversation, she stood abruptly and forced a smile. "Time to go," she said. "I think Dad needs me."

Greg glanced over his shoulder, waved at her father and squeezed her hand. "I admire you, Robyn. You're one fine woman."

GREG BOUNDED UP the steps to his house. He felt good all over. Good about meeting his new neighbors. Good about helping them. And especially good about Robyn.

He grinned as he opened the door. For some reason he had energy to burn tonight. He turned on his portable stereo and clicked in a heavy-beat soul cassette. Singing to the music, he unpacked one box, then another of the dozen he'd stacked in his living room.

He'd have to remember to send his realtor a plant or something. A bonus for finding this house, this neighborhood. These people were friendly, they were caring and they were...damned good-looking! He bent to look out the living room window toward Robyn's house to see if he could catch a glimpse of her.

A stroke of genius you had there, old boy, asking her to become a mentor. Once you get the unpacking done and get through this week's evening meetings to promote recycling, you'll have excuses to spend time with her.

Wait a minute, he thought. What if he asked her to organize the fund-raising instead of being a mentor? He'd have to confer with her about all the fund-raising possibilities, of course. They'd make public appearances together. Have lunch. Dinner.

The more he thought about it, the more excited he got. He'd talk to Wanda Richley, coordinator of the gifted program at the Bethany schools, as soon as she got back from her trip. If Wanda had no objections, he'd approach Robyn with the idea.

He reached into another box, and his hand closed over something hard and flat—a picture frame. Slowly he unwrapped the picture of him and Chelsea, then reached into the box for the one of him and Brad. Did he want the pictures in his new home?

Yeah, he did. Maybe someday he'd feel like putting them away, but not yet. He propped them up on the table that backed up to his sofa and briefly wondered if Robyn had ever been married or had children. Judging from what Lillian said, he was sure she hadn't. But Robyn had certainly got a strange expression on her face when he mentioned he hoped someday he had a daughter as devoted to him as she was to her father. What emotion had triggered that expression?

Oh, well. That was the fun part about meeting new people—getting to know them. And he intended to get to know Robyn Woodson well. Very well, indeed.

LILLIAN LET the sheer peach curtains at her dining room window fall into place, feeling smug, satisfied and challenged all at the same time.

What luck that nice young man had moved in next door to Robyn. He was a looker, that Greg. If she was twenty years younger, she might give Robyn a run for her money.

His presence in the neighborhood gave her plans a decidedly new slant. That he and Robyn were attracted to each other was as obvious as the June heat in Oklahoma.

If Lillian played her cards right, she might be able to get those two young people together while she kept her promises to Carol Ann.

The big hitch in her plan was Jonathan. Now that he'd bunged up his arm, she was going to have a job on her hands getting him to do what he should have done years ago—grow a little. He hadn't begun to use the intelligence God had blessed him with.

Any man who could design and build his own house could certainly learn to do for himself so his daughter could live her own life. If he wanted to waste his life, that was his business, but he was wasting Robyn's, as well. That was something Lillian could no longer allow him to do.

She was sure everyone in the neighborhood would call her a busybody, accuse her of meddling in people's affairs again. But someday they'd thank her for what she planned to do.

First thing tomorrow she'd make that phone call and set the wheels in motion.

CHAPTER FOUR

THURSDAY EVENING Robyn plopped down next to her father on the living room sofa, tugged off her tennis shoes and made wide circles in the air with her tired, aching feet.

One more day until the weekend, one more day planning the meals and supervising the cooking, cleaning and deliveries for Meals for the Heart—all work she could live a lifetime and never miss doing.

Saturday, though, was Greg's party. *A party.* She could hardly wait. A hint of the old Robyn bubbled inside her—the woman with endless energy who used to scramble out of bed every morning, anxious to go to work. The woman who teased her boss out of his dark moods, whose optimism rarely faltered. What had happened to that woman?

Her fatigue faded in anticipation of Greg's party and the opportunity to mix with people involved in challenging careers. People like ... Greg.

Hmm. Greg. How would she have described him to her mother? A nice man. Helpful. Energetic. Firm hips and a dusting of blond on his thighs. No, no, that's not the way she'd describe him to her mother! But she'd say pushy. Too pushy for his own good. She had a hunch she'd be smart to drop off the food Saturday night, feign a headache, stay out of his life and keep him out of hers. She didn't need his guilt trips. She manufactured her own, thank you.

Beside her Jonathan flipped on the television and skipped from station to station with the remote control, breaking her train of thought. Robyn watched the impatience play across his face and prayed the next week would pass quickly. Then the sores on his hands would be healed, and maybe she could make progress with him on his computer.

If she couldn't get him to take that one step toward independence, the rest of her plan was probably doomed, and she could forget about returning to Washington by late September. First she had to nudge him out of the house, persuade him to make new friends, help him learn to communicate better. Then she had a Herculean task ahead of her—to talk him into living in Washington with her until his number came up at the kennel for a hearing dog.

The little detail she hadn't worked out was how long he'd have to twiddle his thumbs in Washington, waiting for his dog. As things stood at Kendra's Kennel, the wait could be three years. Her father would never leave if he thought he'd have to stay away from home that long. Six months? Maybe. Three years? Never!

She had to find a way to help Kendra expand her training facilities.

The light above the front door flashed. Thinking it could be Greg, she popped up and waved her father back to the couch. "Don't worry, Dad," she signed. "I'll get it."

When she opened the door and found Lillian with a folded newspaper tucked beneath her arm, she smiled over her disappointment. "Oh, hi, Lillian."

"Hi." She peeked around Robyn's shoulder, fluttered her hand and frowned at Jonathan. "I was beginning to think you two weren't home. You should be so lucky, right?"

Robyn glanced over her shoulder and sucked in a smile. Her father had turned his back to the door. He lay on the couch, his unbroken arm slung over his eyes, playing possum.

"Jonathan have a bad day?"

Robyn stepped outside to join Lillian on the front porch. At sunset, the day was only beginning to cool from a sweltering one hundred degrees. "He's just frustrated. Since he can't work, he's been going with me to the office this week. Today he inspected the building. He's stewing because he can't do all the repairs that need to be done."

"He never was a patient man, your father."

"Boy, how I know it!"

"Robyn, dear, I didn't come here to discuss Jonathan's cantankerous ways. I came to ask if you read the travel and entertainment section of the *Sunday Oklahoman*." She whipped the newspaper from beneath her arm and quickly unfolded it.

"Afraid not," Robyn said with little interest. The only trip she wanted to take was to Washington, D.C. "Why? What did you find? Another good deal on a cruise?"

"My, no! Two a year's enough for me. But there's an article I can't wait for you to read."

"Why don't we sit on the bench?" As she descended the steps, Robyn let her gaze drift to Greg's house, wondering if she might see him this evening. Although he had phoned to check on her father daily since Sunday, she hadn't seen him for more than a neighborly hello. She guessed that was for the best. Still . . .

"If you're looking for Greg, he just got home," Lillian said, joining Robyn on the bench beneath the tree. "He's early this evening. Usually pulls in about ten o'clock. My sources tell me he's having a party Saturday night. Are you invited? I'm not."

"Yes, but probably because I agreed to help him with a volunteer program he's working on with the schools." She told Lillian about Greg's mentorship program and the nature of the party. "What is it you wanted me to see in that newspaper?" Robyn asked, ignoring Lillian's nosiness.

"Have you ever been to the KRMG Great Raft Race on Labor Day?"

"Once, when I was in college." She and her friends from Oklahoma State University in Stillwater had driven east for the annual holiday frolic down the Arkansas River from Sand Springs to Tulsa. She remembered wishing they had taken the time to put together a raft. Although thousands of people came to watch the zany race, the ones who had the most fun were the ones who manned the hundreds of colorful rafts.

Robyn and her friends did take part in the weekend partying in Sand Springs and Tulsa. That year there had been parades, goat-roping contests, square dances, concerts and a fireworks display over the Arkansas River in Tulsa.

"How would you like to go this year?" Lillian asked.

"Well, I might." She and her father hadn't spent a weekend away together in as long as she could remember. "If I could talk Dad into it." Then she asked the loaded question. "Are you going?" Her father would veto the trip if he thought Lillian was included in the plans.

"Never mind me. You'll want to go after you read this." Lillian thrust the paper into Robyn's hands and stabbed a finger at a feature story that bore the headline "KRMG Great Raft Race Garners Million Dollar Pot."

Lured by the thought of a million dollars, Robyn, in the waning light of day that filtered through the leaves, scanned the article Lillian had circled.

Two paragraphs into the story, Robyn sat up with a start. A wealthy Tulsa businessman, who had made his fortune by adhering to the teamwork ethic, was launching a new division in this year's race down the Arkansas River from Sand Springs to Tulsa. In addition to the division for the serious racers—the ones who wanted to finish the eight-mile course first—and the Pokey Okies—the fun seekers—there would be a division for nonprofit groups.

The team that accumulated the most points during the weekend, as decided by the wealthy benefactor and his employees, would win a whopping million dollars for its charity.

Robyn smoothed her hands over the newspaper, her hopes mushrooming into fantasies. "Imagine—a million bucks! If we could put together a team for Kendra's Hearing Dogs and win that race, the kennel could have their buildings and their help and tons of dog food. Dad could get his hearing dog a whole lot sooner."

"Yes, my dear, and if you win, you could have your freedom. You wouldn't have to stick around forever and play nursemaid to your father. You could pack your bags and move to Washington. How long did your boss say you had until you needed to be back at work?"

Robyn's pulse kicked into high gear. "About three months. I need to be there by September 25."

"Evening, ladies."

Hearing the rich timbre of Greg's voice, Robyn pivoted on the bench and smiled. "Well, hi. Home early tonight?" His tie, pulled loose, hung at a jaunty angle beneath the open neck of his dress shirt. He looked bone tired and a fit candidate for a hot shower, a cold drink and a soft pillow. Smiling into her upturned face, he gave her shoulder a light squeeze that carried a hint of something more than friendship.

"I think we're finally getting the bugs out of that new equipment," he said. He circled the bench, leaned his hips against the tree trunk and folded his arms over his chest. "Where do you have to be by September 25?"

"The East Coast," she said.

"Going on a vacation?"

She thought of her eighteen months working to help her family and decided yes, the trip could be considered somewhat of a vacation. "You might call it that," she said.

Lillian shot Robyn a questioning glance. Robyn folded her hands over the newspaper in her lap, wishing Greg would drop the subject. Then she realized she was allowing Greg's question to make her feel guilty for no good reason. She lifted her chin, smiled with self-assurance and tried to decide how much to tell Greg about her plans.

Good old perceptive Lillian stood, turned her back on Greg and waggled her brows at Robyn. "Well, if you young folks will excuse me, it's time for my evening bubble bath."

As Lillian walked across the lawn with a smug look on her face, Greg said, "A vacation would be wonderful for your father. I took one after my brother died, and it helped."

Not one to lie, Robyn decided to set him straight then and there. "We're not going on a vacation, Greg."

He frowned. "But you said—"

"I'm afraid I misled you," she said, steeling herself for the disapproval she sensed would come. "When you walked up, I was telling Lillian I have to be in Washington by September 25."

"Oh? How long will you be gone?"

"Permanently, I'm afraid."

"Permanently?" He crossed to sit beside her.

"That's right. I'm going back to my job in Washington."

Greg's mouth fell open so wide he could have swallowed the big mosquito that hovered before his face. Ridding himself of the buzzing pest with a broad sweep of his hand, he regarded her as if she had told him she were planning to abandon a houseful of infants. "You're moving back to the East Coast?"

"That's right. I am."

Bristling at Greg's tone of voice, she stood, crossed her arms and met his demanding gaze. Unless she was a poor judge of body language, he was about to subject her to his version of what the dutiful daughter should do for her father. Tonight she was fresh out of patience for his know-it-all attitude. She was tired. She was hungry. She ached from a twelve-hour workday, and she was anxious to sink into a hot tub for a long, soothing soak.

Besides, after eighteen months of caring for her parents—and not that she minded the sacrifice—she had a glimmer of hope that she might be able to resume her career again. If somehow she could figure out a way to win that raft race prize pot, her father might be able to stay in Bethany. Greg had no right to question her judgment—even if a little voice kept telling her she shouldn't push her father to do too much too soon.

Expecting emphatic disapproval of her plans, she puzzled at the half smile that crept over his face. "There goes my luck again," he said. "I've been telling myself all week how lucky I was to move next door to such a good-looking woman. Now you're going to move away."

He stood and with a solitary finger slowly traced a path across her forearms crossed at her breast. Regret showed in the husky tenor of his voice. "I'll miss you, Robyn. We've known each other less than a week, but I already think of you as a friend. A special friend."

So, she must have imagined that his reaction to her plans was critical. Before that moment, three months had seemed an interminable period of time. But with Greg standing there, making goose bumps dance on her arms, three months seemed more like a pleasurable interlude than a period to be endured. Maybe her luck was beginning to change.

"I'll miss you, too. If you're ever in Washington, you'll have to come see me."

"Where will you and your dad live? In the suburbs?"

Greg's words flattened the goose bumps that had been dancing on her arms. He assumed her father would be moving to Washington with her—permanently.

She remembered what he had said Sunday—that she was too devoted a daughter to put her career before her father's welfare. His words ate at her insecurities, and she prepared herself to tell the truth and face his disapproval. "We're not moving to Washington, Greg. I am."

"You mean Jonathan's staying here? All by himself?"

She swallowed hard, not liking the way Greg made her plans sound to her own ears. "That's right. Dad will stay here in Bethany."

"How can he possibly live by himself so soon?"

"I have plans for him to stay with me for a few—"

"He must be pretty upset over this."

Robyn's gaze flicked over Greg's shoulder, to the light that burned in her father's bedroom. "I—I don't know how he feels about it yet."

"You don't know? You mean you haven't told him?"

"No. I only decided—"

"When do you think you'll get around to telling him? I should think—"

"Wait a minute," Robyn snapped. "You won't give me a chance to explain, and I resent that. Besides, what business is it of yours, anyway?"

He opened his mouth to speak, then shut it, as if he thought better about what he was going to say. He stared at her for a long moment, the firm set of his mouth an indication that the thoughts playing through his mind were disapproving ones.

"How can you do it, Robyn? How can you think about leaving your father—" he paused, glancing away for a second, then back "—only two weeks after he gets his cast off?"

"If you'll just give me time to explain, you'll see that—"

"He'll be lost without you. You said so yourself when we took that walk to the pond." Realization sparked in his eyes. "Wait a minute. Is that why you were so upset that day? Because your father's injuries might interfere with your plans to leave?"

Greg's words ripped a hole in Robyn's composure and snapped the thin line of patience that held her beleaguered self together. "As I recall, you were the one who told me I deserved to have a life of my own."

"That's right, but I didn't mean—"

"And now that I've found a way to do that, you act as if I'm some self-centered, inconsiderate daughter who doesn't care about her father. Who do you think you are that you have a right to stand in judgment of me?"

Her words hit him with the force of a slap. She could see it in his eyes. He stood there, stunned, and she decided a quick exit was in order before he found another reason to criticize her. "I'd better be going. Dad needs me," she said coldly, "and, regardless of what you think, I do respond to his needs."

"You're not taking this the way I meant it."

"You'll forgive me if I don't ask for an explanation."

"I was just trying to keep you from making some of the same mistakes I made."

That, she decided, was her cue to remove herself from his condescending attitude. "Good night, Greg."

She turned, but he caught her arm. "Robyn, wait."

Although the anger still coursed through her veins, she couldn't ignore the unsettling effect his hand had on her composure. A sudden gust of wind rattled the magnolia leaves and stirred up the heady, sweet scent of petunias. "You had no right to talk to me that way. Give me one good reason I should stick around and take more of your verbal abuse."

"I had reasons for saying what I said."

"Well, I'm listening."

"I wanted to warn you to think carefully about what you were doing before it was too late."

"Too late for who, Greg? For me? For my father?"

"For both of you," he said grimly.

"Why don't you tell me what you're really talking about. I have a feeling this isn't about me at all. It's about you, isn't it?"

"Just take care of your father, Robyn. He's a good father, and he loves you."

She stiffened at his comment and tried to pull away, but he held her tightly in his grasp.

"Don't take offense," he said. "I think you're misinterpreting what I said."

"Then why don't you tell me exactly what you meant?" she demanded.

"I meant that when we don't take care of the people we love, it comes back to haunt us."

"Aha! Now we're getting to the heart of our little problem. *You* obviously have some kind of a guilt hang-up. How dare you project it on me? How dare you—"

Full lips descended on hers, silencing her protest. She struggled against the hold on her arms and complained into the warm recesses of his mouth. She would not be bullied.

She would not give in to his kiss. Not now, not ever. Hmm....

The ground tilted beneath her, and she sagged against his chest, palms pressed against firm swells. She felt the thud of his heart beneath her fingertips, and a ribbon of heat unfurled in her abdomen. Dear Lord, had it been that long since she'd been kissed?

To her dismay, Greg was the one who broke the kiss. He draped his forearms over her shoulders and pressed his forehead to hers. "God, woman, you kiss good."

"Not fair. You took advantage of me in a—a—weak moment."

He chuckled. "Didn't seem weak to me. Besides, I merely did what I've been wanting to do all week." He grinned and angled his head for a return trip to her lips.

Again she flattened her palms against his chest, this time pressing hard. "Oh, no, you don't."

"Why not? You enjoyed that kiss as much as I did. And you have to admit, it's a whole lot better than arguing."

"That may be, but I want to settle our argument right here and now."

"Ah, Robyn. Can't you lighten up? It's a gorgeous evening, far too gorgeous to stand here fighting when we could be—"

"Greg..."

"All right, let's hear it."

To keep her hands from roaming over his chest, she fussed with his collar, staring at the top button on his shirt. She knew by the heat of his gaze and the warmth emanating from the thighs that brushed against hers that if she looked up, her lips would ignore the restraint she was trying to show. "You have a nasty habit of sticking your nose in my business."

"True."

"You're not going to argue with me?"

"Uh-uh. But surely you know my intentions are good."

"Whatever your intentions, I'd appreciate it if you'd leave my father's welfare to me." That said, she wriggled free of his arms and turned to walk to her porch.

"Robyn, don't leave, not like this."

"I'll see you Saturday night, Greg, but remember, my father's welfare is my business, and mine alone."

MOONLIGHT FILTERED THROUGH the white eyelet curtains that fluttered over Robyn's open window. She lay on her brass bed in the front bedroom and punched her pillow, resenting Greg's sermon about her father.

Her lips still tingled from his kiss. But what could she expect when she hadn't been kissed by a man in eighteen long months?

The last man had been Phillip, just before he broke off their relationship after learning that her father was deaf and that his hearing loss was genetic. With the finesse of a weasel he had explained he couldn't be seriously involved with anyone who might give him defective children. She could have told him there was no chance of that happening! Children were not in her life plan.

Something Greg had said kept popping into her mind, something about mistakes he had made and people he had loved. Whatever his regrets, she was willing to bet they were troubling him deeply. And he appeared to be punishing himself for something.

Well, everyone had problems. Right? Right. But for the first time in months she was beginning to find solutions to hers. If she could persuade Kendra to form a team for that raft race in Tulsa, maybe they could win the prize money.

Kendra had told her she could move rather quickly to eliminate the waiting list once she had funds and the handlers had completed their training. Kendra said she could haul in a couple of mobile homes to use until permanent buildings were erected. And she was close to a break-through on breeding good dogs for the program. But everything hinged on money.

One point Greg had made was well-taken. Robyn should have discussed the move to Washington with her father. He'd refuse to go at first. But the optimist in her hoped in time she could persuade him to live with her there for several months. The realist in her, though, said she was dreaming.

She scooted to her knees, pulled the curtains aside and peered through the night at Greg's house. One moment she had been furious with him over his accusations about her neglecting her father. The next she had melted in his arms like hot butter. His holier-than-thou attitude still infuriated her. She'd been a good daughter. He had no right to imply that she didn't have her father's interests at heart. Woodsons always cared for their own.

Saturday she'd visit Kendra at the kennel and talk her into entering the Labor Day race. Then she'd persuade Jonathan to organize the raft's construction.

As she refined her plan, the memory of Greg's kiss kept intruding on her thoughts. Still looking out the window at his house, she wondered if he'd like to go with her to the kennel.

GREG PUNCHED HIS PILLOW with his fist and threw it across the room. Sitting up in bed, he rested his forearms on bent knees and stared out the window at Robyn's house.

He wondered where her bedroom was and imagined how she looked lying in bed. By now she was probably asleep, curled into a soft ball like a kitten. Now that he'd kissed her and felt the soft curves of her body molding to his, he couldn't get her out of his mind. If only she hadn't tempted him with innocent brown eyes and soft lips.

Damn! Maybe he should have kept his apartment in the city. In three months Robyn would move back to Washington. With his luck, he would grow to care for her, and he could ill afford another goodbye.

The collective pain of all the goodbyes knifed through his stomach. He hadn't experienced that pain in weeks. By devoting himself to his plant, to his volunteer work with gifted kids, he had finally shifted his focus from the past to the future. Until he'd met Robyn....

He had to find a way to keep his distance from her. After the party Saturday night, he'd be more careful.

FLUSHED AND DRIPPING with sweat, Manuel rolled the push mower into the garage behind the Ortegas' white frame house, shoved the warped door into place and snapped the padlock shut. He had finally finished his Friday chores.

When he had mowed the lawn two weeks ago, he had forgotten to lock the door. One of the twins had toddled inside, played with the tool box latch until she opened it, found a hacksaw and cut a gash in her plump little thigh.

Mr. Ortega had returned from his job at the automobile plant. Seeing eighteen-month-old Rosa with the ugly cut on her leg, he had ripped into Manuel as if he had intentionally hurt one of the youngest of his ten children.

The only thing good about his temporary guardian's tirade was that Mr. Ortega had spewed his anger in his native Spanish. What a welcome sound! After living in the United States six months, Manuel craved the opportunity to speak Spanish as much as he did his favorite Mexican foods. Because they were trying to help their children speak

English without an accent, the Ortegas uttered Spanish in their home only on special occasions.

"Man-uel," a high-pitched voice called from the back porch.

He recognized the voice of the Ortegas' diminutive ten-year-old daughter, Consuelo. She had taken a special liking to him since he had moved in with the family after his parents had disappeared during a hurricane on a trip to Mexico. Whenever he brooded over his missing parents, Consuelo assured him that any day he would find out what had happened to Ramón and Carmen Garcia. "What do you want, little one?"

"Lyndon's on the phone," she said, screwing her face into a frown. "Should I tell him you can't talk?"

"Don't worry," he said, tousling her dark, silky hair as he passed her on the steps. "I won't get caught."

Not talking on the phone to Lyndon was part of his two-week grounding for getting into trouble on Sunday. Mr. Ortega despised Lyndon, but Lyndon was Manuel's best friend. His only friend, really. At least Manuel got to see Lyndon at summer school for a few minutes each morning.

He wished he hadn't accepted Lyndon's dare to drive his new sports car. He couldn't forget the pain on the face of the man he had run into—a deaf man. He had disappointed the Ortegas, too—again. On their day off, they had had to go down to the police station to get him. He was sixteen, but he did not have a driver's license. The police had lectured the Ortegas about disciplining him. Mr. Ortega had warned him that the next time he got into trouble, he could look for another place to live. He almost wished that would happen. He was going crazy living there.

Sounds of siblings arguing in the small living room leaped through the thin walls as Manuel picked up the re-

ceiver in the kitchen. "Hey, *amigo. Buenos dias*," he said
to Lyndon. While Lyndon had spiced Manuel's English
with slang terms, Manuel had taught his friend a few simple phrases in Spanish.

"*Buenos dias* to you, *amigo. ¿Qué pasa?*"

"Nothing much. I can't talk long. Mrs. Ortega will be
back soon and—"

"I know. You're dead meat if they catch you talking to
me. Dad said to tell you he has good news about that man
we ran into."

Manuel gripped the receiver tightly in his hand. "Is he
okay?"

"Yeah, and he's not going to sue. Dad had his lawyer
check."

Sue. In Manuel's village in Mexico no one would have
thought to sue under the circumstances. There he would
have gone to the man's house, apologized formally to the
family and worked in his place until his injuries had healed
and he could resume his responsibilities. Manuel couldn't
help feeling guilty for what he had done.

"Are you still grounded?" Manuel asked his friend.

"Sort of. Dad said if I sign up for that mentor program
that Michaels guy told us about at school yesterday, he
might reconsider. Are you going to sign up?"

"I don't know," Manuel said. The mentorships available through the gifted program were supposed to help
prepare him for college, but he wasn't sure that he'd be able
to go. Since his father had lost his business in the plum-
meting Mexican economy, his family had been struggling.
They had hoped to make a better life in the United States.
His parents had returned to Mexico to make arrangements
to bring back two aunts and a cousin. "So, are you going
to sign up?"

"No way. I think it sucks."

There Lyndon went again, trying to hide his strong vocabulary with crude words. "You should. You want to be a doctor, right?" He sensed Lyndon wanted to sign up for a mentor and would if he would, too.

"Yeah, but—"

"Mr. Michaels said you could work with a doctor in a hospital. You could even watch an operation."

"To tell you the truth, I don't want anything to do with that gifted program. Gifted, jeez! Why do they have to call us gifted? Like we're weird or something. It makes us sound like we think we're better than everybody else. Why don't they just call us smart or intelligent? People comprehend those words."

Manuel knew whom he meant by "people"— Jake and the popular guys who followed him around school. "In my village they didn't call me gifted. When Mrs. Richley called me in and told me I scored high enough on the tests to be in the gifted program here, I felt honored, and my parents were proud. But—"

"Gifted equals nerd in Jake's book," Lyndon interrupted. "And I'll tell you something else—ever since they wrote 'gifted' in their little grade books, the teachers have been expecting me to be perfect or do twice as much work."

Manuel heard the car door slam. "Mrs. Ortega's home. I've got to go."

"Wait a minute," Lyndon said. "I called to ask you to a party at my house next Thursday night."

"A party? But you're grounded."

Lyndon chuckled and lowered his voice. "Dad said I couldn't drive my car. He said I couldn't leave the house at night. He didn't say I couldn't have my friends over."

"But surely when he sees all your friends—"

"He won't see them, *amigo*. Mom and Dad are flying to Dallas Thursday to shop for clothes for their cruise. They won't be back until Sunday."

"But Mr. Ortega would never permit—"

"Permit, hell," Lyndon said. "Make some excuse and get your Mexican bod over here. I've invited Jake and the guys."

"They're coming?"

"Sure. All I had to say was the magic word."

"What was that?" Manuel wanted to know.

Lyndon laughed. "Beer. What else?"

CHAPTER FIVE

ON SATURDAY Robyn rose early, showered and put on a yellow sundress. Ready for her eight o'clock appointment with Kendra at the kennel, she ran her fingers over the telephone and debated whether or not to invite Greg.

"Oh, what the heck," she said, picking up the receiver, "I might as well."

She dialed Greg's number and waited five rings. On the sixth she hung up. Glancing out the window, she saw his car in the driveway. He was probably sleeping late. With the kind of week he'd had, he deserved some rest. Probably just as well she couldn't reach him, she reasoned. Still, she couldn't get him out of her mind as she whipped up a batch of blueberry pancakes for her father.

While her dad was devouring his second stack, Robyn gave him a hug and headed for the door. "I'll be back by nine-thirty," she signed, backing through the dining room. "Lillian's home if you need anything."

He gave her his no-way look and waved her on. Today, she noticed, he was maneuvering his fork with his left hand with almost normal dexterity. Good. If Kendra approved her plan, he would need the use of those fingers.

Other fingers, long, tapered ones that had curled around her arms when Greg had kissed her Thursday night, lingered in her thoughts as she opened her car door. Changing her mind, she slammed the door, crossed to Greg's house and rang the buzzer.

A few moments passed, and still no Greg. Disappointed, she turned to leave. The sound of a door opening infused her with hope, and she spun around.

She momentarily lost her ability to breathe. Greg stood in the doorway, dressed only in a Turkish towel of midnight blue secured low around his hips by a simple tuck of the fabric. The golden highlights in his wet hair caught the sunshine that streamed through the doorway. Water trickled down his bare chest, catching here and there in the mat of golden hair that softened the hard contours of his pectorals.

"Good. You're up already," she said, then cursed herself for her choice of words. She followed a single droplet as it moved down his torso. Her gaze froze on the vertical band of hair that narrowed below his navel and disappeared beneath the tuck of the towel.

"Oh, it's you," he said in a flat voice. "I thought you were the paper boy. He missed me this morning. When I phoned the newspaper they said someone would be right out."

"I'm not the paper boy," she said softly.

He smiled, but only a little. "Obviously." Then he tightened the tuck on his towel and with a frown asked, "Did you need to see me about something?"

Was she welcome on his doorstep or wasn't she? She really couldn't tell. Maybe she should go to the kennel without him. "Well, to tell you the truth, I—"

"Forgive my manners," he said, suddenly a cordial, if not enthusiastic, host. "Come in. Coffee's on."

She balked, gesturing at his towel. "You're obviously not ready for company."

"You're not company. You're a neighbor." He pushed the door open wider for her.

Stepping through the doorway, she made sure she didn't brush against that towel. He smelled of soap and toothpaste. Her wayward gaze lowered to the tuck of the towel, and she worried what would happen if he sneezed or bent over.

Once inside, she turned around and, through sheet self-discipline, forced herself to train her eyes on his face. "I've got to go by the kennel this morning," she said, "The one I told you about that trains hearing dogs."

"So, do you need a ride?" He pivoted, crossed the room, disappeared around a corner and reappeared, from the waist up, in the serving window. Now in the kitchen, he lifted a coffee carafe, filled a mug, sipped from it and grimaced as he burned his mouth on the hot liquid.

"Uh, no, I'm driving. Today the owner—Kendra Lewis—is beginning the bonding process for a dog to a client."

He lifted the carafe to offer her a cup of coffee, and she shook her head.

"I thought you might want to go with me to see it. I'm sure she'd be glad to show you how she picks dogs for the program, too."

Sucking on an ice cube he'd retrieved from the refrigerator, Greg mumbled, "Why not? I'll just be a minute. Make yourself at home."

BEHIND THE CLOSED DOOR of his bedroom, Greg stuffed his shirttail into his jeans and zipped them, with some difficulty. Damned jeans were too tight—this morning, at least.

Way to go, boy. Way to keep your distance. Answer the door in a towel. A wet towel. And make a fool of yourself with the hot coffee. You might as well have worn a neon sign on your chest that flashed, You turn me on!

Keeping his distance from Robyn was going to be harder than he thought.

So why did you agree to go with her to the kennel? You could have played it safe. Stayed home. Spent the time getting ready for the party tonight.

True. He could have done that. But she looked and smelled so... fresh. She'd probably just showered. Hmm. Robyn in the shower. Now there was an inspiring thought.

He ran a comb through his hair and let the grin he'd suppressed in the living room spread over his face. Maybe if he let these feelings show in the privacy of his bedroom, he could act more reserved when he was with her.

Reserved, hell! He wanted to pull her into his arms and... Never mind what he wanted to do next.

Robyn would walk onto a plane in three months, and he'd probably never see her again. If he didn't watch out, he'd be hurting by that time. She was bright, she was energetic, she had a delightful, playful manner and she was... luscious. He could get accustomed to that combination quickly, even if she did have her priorities screwed up as far as her father was concerned.

He tossed his comb onto the dresser and regarded himself in the mirror as if he were lecturing a friend. *No more answering the door in a towel. As for today, keep your hands to yourself and your mind on the dogs. Or you're in for trouble, buddy. Mighty big trouble.*

WHILE SHE WAITED on Greg's living room couch, Robyn could hear him in his bedroom opening and closing drawers. Just being in his house while he dressed made her feel uncomfortable—in an intimate sort of way. She didn't know why. When he'd answered the door he was, for the most part, undressed.

She smiled. It had not been an altogether unpleasant way to start the day.

She glanced around the room, admiring his choice of colors. Navy blue and gray, with a touch of purple here and there. Navy for strength, gray for dependability, purple for... passion. The color mix in the bright, airy room with the cathedral ceiling and full-length windows intrigued her—as did Greg himself. One minute she was sure he was attracted to her, and the next she was positive he was pushing her away.

Two silver picture frames on a teakwood table that backed up to the sofa drew her attention. She stood, crossed the room and looked at them. In one a younger Greg with sun-streaked hair to his shoulders stood behind a diminutive blond woman, hugging her to his chest. Robyn picked up the frame and felt a twinge of envy for the closeness between Greg and the woman in the picture.

"That was my wife. Chelsea."

At the sound of Greg's voice, Robyn turned and saw him lounging against the doorway to his bedroom, his arms folded. "Oh, hi," she said. "I didn't hear you come in."

As he crossed to stand beside her, she looked at the picture of him with his wife again. "She was lovely, Greg."

He took the picture from her and replaced it on the table. She watched his expression carefully and observed that it was peaceful. She decided he must have recovered from losing Chelsea, if one ever recovered from losing a spouse.

"When I lost her and Christopher, I didn't think I'd ever get over it. But time passes, hurts heal, feelings change." He glanced at the picture again. "I guess I should put this away."

His gaze shifted to the second picture. He picked it up, and Robyn noticed the almost reverent way he handled it. That frame, too, bore an image of Greg. Beside him was a

youth in his early teens who had Greg's full mouth and
sparkling blue eyes. Greg and the boy were sitting on a red
brick wall, their arms draped affectionately across each
other's shoulders. If she didn't miss her guess, the young
man was probably Brad. "Is that your brother?" she
asked.

He avoided her gaze. "Yes. That's Brad."

"He was a good-looking young man. He looked a lot like
you."

His thin smile appeared forced. "That's what people
used to tell us. He was a good kid. Someday I hope I have
a son just like him."

"How did he die, Greg?" She imagined a sports injury
or leukemia or some horrible accident that must have devastated his family.

"How?" he asked, regarding her with a stony look. "I'll
tell you how. He committed suicide."

AS SOON AS GREG DROPPED the bomb about his brother's
suicide, he announced he thought they should take separate cars because of errands he had to run after the kennel
visit. While Robyn fought to recover her composure, he
locked his house, started his car and backed out of the
driveway waiting for her to lead the way to the kennel.

As she meandered through residential streets to the in-
terstates that would take them the fifteen miles across town
to Kendra's kennel in northeast Oklahoma City, she kept
hearing Greg's words ringing in her ears.

Suicide. She'd read newspaper articles about teens who
had taken their own lives, but she had never known anyone who had suffered the loss. She was totally unprepared
to offer Greg the comfort, the understanding she imagined
he needed.

Was that why he had moved from Tulsa? To escape the memories? A dozen questions buzzed in her mind.

Exiting the interstate, she took a two-lane asphalt road a half mile before she turned. Kendra's kennel was set back from the road in the dappled shade of native oaks. It was known for flealess boarding and caring hands. Built in the mid-fifties, it consisted of a red brick building that housed the reception area and office, plus half a dozen kennel structures.

The moment Robyn stepped from her car, an alert dog barked, setting off a reaction that swept through the sprawling kennel. She walked to Greg's car and tried to think of what she should say.

"I guess they don't have trouble with burglars around here, do they?" he said, his mood surprisingly light as he climbed out of the car.

"Only extremely dumb ones." Robyn took his easy-goingness as a cue he didn't want to talk about Brad, and she admitted to herself that she was relieved. If Greg wanted to pretend he hadn't just given her earth-shattering news, she would play along with his game.

"How many dogs can they board?"

"Kendra says two hundred. Still, I hear she has to turn customers away on holiday weekends."

"Maybe I'm in the wrong business," he said, then quickly added, "but aluminum recycling is a heck of a lot easier to clean up after than two hundred dogs."

"Yeah. Right. A lot easier," she said, then wrinkled her nose. "And a lot more fragrant." She managed a brittle laugh, and Greg smiled, as if appreciating her effort at levity. She wanted to slip her arm around his waist and pull him close for a comforting hug. But she felt he had erected some kind of an emotional barrier between them. She didn't want to risk violating what could be his effort to remain in control of his emotions.

When they stepped inside the reception area, she welcomed the feeling that she'd entered someone's home instead of a business. The receptionist was cooing to an apricot teacup poodle she held in her arms, while the dog's owner bid her companion farewell. The room smelled faintly of flea dip, a required treatment for all canine guests so Kendra could maintain the flea-free environment.

Kendra was talking on the phone while she processed the paperwork for two incoming golden retrievers. A petite woman in her early thirties with light brown hair, she acknowledged Robyn and Greg's arrival with a broad grin and sparkling green eyes. Placing her hand over the receiver, she whispered, "Give me a minute, and I'll be right with you."

Robyn scribbled a note asking if Kendra could give Greg the same demonstration she'd given her father. Nodding, Kendra waved them into the makeshift training facility, which consisted of two older and smaller kennel areas.

Robyn led Greg through the concrete-floored building that Kendra tried to reserve as boarding quarters for hearing dogs in training. Kennels with outdoor runs lined either side of the narrow, low-ceilinged room. Five dogs with wildly wagging tails stuck their noses through the chain-link gates—a Welsh corgi, a spaniel cross, two half-grown collie pups and Miracle, a sable-and-gold collie and Kendra's hearing dog demonstrator.

The next building was much the same, only the chain-link dividers had been removed. Distributed around the room were an old sofa, an end table, a twin bed with black-and-white ticking mattress and a telephone on a scarred wooden nightstand. A large pegboard was affixed to the wall at the far end of the room.

"This is the sound training area," Robyn explained. "That is, when Kendra doesn't need it to board dogs." She pointed to the pegboard to which a number of electronic devices had been affixed. "The phone company rigged that up so she could simulate the sounds the dogs need to learn."

The door opened and Kendra joined them, an exuberant Miracle on a leash at her left side. The day was young, yet Kendra's long French braid already looked disheveled. Fatigue lines showed around her eyes. Still she managed to look more like a college student than the owner of a labor-intensive business.

Robyn introduced Greg to her. While they shook hands, she bent on one knee and opened her arms. "Miracle, baby," she crooned. "Come here to Robyn."

The collie, ears alert, tail wagging, turned her long, pointed nose to Kendra.

"It's okay, girl. Go ahead," Kendra told her.

Miracle bounded into Robyn's arms, whining an enthusiastic greeting.

Greg knelt beside Robyn and earned Miracle's acceptance with his roughish stroking. He ran his thumb beneath the collie's right eye. "Is she blind in this eye?"

"Yes," Robyn said matter-of-factly.

"And she can still be a hearing dog?"

"She doesn't need her eyes to hear," Kendra explained. "Actually, she's our demonstration dog. But we could have assigned her to a deaf person."

"She's a beauty," Greg said. "I like collies."

"They've worked well for us. We've used others, too—and mixed breeds. We'd train any dog that had the right intelligence, disposition and willingness to work."

"Kendra's rescued some dogs from the humane society only hours before they would have been put to sleep."

"And we're in the process of breeding for the role," Kendra added. "We're getting close. I've applied for a grant, and I really think there's a chance we'll get this one. If we do, I'll hire a couple more trainers and expand the breeding program I've begun here. Screening pups at the pound takes too long."

"How do you know when a dog is right?" Greg asked.

"We give each one a series of tests."

"What do you look for?"

"Alert, friendly dogs. Full of energy, curious. They've also got to be smart and even tempered. We also look for willingness to work and ability to trust a master."

"Trust, huh? How do you test for that?"

"Watch." Kendra bent over and slid an arm around either side of Miracle's body so her arms crossed beneath the dog's stomach like a sling. When she lifted Miracle in the cradle of her arms, the dog thrashed for a moment, then relaxed.

"See, at first she was frightened, but she quickly settled down because she trusts me."

Robyn watched while Kendra demonstrated the other tests for Greg, pleased by his keen interest. Then came the fun part. Releasing Miracle to play with Robyn, Kendra set a wind-up alarm clock on the small end table, walked to the opposite end of the room and turned her back.

The moment the alarm went off, Miracle ran to the clock, then bolted for Kendra, poking her long nose insistently into her trainer's hand. She continued to run back and forth between the clock and Kendra until the trainer walked to the sound and turned off the alarm.

"That," said Kendra, "we call alerting."

"She sure knows her stuff," Greg said. "What other sounds does she respond to?"

"Lots. A telephone's ring, a doorbell, a knock on a door, a smoke alarm. Whatever's important to the client. We can even teach a dog to respond to a baby's cry."

"How long does it take a dog to learn all that?" Greg asked.

"About five months. First we have to obedience train the dog. Then comes the sound familiarization, and finally the bonding with the master."

"Robyn says the training process is expensive."

"Somewhere between twenty-five hundred and three thousand dollars. And we don't try to make any money on them."

"Robyn's father could sure use one of your dogs."

"I know," Kendra said wistfully. "He's on the list. It gets longer every day."

She glanced at her watch. "It's time for Mr. Gilliam's appointment. You and Robyn can sit on the couch and watch us through the window. I'll open the door so you can hear what's going on."

FIFTEEN MINUTES LATER, Robyn and Greg, kneeling side by side on the couch, watched George Gilliam through the glass. A grandfatherly man of about seventy, he stood outside, not ten feet away from them, an open field to his left. Facing Kendra, he looked as if he were a teenager about to get his driver's license.

Greg glanced at Robyn's face, relieved to see that the shock had worn off. He'd known she'd ask about Brad's death sooner or later. Although the question had surfaced sooner than he'd anticipated, he was relieved the truth was out. Hiding the truth was more difficult than dealing with it.

"He sure looks anxious, doesn't he?" he said of Mr. Gilliam. "Look, he's popping his knuckles."

"I don't blame him," Robyn said with one of her sunny smiles he found so appealing. "His whole life is about to change."

Kendra introduced Mr. Gilliam to Crackers, a spaniel cross who sat obediently at her trainer's left. Her tail wagging, her tongue lolling in the summer sun, Crackers looked up at Kendra adoringly, as if anxious to please her by repeating the tasks she had learned during the past six months.

His face alight with anticipation, George Gilliam bent to his knee with arthritic stiffness. Crackers wagged her tail and gave his face a swipe with her moist tongue.

Kendra handed Mr. Gilliam a sturdy rope about six feet long and signed as she spoke that he was to tie one end to his belt and the other to Crackers's collar. For the next twenty-four hours the two were to be inseparable. They were to walk together, run, eat, sleep and play as one. At the end of the period, the dog's allegiance would be transferred from her, the trainer, to Mr. Gilliam. Then the two would work together at the kennel for a week.

Amazing, Greg thought, how quickly bonding takes place. He had held little Christopher in his arms for only a few moments before he died. Christopher would forever be his son.

Mr. Gilliam secured the rope to his belt as instructed, then set off at a leisurely pace across the open field in the heavy gait Robyn said was often seen in profoundly deaf people. At first the dog hesitated, looking over her shoulder at Kendra. When the man tugged gently on the rope, Crackers followed. He rewarded her with lavish petting and vigorous scratching behind the ears.

Greg nudged Robyn with his elbow. "Look. Kendra has tears in her eyes."

"She's been working with that dog every day for six months. I'm sure it's hard to let her go."

Greg's smile faded, and he turned to look out the window again, knowing exactly how Kendra felt. "Saying goodbye is never easy, is it?"

Robyn curled her fingers around his arm and gave him a consoling look. "I'm so sorry about Brad," she said. "It must have been awful for you and your parents."

"Yeah, it was." He draped his arm around her shoulders and kissed the top of her head. "We'll talk about it sometime. But not now. Okay?"

She looked up and smiled. "Okay." She lifted her chin and kissed him softly, sweetly.

If only he had had Robyn to help him through the worst months after Brad had died.

"I guess I'd better be going," he said, standing and extending his hand to help her from the couch. "I have to drop by the office. I'm expecting some mail I need for the meeting tonight. And I've got to make a phone call."

"Can I bring anything besides the food?"

"Bring yourself, and remember—the party starts at seven-thirty."

"What party?"

Greg looked at the man walking through the doorway and recognized him as Joe, the one who had detained the drag-racing teens after they'd hit Jonathan with their car. Later, Robyn had told him Joe was another neighbor, a close friend of Jonathan's and a veterinarian.

Robin gave Joe a hug. "You remember Greg, don't you?"

"How could I forget?" He smiled at Greg and offered his hand. "I sure appreciate the help you gave Jonathan on Sunday."

"My pleasure," Greg said. "What are you doing here today?"

"Checking out some frisky little collie pups. They're fit as fiddles. Ready to train. I hear Kendra showed you the works. What do you think?"

"I'm really impressed. I wish I could do something to help Kendra."

"Watch what you say. She'll have you cleaning out kennels before you know it."

"That's where I draw the line," Greg said with a laugh, then added, "Speaking of help, I could sure use yours."

"You got a sick dog?"

"No, but I'm organizing a mentorship program for the older gifted kids in the Bethany schools. Several want to work with a veterinarian. Think you could spare a couple of hours a week?"

"Oh, I'm sure I could squeeze it in," Joe said in a slow southwestern drawl.

"Great. Then how about coming to a party at my house tonight? You can meet the other mentors there." He slipped his arm around Robyn's waist and smiled at her. "I've persuaded Robyn to help us, too."

And he could hardly wait to talk to Wanda Richley about the expanded role he had in mind for Robyn. He remembered his resolution to keep his relationship with Robyn distant and friendly—*only* friendly. When he had made that resolution, he'd fully intended to keep it. But when he saw her, when she smiled at him...kissed him...he forgot he'd ever made a resolution.

Joe's eyes gleamed with approval. "So that's what you were talking about when I came in. Sure, I'll go to your party. Maybe afterward I'll drop in on Jonathan and say hello."

ROBYN LEFT THE TWO MEN discussing Greg's program. She
found Kendra in her cramped office, frowning over what
looked like a business letter. "What's wrong?" She hoped
it was nothing serious. She had had about all the depressing news she could take for one day.

Kendra thrust the paper into Robyn's hands. "Read for
yourself. We didn't get that grant I was talking about. I was
so sure we would."

"Oh, Kendra, I'm so sorry."

Kendra heaved a deep sigh. "The Goodson Foundation
gave us ten thousand dollars for 'administrative support.'
But I sure could have used that hundred thousand dollars.
I wonder who got it."

"Nobody as deserving as you, I'm sure," Robyn said.
She realized this meant a setback in Kendra's plans to ex-
pand the training program, and she couldn't wait to tell
Kendra her news—her *good* news.

"I don't know what I'm going to do," Kendra said.
"This week alone I've had five calls from people who need
dogs. Five! I hate telling them I can't help them."

"What if I told you," Robyn began, "that I've found a
way we may be able to raise a million dollars for your
training center?"

Kendra's eyes bugged out. "A million dollars! What are
you planning to do—rob the Federal Reserve?"

"No, I'm serious." From her purse Robyn pulled the
clipping Lillian had given her. She showed it to Kendra.

Kendra skimmed the article, then flicked the clipping
with her thumb and forefinger. "A million bucks! What I
couldn't do with a million." She stood, walked to the window and looked into the courtyard. "Instead of one dog
out there training, we could have two dozen at a time."

She turned to Robyn, her eyes bright with hope. "We could wipe out that waiting list in no time. Oh, Robyn, do you think we'd have a chance?"

"A better one than you think. Dad rafted on the Illinois River for the first twenty years of his life."

"I didn't know that."

"And he's quite an accomplished carpenter. I'll bet he knows how to design a raft worthy of that race.'

"Do you think he'd agree to do it?"

"Frankly, I'm counting on it. This is just what he needs to get him moving again."

"Joe told me he was in an accident Sunday. He said he broke his arm."

"He did. But he's a stubborn man. If he decides this is what he wants to do, he'll find a way to do it."

Kendra picked up a pencil and tapped it against the desktop, the pros and cons of the idea playing across her mind. Her expression grew solemn. "There's a major problem here."

"Only one?" Robyn laughed, knowing how meticulous Kendra was in her attention to detail.

Kendra regarded Robyn with a challenging gleam in her eyes. "I can't fit another thing into my schedule. I live here as it is. I'll agree to enter that race if you'll help."

"Uh-oh. What do I have to do?"

"Organize our entry—and that includes finding and training the team. What do you say, Robyn? Will you do it?"

Robyn groaned, calculating the number of hours already committed in her day. "I can help, but I don't see how I can find enough time to assume responsibility for all that."

Kendra glanced at the letter again, as if mulling over something. She snapped her attention to Robyn. "What if

I offered to pay you? What if you worked here part-time, say mornings, and relieved me of the administrative duties for the hearing dog program?''

"You know I can't do that. Meals for the Heart takes a full day and then some."

Kendra's eyes danced with enthusiasm. "What if you reported to your office, organized your crew, then left to come over here for three hours a day? Mr. Gilliam's sister used to be a nutritionist for the public school system. She's always bringing me goodies. I'll bet I could talk her into filling in for you at Meals for the Heart three hours a day so you could work here."

"Wait a minute," Robyn said, holding up her hands. "You're going too fast. Besides, I can't afford to pay anyone to do my job."

"Don't you see? Mr. Gilliam and his sister haven't found a way to cover the expenses for Crackers yet. As you know, I usually help our clients find sponsors to pay for the dogs' training. Mr. Gilliam and his sister could barter for Crackers with time instead of money. You wouldn't have to pay her a cent."

Robyn had continued to manage her mother's business only because it provided the income she and her father needed. She was nuts about dogs, admired Kendra and felt challenged by the request to bring her management savvy to the hearing dog program. Best of all, if she took the job, she could be assured that the hearing dogs program could float a raft in that Labor Day race.

Kendra squeezed her hand and spoke in a singsong voice. "You want to do it. I can tell by the look on your face."

"Well—"

"Hallelujah! Now I'll have more time to spend training the dogs."

"Does that mean you'll be able to work your way down that waiting list a little quicker?"

Kendra cast her a wary glance. "I'm afraid not quick enough to get to your father's application anytime soon. But, yes, I'll probably be able to work with at least two or three more dogs at a time now that you've accepted the job."

She gave Robyn an enthusiastic hug. "It's going to be fun having you around here." She lowered her voice. "And you can bring that sexy boyfriend with you anytime you like."

Robyn grinned. "He isn't my boyfriend. He's my neighbor. But he is nice looking, isn't he?"

"*That's* the understatement of the year. And don't tell me you're not interested."

"Well..."

"I thought so. I guess you know you've got his undivided attention. You should see the expression on his face when he looks at you."

Robyn found Kendra's observation strangely unsettling. This morning Greg had confirmed what she had suspected—that he wanted children. If she didn't miss her guess, he wanted them to fill the empty spaces left in his life by Chelsea and Christopher...and by Brad. That eliminated any possibility that she and Greg could ever be serious about each other. Although she loved children, she didn't plan to have any of her own—ever.

"Don't get carried away," she told Kendra. "Greg and I will never be more than friends. Close friends, maybe, but only friends."

"Why do you say that?"

Robyn fiddled with the amethyst ring she wore on her right hand, the ring that had been her mother's. "Several reasons. The main one is I'm leaving in September to go to Washington. I guess you should know that before I accept the job here. I can only work two or three months at the most.''

"Why are you leaving?"

"My old job's opened up."

"But how can you leave your father?"

Robyn groaned. "Not you, too!"

"I take it someone has been bugging you about your plans. Greg, maybe?"

"You guessed it."

"Maybe he just doesn't want you to move away from him. Maybe he has ulterior motives for wanting you to stay."

"No, he's been pointed about his reasons. They all have to do with my father. We've already argued over our differences of opinion. But I think we have all that behind us now. We're going to be good friends from now on."

Kendra smothered a grin. "I'm betting you two wind up more than just friends."

"Don't count on it," Robyn said, wishing Kendra could be right. She slung her purse strap over her shoulder and started for the door. "Call me after you talk with Mr. Gilliam's sister."

"Just suppose," Kendra went on, as if she hadn't heard Robyn, "that you and Greg become close—very close—by the time you're supposed to leave. Then would you stay?"

Robin considered the possibility, but her thoughts hit that major obstacle in her mind. "I don't think so, Kendra. He wants kids. I don't."

"Why don't you?"

"With my kind of career, whether I work in D.C. or someplace else, I have to travel lots. I work late most nights, even weekends sometimes. Not the kind of life conducive to raising well-balanced kids."

"So, Robyn Woodson's a career girl, for now, for-ever?"

"Is that so hard to understand?" Robyn spread her arms and dropped them to her sides. "Look at you."

Kendra glanced around the room rather wistfully, Robyn thought. "I'd trade this joint in a flash for the right man and a chubby-cheeked kid with a snotty nose."

Robyn smiled. "Then I hope you get that chance."

"Me, too. Good luck persuading your father to help us. When do you plan to ask him?"

"Just as soon as I get home."

CHAPTER SIX

ROBYN FOUND her father a half hour later in his bedroom, struggling to tie his shoes.

"Here, let me help you with those," she signed, kneeling before him on the rug her mother had hooked.

She knew Jonathan hated for her to do menial tasks for him, such as tying his shoes, but she ignored his look of annoyance. "Dad, I have news."

"Good news?" he finger spelled with his left hand.

She forced the day's bad news—the facts of Greg's brother's death—from her mind and concentrated on the task at hand. "Very good news. Come into the kitchen." All the way home she had rehearsed how she was going to tell him about the race. She had to convince him that the entire project hinged on his agreeing to help.

Over coffee she outlined the idea for the hearing dogs raft and watched for signs of interest in his eyes. The moment she mentioned river rafting, his eyes misted over, and she caught him looking away. She knew he was reminded of her mother and the day they had met.

She paused, took a deep breath and plunged on. "We need someone to design the raft and oversee construction. I was thinking, with your skills and your experience on the river—"

Vehemently, Jonathan shook his head.

"Dad, we have to have your help. Don't you see? If we win that race, you'll get your hearing dog a lot sooner."

Her hands flew in accompaniment to her voice as she gave him an enthusiastic account of Mr. Gilliam and Crackers.

This time Jonathan's refusal did not bear the same unqualified vehemence. She could tell she was getting through to him.

"You're the only one who can do it, Dad. You were rafting on the Illinois not long after you learned to walk."

The light flashed over the front door, interrupting their conversation. Robyn rose to answer it. She found Lillian waiting outside, and not too patiently.

"About time. I've rung at this danged door six times this morning. Jonathan was here. I know he was. But he wouldn't come to the door." She stuck her head inside. "There you are, you stubborn old—"

"Won't you come in, Lillian?" Robyn asked dryly. "I'm sure Dad was just busy."

"No, as usual, he was ignoring me, weren't you, Jonathan? Jonathan?"

Robyn's father had planted himself on the couch and deftly presented his back to Lillian. He was reading the morning newspaper he had apparently snatched from the coffee table.

"What was it you wanted, Lillian? Perhaps I can help."

"I wanted to speak with your father, but that can wait. Did you see that woman at the kennel about the race?"

"I was just telling Dad about it," Robyn said. She didn't really want to share her news with Lillian until she'd secured a commitment from her father. But since it was Lillian's idea in the first place, she extended the invitation. "Why don't you join us, and I'll tell you both together."

"Well, I'm glad someone around here has some manners." Lillian perched on the edge of a straight-back chair and poked Jonathan none too gently on the arm.

He dropped his newspaper and glared at her.

"I rang the doorbell six times this morning, and you didn't answer it," she signed.

Jonathan retreated behind his paper.

Lillian scooted over to the couch, where she had a clear view of his face. "You were avoiding me, you—you—"

"Lillian, please, leave Dad alone."

"I got worried when he didn't answer," Lillian persisted. "What if he'd hit his head? What if, God forbid, he'd had a heart attack?"

Robyn arched a brow, surprised at the concern she heard in Lillian's voice. "As you can see, Dad's fine. What was it you wanted to speak with him about?"

Lillian tilted her chin and looked away. "It isn't important anymore." She snapped her attention to Robyn. "So tell me about the race. Are we on?"

Robyn smiled. "We're on. I was just trying to persuade Dad to agree to design and oversee the construction of the raft."

For some reason Robyn couldn't define, Lillian didn't appear surprised to hear her plans for her father. Lillian turned to Jonathan, looking as if she didn't care if he took on the project or floated to hell in a hand basket.

"Well," Lillian asked him, "are you going to do it?" Then, before Jonathan had a chance to answer, she said to Robyn, slowly, distinctly, "Of course he's not. A man with his handicap couldn't possibly take on such responsibility."

Jonathan bolted from the couch, his face twisted in a dark cloud of fury. The tops of his ears colored bright red, like the time he sunburned them while working in the garden. He turned to Robyn, pointed at his chest and, with a jerking nod of his head, conveyed his silent consent.

Jonathan Woodson, egged on by Lillian Chatwell, would definitely be in charge of the raft.

This time the hen outsmarted the fox, Robyn thought as she watched her father stalk off to his bedroom. Lillian knew what she was doing every step of the way.

"Nice work," she told Lillian with a chuckle. "I was having trouble until you pitched in."

"You don't think Jonathan would do what you ask because you want him to, do you?" She rolled her eyes and shook her head. "Sometimes you have to help these men along, Robyn."

Robyn recalled how her mother had maneuvered her father at times, but in a less abrasive and obvious manner than Lillian's. Robyn had never been good at maneuvering the men in her life. If she had been, Jonathan wouldn't have hidden in his workshop for eight months.

"Robyn," Lillian prodded, "what's your next step with this raft business?"

"A crew. I've got to find some experienced hands."

Lillian patted the back of her beehive. "I white-water rafted in Colorado in my younger days."

"No offense, but I think we need bigger bodies. Male bodies, actually."

Lillian sat up straight in her chair, and her eyes danced. "Why don't you ask Greg?" She leaned forward, as if she were afraid someone would hear what she was saying. "In case you haven't noticed, he has a terrific body."

Robyn laughed. "He did tell me he and his brother used to go camping a lot. Maybe he has some experience. I think I'll ask him tonight at the party."

Lillian sat back in her chair, a smug look on her face. "Why, Robyn. What an absolutely marvelous idea."

THAT EVENING, Robyn, acting as Greg's unofficial party hostess, greeted the guests and kept the table stocked with the hors d'oeuvres she had prepared for the occasion.

She was in the kitchen pouring coffee into the silver server when she felt his hands at her waist and smelled the distinctive vanilla of his cologne. She glanced over her shoulder and smiled. "About time to start the meeting?"

"In a minute or two," he said, pulling her close to his chest. "You're terrific, you know it?"

His words whispered through her hair. He crossed his arms over her chest and nibbled at her neck. Trying to appear unaffected by him, she joked about his remark. "You're just saying that because I've kept you out of the kitchen tonight."

He turned her in his arms and pulled her hands to his chest. "Well, that's part of it, but you also look terrific in that dress."

She had worn the periwinkle-blue silk, a garment from her professional wardrobe she'd long ago shoved to the back of her closet. "Glad you like it. I used to wear it to work."

His smile faded as she turned to the counter. Ah, yes, she had touched on a sensitive subject when she mentioned her work. She busied herself with wiping down the tile counter with a sponge while he picked up the carton of coffee creamer and returned it to the refrigerator.

He asked, "Are you sure Jonathan's going to be okay this evening?"

Robyn let her gaze drift to the window overlooking the driveway between their two houses. "He'll be okay."

"You don't sound so sure. Did you tell him about Washington yet?"

"Not yet. I will...soon. He's been missing Mom a lot lately. And he hasn't been sleeping well since the accident. He wakes up with terrible nightmares."

"Do you have any idea what's causing them?"

"For one thing, he keeps seeing the face of that boy who ran into him."

"I'm sorry, Robyn."

"Don't be sorry. It wasn't your fault those two boys were so reckless and irresponsible."

"Is he alone tonight?"

Robyn chuckled. "No, but he may wish he was before the evening's over. I asked Lillian to pop in on him from time to time."

Greg groaned. "Poor Jonathan. I'll have to thank him for his sacrifice. I really needed you here tonight. I couldn't have done this without you."

He took the sponge from her hands, tossed it into the sink and said, "Come here a minute, will you?" He angled his head.

Just when she thought Greg was going to fit his lips to hers, just when she was sure she wanted him to, a muscle in his jaw flexed, and his kissed her forehead, instead.

There he went again, giving her those damned mixed signals! Did he want to kiss her or didn't he? She heard laughter on the other side of the kitchen door, and she used it as an excuse to disentangle herself from the awkward situation.

Picking up the tray containing the tea and sugar, she headed for the door, then remembered she'd promised herself she would secure Greg's commitment tonight about helping her with the race. Turning around and finding him right behind her, she said, "When the meeting's over, can we talk?"

"Sure," he said, letting his gaze fall momentarily to her lips. "What about?"

"I talked to Kendra and—"

Wanda Richley stuck her head around the kitchen door. "Anytime you two are ready, we'd like to start. Some of these folks need to get home to their families."

ROBYN SAT ON THE SOFA while Greg explained the concept of mentoring. A discussion ensued about a pet project of Greg's—a special school for gifted students designed so they could work to their potential. A school with emphasis on counseling and parent involvement.

The earnestness in his voice when he emphasized the need for counseling was another clue to Robyn that Greg was pouring himself into his volunteer work to help him cope with Brad's suicide.

"I have some great news," Greg said. "As I told many of you, I applied for a grant for innovations in education with the Goodson Foundation."

Robyn's head shot up, and a sickening feeling pooled in her stomach. *The Goodson Foundation?*

Greg waved a piece of paper in the air. "I heard from them this morning." His face broke into a broad grin. "They've granted us one hundred thousand dollars as a down payment on an abandoned school building that's up for sale."

He was the one who got the grant Kendra had counted on!

While the others met Greg's announcement with enthusiastic applause and congratulatory comments, she stared at him, numb with disbelief. Instead of helping people like her father survive as independent citizens, the Goodson Foundation money would go to buy a run-down building for kids who had all their faculties—and then some!

The phone rang, and Robyn rose to answer it. Greg's plant manager insisted he come to the phone to unravel a problem the weekend crew was having with the new equipment. She stepped through the kitchen doorway and, unsmiling, signaled Greg with a sharp jerk of her thumb that he needed to take the call.

He looked at her questioningly, but she glanced away, needing to work through her anger before she spoke.

His call lasted several minutes, giving her the opportunity to step onto the front porch, where she could vent her anger.

"I can't believe it!" She slammed an open palm against the brick wall. "What kind of justice is there in this world?"

She heard the door open behind her and felt a hand on her shoulder. "Robyn, something's wrong. What is it?"

Containing her resentment, she turned to face him. "Your announcement in there was rather disconcerting, I'm afraid."

"Why?"

"Guess who your competition was for that grant."

"I don't know, Robyn. Lots of people, I guess."

"When I spoke with Kendra this morning she was in a blue funk. She'd just received notification from the Goodson Foundation—" she opened her eyes wide for emphasis "—that they had declined her request for funds to expand the hearing dog facilities. Guess who got the money, Greg? You!"

"Robyn, I had no idea—"

"Of course you didn't, but I can't help resenting the foundation's choice. Look, I know you're wound up in your volunteer work for gifted kids ... and I'm sure it's a worthwhile cause, but—"

"But what?" he said, his eyes narrowing suspiciously.

"But those kids already have so much going for them," she blurted out. "When people like my father really need help."

His expression hardened. "I should think, after what I told you about Brad this morning, you'd know these kids have needs every bit as important as your father's. I thought you were a compassionate woman. I guess I was wrong."

"Oh, Greg," she said, sagging against the wall. "It isn't that I don't think gifted kids have needs, but at least they can live by themselves when they mature. A good part of their potential isn't locked inside their bodies because they can't talk."

"You're assuming because they're brilliant, their lives are a breeze. Don't you know being gifted can be as much of a handicap to some kids as being deaf is to others!"

Robyn reached for the railing by the steps, knowing Greg was thinking of his brother. She felt guilty for being resentful. "I'm sure you're right. I'm sorry. It's hot. It's been a long day. Maybe I should go home. We can talk about this later." She turned to go.

He put a restraining hand on her arm, but the warmth of moments earlier was gone. "I need you to stay. There's a report you need to hear—something that involves you. Stay, Robyn."

He sounded as if he were giving an obedience command to one of Kendra's dogs, and he looked at her as if his request were a test. A test of their friendship. "Well, I guess I could stay," she told him reluctantly.

He released her arm and opened the door. "You won't be sorry, Robyn. Promise."

AS SOON AS SHE WAS SEATED, Greg smiled and called on a short, stocky man named Sam who owned a string of building-supply houses.

The balding man in his mid-fifties puffed out his chest, obviously enjoying the attention focused on him. "One thing Greg told all of us when he called was that he expected this mentoring business to work both ways. As members of the community, we'll help these bright students. They, in turn, will be expected to give back to the community.''

Robyn was aware that most eyes in the room were trained on her. She checked the hem of her skirt to see if her slip was showing. Finding it in place, she willed herself to concentrate on what the businessman was saying.

He looked straight at her and smiled. ''Robyn, we understand your father's come on some bad times with his injuries and all.''

She blinked slowly, wondering what was coming next.

''Greg here told us about those furniture contracts your father can't finish because of his accident.'' He glanced around the room and smiled, and the others smiled with him.

''While you were in the kitchen, we took a straw vote and decided to make your father these kids' first community project. With the aid of those of us who are pretty darned good carpenters, we're going to finish the hope chests and clocks for your father.''

Robyn's mouth dropped open while the men and women in the room applauded and smiled with the good feelings that came with helping others.

''I—I don't know what to say,'' she said, rising to her feet, ''but I know my Dad will be relieved.'' She looked at Greg and felt ashamed for her behavior on the porch. She tried, as best she could, to convey her appreciation to him for his sensitivity to her father. He smiled, and there wasn't a hint of malice or resentment toward her—only joy.

''It'll be a good lesson for these kids to learn—that a deaf person can lead a productive life,'' Sam said. ''Your father's built quite a reputation in this community for his carpentry. I'd say this project was made in heaven.''

"My dad's been worried about his contracts," she said, glancing around the room. "I can't tell you how much this will mean to him." She paused, then added, "If there's ever anything I can do to help you all with any of your projects, please, let me know."

She took her seat again to the sound of applause.

"You shouldn't be so quick to offer," Greg said, "because—" he handed her a stack of papers clipped together "—we have something in mind already."

Someone in the group chuckled. Robyn's gaze moved to the top page, and she read, "KRMG Great Raft Race." Puzzled, she looked up. Greg must have spoken to Kendra and volunteered the mentors to help with the hearing dogs raft. With that formality out of the way, she could ask him to skipper the crew.

Feeling the warmth of a sense of community, she directed her words at those seated in the room. "What are you wonderful people going to do now, as if I can't guess?"

"I'll tell you what we're going to do," Greg said. "We're going to enter that raft race."

"Yes . . ." she said, smiling.

"And we're going to win!"

More applause, loudest and enthusiastic, filled the room. Robyn joined in, delighted so many would be helping her with the hearing dogs team. "Oh, Greg, that's wonderful. I couldn't have asked—"

"And," he went on, silencing the applause with his hands, "we'd like to have the kids help us build our raft in your father's workshop, if he doesn't mind."

Our raft? Robyn puzzled over his choice of words. "Our raft?" she repeated.

He nodded. "And we'd like you to be in charge of the organization."

Now she was confused. Kendra had already asked her to be in charge. "I'm afraid I don't understand."

"Robyn, please say yes. If we win this race, we'll have enough money to open our school."

To open our school? No! She stood, spilling her iced tea onto the coffee table. "I—I can't do that. I don't want you to think I don't appreciate you, but . . . but . . ."

"But what, Robyn" Greg looked at her strangely, obviously confused by her behavior.

She lifted her chin. She had no reason to be ashamed of what she was doing. Somehow she would find a way to repay Greg's mentors for helping her father, but she would not give up her right to compete for that million dollars for Kendra's hearing dogs. "I'm afraid I've already agreed to head up another team."

"Another team?" Greg said. "What other team?"

"That's what I was trying to tell you in the kitchen," she said. "Kendra's is going after that prize pot so she can expand her training facilities for hearing dogs. I'm sorry I can't help you, but I'm already committed."

SOMEHOW ROBYN made it through one more matter of business. Then, while Greg was tied up in conversation, she politely excused herself to go home. Her head ached, she had a knot at the base of her neck, and her stomach felt like curdled milk.

Her foot hadn't hit the first step on Greg's porch when his hand snagged her arm. "Robyn," he said, "we need to talk."

She shook her head, not wanting to argue with him again. "I'm sorry about the way things have turned out," she said. "I'll find a way to pay you back for what you're doing to help Dad. I promise I will. But you have to understand I've got to help Kendra."

"I had no idea you were planning to enter that race."

"I probably would have said something about it this morning after I cleared it with Kendra—if you were still around."

"I wish for once we weren't at odds with each other."

"Well, it appears we are." She turned to leave again.

"What do I have to do to get you to stay?" he said. "This, maybe?" He halted her with a hand on each shoulder and massaged her knotted-up muscles.

Closing her eyes, she gave in to the massaging motion, to the pull he had on her, then felt him draw her against his chest.

"Ah, Robyn, what am I going to do with you?"

Turning, she saw the hard set of his jaw, the hurt flashing in his eyes. She leaned into his chest, into contours made for her cheek. "I hope your friends in there understand why I had to say no."

He tilted her chin until she looked into his eyes. "I'm sure they do."

"And how about you?" she asked.

"Part of me wanted to work with you on the race so we could spend time together. But another part of me kept saying I was a fool."

"What a strange thing to say," she said, feeling more than a little insulted.

"What I mean is I want to be with you. I think about you at night. I think about you when I'm at the office. I can't wait to hold you like this."

He urged her closer, and letting her emotions take over, she complied. She felt her insides tingle, felt him, aroused, pressing into her abdomen. "Would you be surprised if I told you I feel that way, too?"

"But you know as well as I do," he said, "that almost every time we get together we wind up arguing about something. I get the feeling we really don't think the same. That we don't share the same dreams.''

''Maybe we'll just have to settle for being friends,'' she said, hurting as she said the words.

''If you think we can manage that, you're a bigger fool than I am.''

She started to slip from his arms, but he pulled her tight against him.

''I've been smelling that damned honeysuckle perfume of yours ever since you got here. Do you have any idea how that drives a man wild?''

He sifted his fingers through her hair and cradled her head in a hand that was insistent and trembling. ''I may make you mad by what I'm going to say, but I can't help it. You've got to know how it is with me. I want you next to me. I lie awake at night and think about you sleeping next door, and it drives me crazy.''

Robyn opened her mouth to speak, but he dipped his head, taking her words into his mouth.

When their lips touched, he groaned, drawing her even tighter against him. Robyn gave in to his kiss, gave in to it and deepened it. She closed her eyes to the night and her mind to the forces that pulled at them, feeling only at that moment the need to want and be wanted.

Afterwards Greg pressed his forehead to hers and grinned. ''God, woman, you make me feel alive. I haven't felt this way in months. Too damned many months.''

Hearing a voice at the door, she pushed away from him. ''I—I've got to go.''

He reached for her hand. ''Robyn, please, stay. You wanted to talk to me—remember?''

''It doesn't matter anymore,'' she said softly. ''I'll have to find someone else for the job.''

SEEKING THE SOLACE of home, she left Greg standing on his porch. She felt like a truck had driven over her, at least twice. She dragged her feet up the front steps to her house, opened the door and stepped into the living room.

She could have chopped the atmosphere with an ice pick. Lillian sat on one side of the room in an overstuffed armchair, her feet curled beneath her, filing her fingernails. On the opposite side of the room, her father sat in his favorite chair, a hunter green recliner, his arms plastered to the upholstery. Robyn shivered at the icy stare he was leveling at Lillian.

Robyn touched his arm and he jumped, unaware she had entered the house.

"Dad, what's going on here?" she signed. She turned to Lillian. "What did you argue about this time?"

Lillian uncurled her feet, stood and tucked the fingernail file into her pocket. "Nothing. Your father's just being stubborn again, that's all."

"Stubborn?"

"Yes." She looked down her nose at Jonathan and headed for the door. "What did Greg say about the raft race?"

"He can't do it," Robyn said dejectedly.

"Why not?"

Robyn heaved a deep sigh. "Before I had a chance to ask Greg to be on the hearing dogs team, he announced at his meeting that they're competing in the race."

"The mentors?"

"Yes. They're going to have the kids help them build the raft. They wanted me to be their Girl Friday."

"No!"

"I was so embarrassed I could have cried." She told Lillian about the mentors' generous offer to complete her father's furniture contracts and how she had volunteered to help them.

"That's too bad," Lillian said. "I was hoping you two could work together on this thing. Think how much fun it would be spending the weekend with him come Labor Day."

The thought of spending a long weekend in Greg's arms made Robyn's pulse race. "We'll be there, all right, but we'll be competing against each other."

"That just makes for more fireworks on our little block. You should have seen your father tonight. He was madder than a hornet."

"Over what this time?"

"I'll let him tell you about it." She smoothed the errant strands of her auburn beehive into place. "With your plans, somebody's got to push that man. Tell your father I'll see him Monday at one, and tell him not to be late."

After Lillian left, Robyn settled herself onto the arm of the couch, wanting only to go to her room and think about Greg's kiss. But she had to deal with her father.

"Do you want to tell me what that was all about?" she signed, the pace of her gestures indicating her fatigue and irritation.

Her father clammed up, curling his left hand into a fist.

"Okay, Dad," she said wearily. "It can wait. I've had a rough evening, anyway. We'll talk about it over breakfast." She leaned over, kissed his forehead, then retired to her bedroom. For once her father's problems took a back seat to her own.

THE NEXT MORNING over breakfast Robyn learned that Lillian had arranged to have the hospital social worker call on her father during the party.

That sneak, Robyn thought. *She knew I'd be next door at Greg's.* The social worker had told Jonathan about a clinic where he could go for an updated analysis of his communication difficulties. She said the clinic taught something called Visual Phonics that she thought might help him learn to speak.

Her father had reacted to Lillian's plan with his stubborn streak, which sometimes was merely a cover for his fear of failure. But before he could let the social worker know that he wanted no part of any analysis and that he didn't want to learn to talk, Lillian had outmaneuvered him. She had promised the social worker she would deliver Jonathan to the clinic Monday, and to therapy sessions. Then Lillian had whisked the woman from the house.

"Dad," Robyn said, offering him another biscuit, "would it hurt to give it a try? Things have changed a lot since you were nineteen."

"I don't need help!" Jonathan replied, his cigarlike fingers spelling out the words in jerky movements. He pushed away the plate of biscuits and slammed back in his chair.

That was all Robyn could take. She stood, snatched his plate and went to the sink. Through the window she looked at Greg's house. While the hot water washed the margarine from the plate, she debated whether or not to tell her father that she desperately needed him to go to that clinic.

No, she thought. *He has to go because he wants to do it for himself. It won't work if he only does it for me.* Slowly she turned, wiping her hands on a towel.

Jonathan was staring at her, the hint of stubbornness still clouding his gaze. "Dad," she signed, "it's just possible that for the first time Lillian might be right."

SEEKING HIS OWN DOMAIN, Jonathan stomped off to his workshop, flipped on the light and slammed the door shut behind him. Here he was the boss. No man, woman or child was going to tell him what to do in his workshop.

What was it with Robyn these days? Ever since his accident she had needled him almost as much as Lillian. Try this. Consider that. He thought she understood how he felt about therapy and trying to speak.

His gaze drifted out the window. He saw Greg, alone on his front porch. He was leaning against a porch post, his fists stuck in his pockets, his broad mouth set in a grim line.

Nobody seemed happy these days.

Jonathan followed the direction of Greg's gaze to the window in the kitchen, where Robyn was slamming pots and pans around in her fit of anger. He looked at Greg and studied him for a moment. He might not be able to hear people speak, but he was good at reading the emotions on their faces. There was a longing in Greg's gaze.

Maybe that was it! Robyn and Greg must have fought over something last night. When she had returned from the party, she was already upset. A lovers' quarrel? The thought of them being lovers shook him. Robyn hadn't known Greg long enough to be intimate with him in the biblical sense. From what he'd seen, though, his new neighbor would make a fine match for his daughter. And Greg was interested in her.

He couldn't deny that his daughter needed a man to love. He'd watched her during the past eighteen months. She'd unselfishly cared for Carol Ann, then handled the funeral arrangements. After that, she'd been there when he needed her, which was constantly.

He was lucky he had such a loving daughter. He hoped someday she would have a little girl who would love her with the same fierce devotion. He studied her as, unsmiling, she worked in the kitchen. Fatigue was written on her lovely face. If she planned to have children, she needed to get started soon. She was already thirty-one, with no husband in sight.

He studied Greg closely and again noted the yearning in the young man's face as he gazed at Robyn.

Well, well, he thought, rubbing the morning's growth on his chin. Maybe there was hope for Robyn yet.

But what was wrong between her and Greg? His own dependence on Robyn, maybe? That thought shook him to the toes of his leather work boots. No daughter of his was going to miss out on a fine man like Greg because of her father's stubbornness.

Robyn's emotions had been running high lately. She was interested in Greg, all right. Was it possible she was in love with him already? He smiled, remembering how he and Carol Ann had fallen instantly in love that day he'd pulled her from the river. He'd loved her so much he'd been afraid she'd leave him there in the woods to suffer his life without her.

Frowning over the problem that could be keeping them apart, he wondered if Greg might have a move in mind for the future. If so, he could want Robyn to go with him, and that would explain the tension between them now. Robyn couldn't go if she felt obligated to take care of a dependent father.

The bloody hell she couldn't! He'd show the both of them, no matter how hard it was for him, no matter what embarrassments he had to suffer. He'd go to that appointment Lillian had set up for him Monday. And he'd design the best darned raft those two kids had ever seen. They'd win that raft race, he'd get his dog and he'd set his daughter free.

The thought of losing her squeezed at his heart. He was scared of living alone, even if he wouldn't admit his fears

to anyone. But a man couldn't hold on to his daughter forever, not if he truly loved her.

He thought of the children in the neighborhood who
dropped by to brighten his day. If he ever hoped to have his
own grandchildren, he had to learn to make do for himself.

CHAPTER SEVEN

WHEN JONATHAN AGREED to go with Lillian to the speech and hearing specialist on Monday without complaining, Robyn was convinced he had slipped in the shower and knocked himself silly.

Not questioning a kind rendering by the fates, she hurried home after work, anxious to learn what the doctor had told him at his session.

She found him in his workshop, perched on a high stool at his drafting table, the sunlight slanting through the window before him onto sketches of rafts. Scattered around his work surface were entry forms, raft specifications and an enveloped addressed to him from the Tulsa radio station organizing the race.

He looked up from his sketches, gave her a peck on the cheek, then resumed his work.

Moving to stand with her back to the window, she tapped his arm until she had his attention. "Dad, what did the doctor say?" she signed.

He tossed his pencil on the drawing board and scowled at her. "She wants me to wear hearing aids. Seven-hundred-and-fifty-dollar hearing aids."

He signed with his left hand, the one he had injured as a child, his gestures slow, crude, deliberate—but for the most part understandable. Amazing what a person could do when he wanted to, she thought with relief. "You have the money in savings," she reminded him.

"That's where it'll stay. No piece of plastic will ever make me hear."

She regarded the defiant tilt of his chin with silent resentment. He was handicapped more by his stubbornness than he was by his deafness. She was tempted to sic Lillian on him, but he was her father, and she would deal with him. "Maybe there's a new kind of hearing aid. You'll give them a try, won't you?"

He deepened his scowl, puffing out his chest as he used to do when her mother wanted him to wear a suit and tie to church. Then his gaze slid over her shoulder to the window, and the irritation faded from his features.

Following the direction of his eyes, Robyn saw Greg in his driveway, unloading groceries from his van. As she watched the muscles play over his back and shoulders, she felt the familiar quickening in her abdomen. Torn by the different paths they were pursuing, she considered not asking him to the party she was planning. But that would be rude. He was, after all, her neighbor. She couldn't ignore him. Nor did she want to, she admitted. Reluctantly she tore her gaze away from him.

Her dad was watching her, the hint of a smile on his lips. "Greg's home early," she said, fluttering her hand over her shoulder self-consciously.

His smile broadened. "So I see."

"I need to talk to him. I'm planning a backyard party for the Fourth of July. You don't mind, do you?"

He slid his unbroken hand over her shoulder and gave her a fatherly squeeze. His brown eyes twinkled his silent approval as he leaned over and kissed her forehead.

THERE HADN'T BEEN A PARTY at the Woodson house since Robyn could remember. She took her father's willingness to invite Greg, Lillian, Joe and his wife, Audrey, for an evening cookout as another sign that he was adjusting to the loss of her mother.

Visions of Washington drifted through her mind while she decorated the backyard for the party. Washington was beautiful in September after the summer crowds of tourists had thinned—a perfect time to introduce her father to the big city. Maybe Lillian would watch the house for him during the months he'd spend there waiting for his dog. Not too many months, she hoped.

Jonathan steadied the stepladder while she stretched high to string twisted red, white and blue crepe paper from the peach tree to the pine to the oak. Tiny U.S. flags she had strung from the house to her father's workshop fluttered in the light breeze, adding another festive touch. She wheeled the double-size charcoal grill from the garage, spread quilts on the lush grass and filled a tub with soft drinks and a plump Rush Springs watermelon.

Vibrant ribbons of rose and cerise streaked the evening sky as she met Greg at the front door in her flag-blue shorts and red tube top. Determined to keep the mood between them light and playful, she opened the door, rose to her toes and kissed him as she would a good friend. "Hi, handsome."

Carrying a hand-crank ice-cream maker, he took one look at her, then set the wooden tub on the porch with a thud. "You look delicious."

"Thanks." Without meaning to, she let her gaze drift to the soft swirls of golden hair that peeked through the neck opening of his navy shirt. "You don't look so bad yourself, fella."

He reached for her hand, then spun her slowly as if they were dancing. "You look like the holiday sherbet I saw in the store." He fixed his hands at her waist, and a muscle twitched in his jaw. "With scoops in all the right places."

His blue eyes warmed to a heated glow as his gaze dipped from her lips to the bare skin above her breasts.

She boxed him in the chest, spun on her heel and flung over her shoulder, "Didn't your mother ever tell you dinner before dessert, my dear man? Dinner before dessert!"

BY DARK the six adults—and four neighborhood children who had sniffed out the party and invited themselves for the fun—had polished off several pounds of southern-style ribs, a bucket of fresh corn on the cob and a big pot of Robyn's baked beans.

"I think I'm going to explode," Greg complained, lying spread-eagled on his back beneath the trees.

"Any man who eats three helpings has no right to complain," Robyn teased him.

Groaning, he rolled over and propped his chin on his fist. Robyn sat across from him on a quilt, her back against a tree, her legs stretched out before her, crossed at the ankles. Very shapely ankles, he noted. Her tube top had submitted to the laws of gravity and shifted low enough so that a hint of creamy-white skin showed below her tan line. As he stared at her, twin beads poked at the knit fabric covering her breasts.

"I ate my dinner like a good boy," he said. "Now can I have dessert?"

Robyn perpetuated that coy attitude she'd greeted him with when he'd arrived, an attitude meant to keep him at a distance, no doubt. "Exactly what did you have in mind?"

"Well…" he said, clearing his throat. "You mean I have to tell you?"

Lillian plunked a bowl heaped with ice cream and her blueberry-strawberry swirl cake into his hands. "Better keep your beady eyes off that ice cream. The way you're looking, you'd melt it in two seconds flat." She winked at

Robyn, handed her a bowl with smaller portions and joined Joe and Audrey on a blanket under the pine tree.

Greg chuckled under his breath and sat up to eat his dessert. His gaze drifted to Jonathan, who sat on the back porch, lighting fireworks for the children one-handedly with a slow-burning punk. Greg found the same liquid warmth in Jonathan's brown eyes that was so appealing in Robyn's. He wouldn't mind having a child with her coloring. Wouldn't mind at all.

"You and your father are sure a lot alike," he said. He shoved Lillian's goopy cake around in his bowl to get at the ice cream. "You're definitely your father's daughter."

Robyn's smile, which had lingered from Lillian's teasing, faded. "Why do you say that?"

"Your eyes, for one thing."

"My mother had brown eyes, too."

"Ah, but you and your father both have the devil in your eyes, and—" he reached over and ran his finger along the smooth curve of her chin "—this is the same, too."

She set her bowl on the quilt and poked at its contents with her spoon. "Most people say I take after my mother."

"Could be. Still, you favor your dad in more ways than one."

Robyn glanced at Jonathan, who was scooping seconds of ice cream into the children's bowls. "I suppose I'm like him...in some ways." Then, as if a bee had bitten her behind, she popped up, stacked their dishes and disappeared into the house without another word.

He was still puzzling over her strange behavior when the first burst of fireworks glittered in the night sky over nearby Eldon Lyon Park. When she walked by, he grabbed her hand and pulled her down beside him on the quilt.

He no longer fooled himself that he could ignore the feelings growing between them. He knew he was asking for trouble, but he pulled her against his chest, and looped his arms casually over her shoulders. Her chin rested on his forearm, his hand on the curves of her bare shoulders. "How about dinner and a movie tomorrow night?"

She rubbed her cheek, her *very soft* cheek, against his forearm and turned to smile up at him, the coyness gone. Thank goodness he didn't have to put up with that act any longer.

"You're asking me to dinner?"

"If you'd rather, we could go to a baseball game." *Or maybe to bed.*

"There's a concert at the zoo amphitheater Friday night," she suggested, still acting surprised he was asking her out.

"But that's two days away." *And two nights.*

She smiled. "We both have to work—remember?"

"Oh, yeah, work." Today he had gone in to the plant to check out a machinery problem and wound up spending half the day there. This wasn't what he'd had in mind when he bought the plant. The operation was a fairly simple one, an intermediate step in the recycling process. Once he had the plant rolling, he figured he'd have a halfway normal schedule. And more time to spend with Robyn—time he couldn't afford to waste, considering her plans. Last night he'd finally decided he would try to persuade her to stay in Oklahoma.

He buried his nose in her hair and sniffed her perfume, then struggled to stem the tide of his masculine urges. Even though his hormones were flowing, he wanted them to know each other as people before they became lovers. Still, at times like this, when she was near to him, smelling sweet and feeling incredibly soft, he had trouble keeping his hands to himself. A lot of trouble.

A loud boom reverberated overhead, making the children shriek with joy. Robyn laughed, causing a gentle swaying of her breasts. Oh, boy!

"I'm glad those rascals stayed," she said.

"Yeah, kids do make a holiday special."

"Depends on the kids. Some of them can be a royal pain."

"I'd love to have two, maybe three someday," he said. "A boy and a girl, anyway. How about you?"

Her shoulders tensed immediately. "Oh, I think I'll pass."

"You mean you don't want kids?"

"Nope."

"Not ever?" He turned her to face him, sure she was joking. He'd watched her playing with the kids tonight. He could tell she was at ease with them. One five-year-old girl had followed her around with adoring eyes and been rewarded with Robyn's gentle touch and teasing manner. It suddenly occurred to him that maybe Robyn couldn't have children. He'd dated a woman once who couldn't, and it was a source of constant sadness for her. Was that how it was for Robyn?

The way he was beginning to feel about her, he decided he'd better resolve the question now. Having children was too important to him to ignore her answer. "Do you mean you don't want to have children—or you can't, Robyn?"

"I don't want to."

A barely perceptible hitch in her voice hinted at some unspoken problem. "Why not?"

She regarded him with a half smile, then looked away. "I told you about my job."

Her job again! "What does your job have to do with it?"

"I travel—lots."

"But there are ways—nannies, nurseries—"

"I'm sorry. I just don't believe in shuffling kids off to nurseries."

"I can't believe you're serious," he said.

"Why?" she shot back. "Because you want kids so much?"

"Maybe. And other reasons." Bits and pieces of conversation fit together like a puzzle in his mind. He wondered if there was more to Robyn's not wanting children than she knew herself. Perhaps something to do with her father. Before he could draw any conclusions, though, he needed more pieces of the puzzle.

After giving her irritation time to ebb, he drew her loosely into his arms, with her head nestled beneath his chin. When he felt her relax, he posed another question. "Was anyone else in your father's family deaf?"

She pulled away and looked at him indignantly. "Did anyone ever tell you your timing's lousy?"

"Well," he persisted, "was anyone?"

"If you must know, yes, Dad's mother—my grandmother."

"Did you know her well?"

"No. She died when Dad was a young boy."

A volley of explosions caused them to cover their ears, and the air seemed to vibrate around them. In the flashes of light, Greg studied Robyn's face and had a gut feeling that what they were talking about made her uneasy. Still, he needed more information. "Anyone else?"

"What is this?" she asked resentfully. "The Spanish Inquisition?"

"I'm just curious. Was anyone?"

She glanced away. She had been doing a good bit of that tonight. "My father's aunt—his mother's sister—and their mother and I think a couple of other relatives way back."

"So, your father's deafness is definitely genetic."

"Yes," she snapped. "Exactly what are you trying to get at?"

"If you had children, would they be deaf?" he asked boldly.

She folded her arms. "Maybe. Maybe not. What difference does it make? I'm not going to have children."

"Well, just supposing you were. What would the chances be?"

"Fifty percent. One in two. Most likely."

"Who told you that?"

"A doctor."

"A genetic counselor?"

"No, my father's doctor."

"Someday you ought to see a geneticist," he said, his hunch growing stronger "You might be able to get a more definitive answer."

WHY WAS IT MEN ALWAYS pressed the issue of having children? Robyn wondered as she shoved the leftovers into the refrigerator.

Biting back her disappointment, she accepted the fact that she couldn't pretend anymore that things might work out with Greg. He wanted children too much to waste his time with someone who didn't. Another Phillip...in a way. At least Phillip had had the nerve to be direct with her about his feelings.

Better she find out now about Greg's priorities while she could still handle the hurt of his rejection. But already she knew that wouldn't be easy. She cared too much for him to brush off what they had shared as something casual and easy to forget.

She needed to get a strong grasp on the future. Get organized. Prepare her father to live in Washington for a few months. *Prepare herself for the heartaches.* There was no time like the present.

She pulled her father in from the front porch, sat him down on the sofa and began with an account of her boss's phone call, which had come a few weeks ago. She told him she needed to be in Washington by late September and that she wanted him to go with her and stay until he could get his hearing dog. Then, feeling like a teenager who had just confessed to wrecking the family car, she waited for his reaction.

The cuckoo clock on the dining room wall heralded the new day with twelve calls while her father stared at her, his eyes brimming with tears.

Reaching for his hand, she said, "Dad, I—"

He shook his head vigorously and brushed away her hand, then rose from the couch. Snatching his folder of raft sketches from the dining room table, he headed for the back door.

The hurt in his expression, the hurt she had put there, tore at Robyn's heart. She didn't know whether to go after him or to leave him alone, so she followed her heart. She found him in his workshop, leaning over his scarred wooden bench.

She touched his shoulder, wanting to console him, to make him understand that she didn't love him any less because she wanted to make a life of her own. He refused to look at her. He stared out the window over his workbench as if she had already left him.

Finally he turned to her, pride and pain and love, too, all mixed up in eyes the same warm brown as her own.

"I won't be gone forever," she signed. "I'll come home every three or four months.... Wait until you see Washington. It's wooded, and the flowers are beautiful and—"

"Stop it!" he signed in an abrupt gesture with his left hand. "I won't go, and that's final. I'm not leaving this house."

"Dad, be reasonable," she said, determined not to let his stubbornness affect her. "I can't leave you here alone."

"I'll be fine."

"No, I won't hear of it. You'll have to come with me. We'll fly back when your dog is ready. The two of you can fly up to see me whenever you like. I'll send you tickets and—"

"I can't fly, and you know it!" he said defensively, and she sensed his insecurities, his fears.

"Of course you can," she assured him. "Lots of deaf people do. And arrangements can be made to have a flight attendant on board who knows sign language."

With a rough finger he traced the curve of her cheek. "Washington's too big. I don't want to go there. I don't want you to live there." He pointed a stiff, insistent finger at the floor. "You belong here, in Bethany."

"I'm not a little girl anymore, Dad. I'm a woman, and Washington is where I choose to live."

"You're just upset. You haven't been yourself lately. Probably because of that young man." He lifted his chin and glanced out the window, in obvious reference to Greg.

Greg's probing questions about having children still stung her heart. "He's been part of it."

"Do you care about him? The way a woman cares about a man?"

This time it was she who glanced out the window. She saw the light in Greg's bedroom window flick off, and she felt the fire of longing deep in her abdomen. "Yes, Dad," she signed, looking at him. "I'm afraid I care about him."

Hope kindled like embers in his eyes. "A lot? A little?"

She gave her answer in slow, fluid movements like those of a hula dancer. "I care for him a lot."

He smiled, brushing away the tendrils of hair from her forehead. "Do you love him, Robyn?"

"I—I don't know," she signed haltingly. "It's awfully soon. We haven't known each other that long."

"I think you know," he told her. "I think you already love that young man, as I loved your mother. If you won't stay for me, stay for him and what you two might have together."

She thought of her father's logic and wished things were that simple. "To tell you the truth, I might stay for him, if he asked me, if we had known each other longer and knew that what we felt was love. But he won't ask me to stay."

Through the window Robyn saw a skyrocket ignite in the night, dusting the darkness with glittering crimson and gold stars.

"Why wouldn't he ask? You're a beautiful young lady. You're intelligent." He grinned teasingly. "You can cook."

She hesitated before she continued, not knowing how her father would take her admission. "He wants something else, Dad. Something I can't give him."

"What?"

"Children."

Jonathan's eyes widened in surprise, then teared, breaking her heart. "I didn't know you couldn't have children."

"It's not that I can't have kids." She paused, uncertain if she could tell him the rest. "I just don't want to."

"Don't want to?" He gave her a puzzled look and shook his head as if he were regarding an impulsive child. "Why not? You're wonderful with the kids around here. You told me how much you enjoyed taking care of your friends' children in Washington."

She held his work-roughened hand between her smaller ones, needing to touch him before answering him, hoping that by doing so he might understand what she had to say. "Don't you see, Dad? I loved my job. I loved every single day. Even when I had to work until midnight and get up at six the next morning to go into the office, I jumped out of bed with a smile on my face."

"You could work and have children. Lots of women do."

"Not with my kind of job. I've told you how much I travel. Sometimes I'm gone a week at a time, sometimes two. My last year in D.C. I was gone more than I was home."

He yanked his tall frame to attention. "Home is not Washington. Home is here, in Bethany."

"Oh, Dad." She ran her fingers lovingly over the dried, cracked skin between his knuckles. "This will always be my home. My real home. But I have to make a life of my own. Someday you'll be with Mother, and I'll have to have something for myself."

"You'd be happier with a man."

"Maybe I would, and I'm not telling you that I won't get married...someday, if I find the right man."

"Greg's a good man," he persisted.

But I won't measure up to his expectations, she wanted to say. She tempered her thoughts for her father. "But he isn't the right man for me. He desperately wants children. He was married once and lost his wife and baby in childbirth. He deserves a woman who wants the same things out of life. I'm just not that woman."

Her father's left arm, with which he had been signing with difficulty, hung limply at his side. When he finally raised it to sign, his movements were slow, speaking powerfully of his feelings. "Then I'll never have grandchildren, will I?"

"I'm sorry I won't ever give you grandchildren, Dad."
She choked on her next words. "But I'll always give you my
love."

His brown eyes shimmered with fresh tears. He drew her
to him and caressed her hair with his hand. A huge, burning knot formed in her throat. While a whole package of
firecrackers ignited somewhere outside in a brisk, popping
chain, she leaned into her father's chest. Her heart ached
with love for him. When the time finally came to say
goodbye, would she be able to say the words?

She glanced through the window at the silhouette of the
house next door. Would she be able to say the words to
Greg?

THE NEXT DAY Robyn arose before dawn, awoke her father for an early breakfast and left for Meals for the Heart.
A few minutes later, Mr. Gilliam, driving with his hearing
dog on duty in the back set, dropped off his sister.

Robyn gave Mrs. Gilliam a tour of the modest facilities
and a list of the day's menus. After checking in the food
deliveries, she introduced Mrs. Gilliam to the three cooks
and two delivery boys. Appearing confident and capable,
Mrs. Gilliam shooed Robyn from the kitchen. That gave
Robyn until four in the afternoon to work at Kendra's kennel.

Thirty minutes later, Robyn settled into a windowless
cubbyhole of an office Kendra had converted from a broom
closet. Her thoughts drifted to her father and their tears of
the night before. First she had hurt him with the news of her
leaving, then with the knowledge that she would never
provide him with the grandchildren he wanted.

She thought of Greg's probing questions and tried to
imagine herself with children of her own. She had enjoyed
caring for her friends' little angels. Oh, there had been a

couple of devils in the pack, but she'd managed to divert their destructive energy into something fun and acceptable by adult standards.

She warmed to the memories. Yes, she could be a good mother. A shiver darted up her spine. But she wouldn't have children. She chose to exercise her right not to follow the traditional path of wife and mother.

She wondered what kind of woman Greg would marry. The thought of him marrying someone else was more than a little disturbing. She didn't want to think of someone else in his arms...someone making love to him...bearing his children.

"Luck," she said out loud. "Why aren't I lucky enough to care for a man who doesn't want children?"

Those thoughts disturbed her throughout the day and accompanied her to bed. While her father thrashed in the room next to her, she flopped onto one side, then the other, repeatedly turning her pillow over for the cool side in an effort to relax and drift off to sleep.

The last time she glanced at the fluorescent alarm clock by her bed, the little hand was on the two. When it seemed she had been asleep for only a few precious minutes, she heard a pounding noise resounding in her head. Reasoning, in her groggy state, that she had a whopper of a headache, she fumbled for the aspirin in her nightstand.

A sharp rap at her window shot fear through her like lightning. Moving slowly, her heart slamming around wildly in her chest, she reached for the telephone.

Before she could call the police, a voice, a very familiar voice, called to her through the partially open window. "Ro-byn. Robyn. Are you in there?"

She jerked open the white eyelet curtains. "Greg? What are you doing here?" She glanced at the clock. "At three o'clock in the morning?"

"Can you come to the door?" he asked. "It's important."

"Sure. Give me a minute."

She grabbed a light robe and stumbled down the hall, through the living room and to the front door. When she opened it, she found Greg pacing the porch, his sun-streaked blond hair appealingly disheveled. Dressed in a maroon cotton jogging suit, he jiggled his keys in his pocket as he paced.

"Something wrong?"

"Plenty. How soon can you get dressed?"

She ran her hand through her hair. "Two minutes. Why the rush?"

"Do you remember during the meeting at my house you said you'd find a way to repay us for helping Jonathan?"

Robyn groaned. "Yes.... But right now?"

He nodded and started for the porch stairs. "Get dressed and meet me at the van. Leave a note for your dad and tell him we're going to the police station."

"Why the police station?"

"Tell him we're going to help a...a friend."

"Okay. But what can I do to help? I'm not a lawyer."

"This...friend doesn't need a lawyer. He needs someone who can speak Spanish, I think."

Robyn sighed. "Then I suppose you've got the right person. I'll be out in two minutes."

She scribbled the note to her father and attached it to the refrigerator door with a magnet before darting to her bedroom to dress. She threw on slacks and a cotton sweater, pulled a comb through her hair and grabbed her tennis shoes before running out the door. She hopped into the passenger seat next to Greg and looked to him for an explanation.

He leaned over, gave her a quick kiss on the lips, shoved his car into reverse and gunned out of the driveway. "Thanks. I won't forget this."

"Why are we going to the police station?"

"I got a call from Wanda Richley."

"*She's* in jail?"

"No, but two of her students are."

"Good grief! What did they do?"

"I don't have the whole story, but they went to a party at some kid's house, and there weren't any parents at home."

"Ah, and someone called the police, I'll bet."

"Apparently the boys raised quite a ruckus. Beer. Loud music. Broken windows."

"Where were the parents?"

"Some rich kid's parents left him alone for three days while they flew to Dallas. Now I ask you, what kind of parents would leave a sixteen-year-old alone that long?"

"I suppose some kids are mature enough to handle it," she allowed.

"Well, this one wasn't."

"What does my speaking Spanish have to do with this?"

"The second boy immigrated from Mexico six months ago. His parents recently disappeared on a trip home to visit relatives. Something about a hurricane. He's living temporarily with his family's immigration sponsors until they find his mom and dad. The sponsors apparently have had it up to here—" he sliced a horizontal line beneath his chin with his forefinger "—with this kid getting into trouble."

"I see," Robyn said. "So the boys called Wanda. Nice. It isn't enough she works for half what she deserves. She's got to be responsible for the kids when their parents aren't around, too."

"Someone has to be. I remember getting into trouble once when I was a kid. If it hadn't been for Mom and Dad, I would have cooled my heels in the juvenile detention center for the weekend."

"Seems to me that might be good for these two boys. Teach them a lesson."

"You can't be serious! Do you have any idea what can happen in a place like that?"

"Well, no," she admitted. "I guess I've led a rather sheltered life."

"Take it from me. You wouldn't want any kid of yours in that place. Oh, sorry. I guess you won't ever have to worry about that, will you?"

Robyn chose to ignore that comment and the note of sarcasm in his voice. "Since Wanda called you, I take it these are kids in the gifted program."

He whipped around a corner and glanced in the rear-view mirror. "Yes, I'm afraid they are."

"Somehow I can't picture that kind of kid getting into trouble with the police."

"They're not saints, Robyn. They're gifted. Besides, sometimes these kids get so sick of being put up on pedestals they rebel against the pressures people put on them. And sometimes they get in trouble just to make the other kids think they're cool."

"Some kind of cool." She grabbed the dashboard as he squealed around another corner. "Be careful or you'll wind up in jail yourself."

"I've got to get there before something happens to those kids. They're in a holding cell with God knows what kind of people."

Robyn studied his profile in the glow of the street lamps that whizzed by. She listened while he continued.

"These kids are damned vulnerable, and they expect too much of themselves. When they don't live up to their own expectations and those of their families and teachers, they feel like they've failed. Many of them need help." He looked away, and his voice dropped. "Brad needed help, and I . . . we . . . didn't know to give it to him."

And, Robyn guessed, Greg probably blamed himself for not recognizing his brother's need. "How long has it been since you talked to anyone about Brad?"

"A long time. Since Mom and Dad moved to California."

"Is that why they moved? To get away from the memories?"

He nodded. They were ten minutes from the police station, moving from stoplight to stoplight on Classen Boulevard. The streets were deserted, except for an occasional car or a cat on the prowl.

"What did you do . . . afterward? How did you deal with it?"

"At the time I was an environmental engineer for Spectre Oil. I tried to go about my routine, but I couldn't concentrate. So I quit my job."

"Then what?"

"I wandered around the country for a couple of months. I needed time to think. Time to make sense of what had happened. Brad was three when I lost my wife and little Christopher. Brad filled a void in my life. As the years went on, we got closer and closer." He made a valiant attempt to smile but the corners of his mouth slanted upward for only a moment. "That's what made it so difficult, the way he did it.'

Robyn sat quietly, figuring he would tell her more when he was ready.

"My first car was a 1965 Corvette, red and white," he went on. "I was saving it for Brad in Mom and Dad's garage until he turned sixteen. They came home one evening from a dance at the country club and found him slumped over the steering wheel. He'd stuffed rags up the exhaust pipe."

Robyn reached for Greg's hand. "You can't blame yourself. Your brother had a choice. He just made the wrong one."

"I know," he said. "But I can't help trying to stop some other kid from making that same choice."

CHAPTER EIGHT

ROBYN AND GREG walked into the Oklahoma City police
station and asked for the officer on duty. When they told
him the purpose of their visit, he checked his records and
led them down a hallway and into a small office containing a metal desk, a telephone and two wooden armchairs.
A stubbed out, stale cigarette in an ashtray gave the room
a putrid odor. Fluorescent tubes that needed replacing
flickered overhead as Robyn and Greg waited for news of
the two boys who had phoned Wanda Richley.

After a fifteen-minute wait, a young police officer met
with them. He explained that Lyndon Joiner and Manuel
Garcia had been picked up on complaints of disturbing the
peace. Because there were no parents available who would
accept responsibility for them, the patrolmen had brought
them down and put them in a holding cell.

"Good of you to haul your...selves out of bed in the
middle of the night to help those boys," the young officer
said.

"Glad to do it." Greg showed momentary amusement at
the officer's near slip of the tongue. "What are you going
to do with them?"

"Scare them, for one thing. Make them think they're in
big trouble."

"Aren't they?"

"The one boy's parents are as much at fault as the boys.
These damned parents who won't take the time to be there

for their kids make me want to puke. Oh, sorry, miss. Excuse the language.''

"That's okay." She said the words to the officer, but she focused her eyes on Greg's. The policeman was only underscoring a point she had tried to make with Greg about herself. She didn't have the time to be a good mother to a child. Maybe now Greg could understand what she'd been trying to tell him.

"But sooner or later," the officer went on, "these kids have to learn to make the right choices."

Robyn studied Greg's face, wondering if he was thinking of the fatal choice his brother had made.

"We're trying to reach family members. Aunts. Uncles. Anyone," the officer continued. "We don't like to keep kids overnight for disturbing the peace. If we don't make some arrangements soon, though, we'll have to take them to the juvenile detention center. We'd rather not do that. Throws them in with real troublemakers. I don't think these boys are bad, just unsupervised and maybe a little rebellious."

"What can we do to help?" Greg asked.

"We'd like you to talk to them. Mrs. Richley said you're working with her boys on a volunteer project for the gifted program these boys are in."

"That's right. Actually *we* are," he said, reaching for Robyn's hand.

"Good. Maybe they'll listen to you."

"What should we say?"

"Get them to tell you what happened tonight. Maybe help them to see they could have made better and wiser decisions. Tell them they'll have to speak to a juvenile counselor early next week—and maybe a judge. That will keep them out of the holding cell for a while. We'll let you know when we reach the families."

"I speak Spanish," Robyn said. "What if I talk with the Garcia boy, and Greg can visit with the other one?"

"Good idea." The officer turned to Greg. "Why don't you step into the office next door? I'll bring the Joiner kid to you there. And don't worry. While the other boy talks with Miss Woodson, I'll stick around to make sure he doesn't cause her any trouble."

TWENTY MINUTES HAD PASSED since Greg left, time enough for Robyn to cope with her frustration, get nervous, calm down and convince herself that she was ready for anything.

She reminded herself she was about to counsel a scared boy in a strange country who'd probably made the wrong friends. If she handled the conversation well, she might be able to make a difference in his life.

Hearing footsteps in the hallway, she stood, faced the door and prayed she'd have the wisdom to counsel the boy.

The door swung open, and a dark-haired youth, his head sagging between slumped shoulders, stumbled into the room ahead of the police officer. The boy appeared to be suffering from one too many. He reeked of beer, and she suspected he might get sick all over the room.

She was so disgusted she felt like leaving him to suffer the consequences of his actions. But beneath the boy's exterior she sensed panic, and she reminded herself of her obligation to Greg.

"Buenas noches, Manuel. Me llamo Señorita Woodson. Tu puedes sentar aquí," she said, gesturing with an open palm to one chair while she sat in the other.

The boy snapped his head up, his bloodshot eyes wide with surprise.

Manuel's face jumped from her memory. "Dear Lord," she cried, "it's you!"

Robyn's heart sank, and she thought she heard it shatter in pieces on the tile floor.

The officer moved to her side as Manuel sank into a chair. "Is there something wrong, Miss Woodson?"

"N-no. I'm fine. Really."

The youth eyed her suspiciously, narrowing his bleary-eyed gaze. She was sure he remembered her from the accident.

If he could think straight, he was probably wondering what she planned to do now that she had the power to cause real trouble for him. She was grateful her father hadn't come with them to the station and wouldn't have to look into the face of the boy sitting before her, the boy who had caused his nightmares.

"I really am here to help you," she told him, this time in English. *But step out of line and I'll leave so quick your head will spin.* "I speak Spanish, so if you prefer—"

"It doesn't matter." He glanced away, but not before Robyn saw the flash of fear in his eyes.

"A teacher in your school—Wanda Richley—phoned Mr. Michaels," she said. "He asked me to come with him to help you and your friend."

When he didn't respond, she decided to follow the officer's instructions. "Why don't you tell me what happened tonight? I understand there was a party. A party without parents."

The boy belched loudly, then dissolved into a fit of hiccups.

Robyn stood and glared down her nose at him. "I guess I'll be going, Officer. I can't help this young man until he sobers up."

The officer took the boy by the arm, yanked him from his seat and reached for the doorknob. "Dumb move, kid."

The boy shrank from the officer. "My friend Lyndon will help me. He's here somewhere. With his uncle."

"Your friend, the blond kid, *was* next door with his uncle. He spoke with Mr. Michaels for a few minutes, then left." The officer gave the boy a none-too-gentle shove through the open doorway.

Perspiration beaded on the boy's forehead and on the skin above his upper lip. "He—he what?"

"You're on your own, pal. You can sober up and be nice to the lady, or you can go back to that holding cell. What's it going to be?"

"I—I'm sorry. That is—"

Seeing the panic in the boy's eyes, Robyn took him firmly by the arm. "Why don't you sit down, and we'll talk."

He seemed to weigh his options, then inclined his head at the door. "Can we talk—without him?"

The policeman shot her a warning glance, but Robyn ignored it. "Leave us alone for a few minutes, will you?"

The officer obliged, pulling the door shut behind him.

Manuel slumped into a chair. "Thanks, Miss Woodson."

His show of manners worked for him. "Why don't you call me Robyn?" she found herself saying.

"Why are you so nice to me? You know I was the one who ran into your father."

"Yes, and I haven't forgotten it," she said. "I'm sorry to say my father hasn't, either. Let's just say I have a friend I owe a favor."

Manuel leaned forward, bracing his elbows on his knees. He wore blue jeans that had seen better days, a black T-shirt emblazoned with the insignia of a popular rock group and tennis shoes. "Mr. Ortega is going to kill me."

"Is he your immigration sponsor?"

"Yes."

"How did you get yourself in this mess?"

He shook his head and buried his head in his hands. "If I tell you, will you tell him?" He frowned in the direction of the door, indicating, she thought, the policeman outside.

"You can trust me."

Manuel told her how Lyndon, knowing his parents would be gone on a long weekend to Dallas, had invited friends over for a party. A beer party. Things got out of hand, Manuel said, and before they knew it, someone had set off tear gas and tossed the canister out the window. With the help of a light breeze, the tear gas had the neighbors clawing at their eyes in a matter of seconds.

"Tear gas? Where did you get tear gas?"

"Lyndon's father. He was in the army. I knew I shouldn't have gone to that party."

"Then why did you go?"

"You wouldn't understand."

"I'll try."

"Mr. Ortega has been trying to get rid of me since I ran into your father. I can't do anything right. And his kids— *¡Dios mio!*—they drive me crazy, all ten of them. No, I take that back, Consuelo is nice. Nine of them drive me crazy. But Lyndon is my friend. He understands me."

Robyn braced her hips against the desk and crossed her arms at the waist, letting Manuel ramble on about the party, about his parents and about some boy named Jake. She guessed Jake was the real troublemaker in the bunch and a person Manuel and Lyndon desperately wanted to befriend.

"Do you feel better now that you've gotten in trouble?" she asked, remembering what Greg had told her. "Will all this make you Jake's friend?"

Manuel's black eyes flashed with resentment.

There was a sharp rap at the door, and Greg entered. He took Robyn's place in front of the desk, and she sat in the other chair, thankful Greg was in charge.

"You have two choices, Manuel," Greg began. "You can stay in the detention center for the night until the authorities decide what to do with you, or—"

"Or what?" Manuel asked. His eyes reflected the expression of a frightened animal.

"Or you can go home with me," Greg said.

Robyn stared at Greg incredulously. "He can do what?"

"I've agreed to sign for Manuel and let him stay with me until we can find his parents or a foster home. He'll have to promise he'll be on good behavior. Go to school. Stay out of trouble."

"You'd do that for me?" Manuel said, moving to his feet. "You would take me to your house?"

Greg pulled his keys from his pocket. "Yep, and if you'll open the door for Miss Woodson, we'll go right now."

"Just like that?"

"It's my guess you could use a friend right now. I'd like to be that friend." He turned to Robyn, his eyes glazed with hope. "In fact, we'd both like to be your friend, wouldn't we, Robyn?"

STANDING AT THE SINK in her kitchen several hours later, Robyn sliced a chef's knife through a juicy, plump tomato for her father's lunch and squinted. Outside the window the sunlight of a hundred-degree day glared off the driveway and made her eyes water.

With the trip to the police station last night and her father's relentless nightmares about his accident, she hadn't had a decent hour's sleep. All morning her body had ached, her eyes had burned, and she couldn't get her limbs to respond to the messages from her tired brain.

She paused, lifted one shoulder to press against her eye and debated how she could explain to her father that the source of his nightmares would be living next door. She heard a car door slam, and her eyes flew open. Bending sideways at the waist, she glanced down the driveway.

Good grief! They were here already— Manuel and Greg. Manuel was lugging a battered suitcase up the front steps to Greg's house with both hands. Greg was right behind him, balancing a grocery sack in one hand and a cardboard box piled high with junk in the other.

She quickly yanked the café curtains shut and turned her back to the window. She couldn't delay telling her father about Manuel staying next door any longer.

Jonathan sat at the table, hunched over his raft drawings. He was frowning as he concentrated on drawing with his left hand. Tonight he and the volunteers Robyn had found were to meet in the workshop to organize.

She resented Greg's insensitivity to her father's feelings. Apparently he hadn't considered how Jonathan would react to Manuel living next door. And Greg expected her to befriend that ingrate who had made her father's life miserable.

Last night Manuel hadn't even thanked Greg for crawling out of bed in the middle of the night to go to the police station to help him. Even worse, when Manuel had realized who she was, he hadn't had the good sense to apologize for what he had done to her father.

Robyn eased a generous helping of chicken salad onto her father's plate, garnished it with tomato slices and took the chair across from him at the table. He shoved his drawings aside and poked at the salad with his fork.

"Dad," she said, touching his hand for his attention. "I have something to tell you."

"You're not eating?" he signed.

"I'm not hungry."

"You're getting skinny." He put down his fork, reached across the table and gave her chin an affectionate pinch. "You didn't sleep well last night, did you?"

"No."

"Then you've got to eat, or you'll get sick. Go." He jerked his head in the direction of the tile countertop. "Fix yourself a plate. I'll wait for you."

"NO FRIENDS IN THE HOUSE unless I'm here. You'll walk straight home from school every day and stay here until I get home from work, unless you make arrangements with me in advance. Is that clear?"

Manuel nodded and waited for Mr. Michaels to continue.

"Once a week you'll mow and trim the law. And no—I repeat—absolutely no alcohol. Is that clear?"

Seated at the kitchen table, Manuel shoved his uneaten hamburger aside and nodded again. With so many rules, he wondered if he would have been smarter to go to the juvenile detention center. His memories of the dirty Mexican jail where his uncle had died dashed that thought from his head.

On the window ledge outside, the thermometer hovered at 105 degrees in the shade. He had walked the two miles from school to Mr. Michaels's house in that heat. Then they had driven to the Ortegas' to pick up his belongings. Perspiration clung to his hair and made his scalp itch, and his T-shirt was plastered to his skin. His stomach felt queasy, his head throbbed, and he smelled so bad he couldn't stand himself. If he never had another beer, it would be too soon. He wanted a hot shower, a cold drink and his parents. How he wanted his parents!

"Why don't you shower," Mr. Michaels said. "End of the hall to your right."

Manuel shoved back his chair and stood. "Where do I put my things?"

"In your room, the blue one across from the bathroom."

"My room?" He had not had a room of his own since he left his village in Mexico. At the Ortegas' he had shared a tiny room with the three youngest boys. There had been no space in the closet, and the boys had constantly rummaged through his things.

"If you take care of it, that will be your room. You can put anything you like on the walls, as long as it wouldn't offend a ninety-year-old grandmother."

Mr. Michaels went to the window that faced the driveway and peered out at the house next door that Manuel had learned was Robyn's.

"You'd better decide how you plan to apologize to Robyn's father," Mr. Michaels said.

Apologize? How could he find the words to make up for what he had done? "But, Mr. Michaels—"

"When you call me Mr. Michaels you make me feel like an old man. Call me Greg, will you?"

"Yes, sir, but I need time. I don't know what to say to Mr. Woodson."

"Something will come to you. And the sooner you do it, the easier it'll be. I think they're eating lunch. While you shower, I'll give them a call. We'll go over after you're through. Oh, and before you see Mr. Woodson, you should know that he has a broken arm. He broke it when you ran into him with Lyndon's car."

Manuel hung his head. Why had he listened to Lyndon?

"He also scratched up his hands and bruised his hip. Because of his broken arm, he can't sign well, so it's hard for him to communicate with people."

Manuel slumped against the wall. "I didn't mean to hurt him. A broken arm!"

"Mr. Woodson may have quite a hospital bill from that accident. I think you ought to offer to pay that bill."

"But I don't have any money."

"You could get a job."

"You know how hard it is for a boy like me to get a job! I'm only sixteen."

"I'll see what I can do to help you find something. What kind of a job would you like?"

Manuel thought of the gardens he would have tended in the summer in his village. Backbreaking labor in the hot sun, but work he knew how to do. "I don't know what I like. Things are so different here."

Greg smiled reassuringly. "Leave that to me. Now, go. Take that shower. I'll make the call to Robyn."

ROBYN SPEARED a cucumber slice, brought the fork to her lips and heard the phone ring. She swiveled in her chair and went to the phone on the desk her father had built into one corner of the kitchen. "Hello."

"Robyn?"

Hearing Greg's voice, she felt an odd mixture of pleasure and trepidation. "Oh, it's you." She turned her back on her father to make sure he couldn't read her lips.

"Do you have a couple of minutes?" he asked her.

"Actually, Dad and I were just finishing lunch."

"Manuel and I'd like to run over for a minute."

Robyn gripped the phone tightly in her hand. "You can't come over here, not with *him*. Don't you remember what I told you about Dad's nightmares?"

"Manuel wants to apologize to your father, Robyn."

"It's too soon. I haven't had time to tell him Manuel's going to be living next door. I'm afraid if he sees him, he'll get awfully upset."

"The boy made mistakes. He wants to make up for them. Won't you give him a chance?"

"He can't erase what he did with a simple 'I'm sorry.' Dad still wakes up in a cold sweat with that boy's face in his mind."

"Tell you what. Manuel and I'll drop over in a few minutes, and we'll explain everything. Then Manuel can apologize. Besides, I need to talk to you about a few things, too."

"You want to talk to me? I'll be right over." She slammed down the receiver. Why couldn't Greg see what he was doing to her father?

BEFORE GREG COULD WASH his hands, Robyn was ringing his doorbell. He hoped she could overcome her resentment of Manuel and cooperate with Greg to help the boy.

As Greg opened the front door, he heard Manuel turn off the shower. "Hi," he said, letting his eyes roam appreciatively over Robyn's body. "Come on in, and let's talk."

"I'm in a hurry. I have to be at the kennel in forty-five minutes."

"It won't take long."

Her gaze darted around the room. "Where is he?"

"In the shower."

"How...is he?"

Greg grinned. "Not too good, I'm afraid. He has one hell of a hangover. I made him get up at seven and go to school. He walked home after that."

"In this heat?"

"The idea is for him not to forget what it's like the morning after."

"You are a sly one, aren't you!"

"Sometimes you have to be with these kids."

"What was it you wanted to see me about?" she asked.

"Can you sit down?" He took a corner cushion of the couch and patted the one next to him.

"Well, just for a minute."

"Good." As she sat beside him, he looped an arm over the back of the couch. When he leaned into the upholstery, he slid his hand beneath her hair and gave her neck an affectionate squeeze. "You look tired, Robyn."

"So do you."

"I stayed up most of the night talking with Manuel." He took her hand and ran his thumb over the soft skin on the backs of her fingers. "He told me more about his parents. The Ortegas can't find them. I was wondering...do you know anyone in Mexico who could help?"

"I might."

"Would you make a few calls and see what you could find out? Hire an investigator if you have to. I'll pay for everything. Manuel's parents are Ramón and Carmen Garcia, and they were visiting relatives in a little village near the Mexican border." He took a pad from the end table and jotted down a few notes. He tore off the top sheet and handed it to her.

Robyn glanced at his notes and frowned. "I'll see what I can do. But no promises. I see Manuel hasn't heard from his parents in quite a while. That isn't good."

"I know. But he has to have some answers. He can deal with the truth better than he can deal with not knowing. I'm worried about him, Robyn."

"Hello, Robyn."

Greg watched Robyn's expression harden as she turned to the freshly showered boy.

"Hello, Manuel."

Greg knew he was expecting a lot from her, considering what Manuel had done to her father. But she was an adult, and Manuel was only a confused, lonely boy. Surely, once she got to know him, she would see he deserved her friendship.

She stood and glanced at her watch. "I really must be going."

Already on his feet, Greg detained her with a hand on her arm. "I need to ask another little favor before you go."

She paused. "What's the favor?"

"Manuel needs a job."

"What do you want me to do?" she asked, taking the bait.

"I was hoping you could help him find one."

"You're not serious!"

He smiled at Manuel. "This young man has some financial obligations, and he wants to meet them himself."

He watched her shift her gaze to Manuel and hoped the sight of the freshly scrubbed youth would weaken her resolve.

"I'll see if I can find something," she said. She looked at Greg and nailed him with an expression that warned him to ask no more favors.

"Thanks. I knew we could count on you."

She gave him a dubious look, then opened the door.

"Oh, and by the way," he said, "I'm sorry, but under the circumstances I guess we'll have to postpone our date for tonight. I'll need a few days to get Manuel squared away before we can go out."

She shrugged. "I guessed as much."

"But we'll pick you and Jonathan up at seven next Saturday morning."

"What for?"

"I have a boat at the plant. I thought we'd go fishing."

"I don't really think Dad will be ready to—"

"Of course he will," he cut her off. "I know he likes to fish. Lillian told me about that little lake in southeastern Oklahoma Jonathan used to take you to." He chuckled. "She also told me the fish love you."

"Maybe later in the summer."

"No, we have to go next weekend. After that, both of us will be tied up with getting ready for the race. Lillian said you plan to start building your raft tonight. Our group meets this weekend for the first time. I want to do this before . . . well, before you leave for Washington."

"Washington."

She said the word as if she hadn't thought about it for some time. But he knew better. She was determined to get back to that job. He wondered what he could say or do to make her change her mind.

"You'll talk to Jonathan?" he asked her.

"I'll try. But until I do, please, keep Manuel away from our house."

"Okay. Let us know when Manuel can come over and apologize to Jonathan. We'll all have a wonderful time next weekend. You'll see."

CHAPTER NINE

FIVE BLACK LINES, like so many spider legs, dipped into Lake Hefner from fishing rods extended over the side of Greg's twenty-foot boat. Robyn and Jonathan sat on one side of the restored teak hull in deck chairs, their feet braced against the side. To block the midmorning sun, they had pulled their hats low over their faces. Greg, Manuel and Lillian, as quiet and sullen as Robyn and her father, fished on the other side of the gleaming white inboard.

While sailboats fluttered across the lake like ladies' silk scarves, the five weekend fishermen rocked at anchor in a quiet cove. The cove was edged with reeds, scrub oak and willow trees, and its water gently lapped at the hull. Overhead, gulls drifted lazily on air currents, calling encouragement to Greg and his party.

Robyn reeled in her line, dipped into the bait bucket and closed her palm around another slippery minnow. As she baited her hook, she felt the sun warm her skin, if not her spirits. She dropped her line in the water, leaned back in her chair and snuck a sideways peek at her father.

He sat beside her, his forehead knitted into a scowl, his left hand clutching his fishing rod. His ball-shaped float rocked gently on the water like the four others. No one had had a decent bite all day. The awkward silence that had settled over them in the morning was beginning to grate on her, and on the others, as well.

The problem was Manuel—or Manuel and her father, to be precise. If only Jonathan had given the boy a chance to apologize earlier in the week. Manuel had tried. He had showed up at their door after summer school one day.

His nervousness had worked against him. Unable to look her father in the eye, Manuel had mumbled words of apology, not realizing Jonathan couldn't make out what he was saying.

She had watched her father's frustration grow until he turned his back on Manuel and left the room. No amount of persuading on her part could convince him to change his mind. Manuel probably thought her father was curt because he still resented him. The truth was she had seen her father act that way before—embarrassed because he couldn't communicate with a stranger.

As if the difficulties between those two weren't enough to darken the day, just before they'd left for the lake, Lillian had scurried across the front lawn. Clutching a yellow plastic food container and a box of homemade gumdrops, she had hinted for an invitation. Too much the gentleman to ignore her, Greg had asked her to come along. Jonathan had been sulking ever since.

What had happened to the friendship she thought was developing between Lillian and her father?

Lillian, to shield her fair skin from the July sun, wore a floppy-brimmed hat atop her beehive. Secured under her neck with a chartreuse polka-dot bow, the hat matched a cover-up that billowed like a painter's smock.

Robyn moved her chair to sit beside Lillian. "I thought you and Dad made your peace."

A flicker of hurt shadowed Lillian's hazel eyes. "Well, you thought wrong."

"Did you argue again?"

"Nope."

"Then why the silent treatment? A person could skate on the ice between you."

Lillian feigned indifference. "Beats me." She handed Robyn her fishing pole and dug around in her cavernous bag until she found a bottle of sunscreen.

"Have you been taking Dad to his therapy sessions?"

"Yes, but I'm not sure they're doing much good. It came as no surprise to me, I'll tell you, when the therapist said your father isn't cooperating worth a hoot."

"Why isn't he?"

"Beats me. Ask your father. Maybe he'll talk to you about it."

That was just what Robyn needed. More bad news. Maybe her father couldn't learn to speak, but he would never know unless he tried. Even though he would have a hearing dog when he lived alone, she would feel better if he could speak.

While she mulled over her conversation with Lillian, her father reeled in his line, then braced his rod between his cast and his thigh. He reached for the box containing Lillian's homemade gumdrops. Aha! He was weakening.

Apparently Lillian thought so, too. She scrambled expectantly to his side. "Here, let me help you with that." She popped open the lid and beamed at him. "Tell me how you like them," she signed. "I'm on a diet."

Jonathan plucked one of the sticky mounds from the box. Using his thumbnail, he sliced it in half. He reached for his fishhook and baited his line with the orange glob.

"Well, I never!" Lillian exclaimed. "I didn't stay up half the night making candy so you could stick it on some stupid fishhooks."

Jonathan shrugged and plopped his baited hook into the water. Almost instantly, his float ducked beneath the water's surface, and he sat up with a start.

"Whooee, look at that!" Greg yelled. "Give me one of those things."

While Jonathan hauled in a flopping perch no bigger than his hand, the others baited their hooks with gumdrops and plunked them in the water. Lines flew, fish flopped, and all signs of restraint dissolved. The five plucked perch from the cove so quickly they didn't have time to thread them on stringers. Instead they tossed the fish into the bottom of the boat, where they flopped around everyone's feet.

Manuel reeled in his line and moved to kneel by Jonathan's side. "You fish," he said, pointing to Jonathan and mocking a casting motion. "And I'll take them off the hook."

Jonathan gave a quick nod and hauled in another perch. They worked as a team, Jonathan catching, Manuel unhooking, until Lillian's candy disappeared.

Once the floats ceased to bob, the five counted their catch and compared tallies. Together Jonathan and Manuel had caught thirty-five perch, half the total take.

"Looks like it's fish for dinner," Greg said. "These little fellows make good eating."

"If you clean those disgusting creatures, I'll cook them," Lillian said, wrinkling her nose.

Jonathan turned his back on her, elbowed Manuel, then poked his finger deep into his mouth as if to throw up. The two shook in silent laughter.

Normally Robyn would have scolded her father for his rudeness, but she was so delighted to see the banter between him and Manuel that she ignored the gesture.

Lillian, however, gave the two a contemptuous look. "Guess Jonathan's cooking dinner."

AFTER A BOUNCY RIDE across the lake to cool off, Greg idled the boat into the cove, close to where he'd parked the van. At four in the afternoon, the sun still beat down on them mercilessly. Manuel vaulted over the side, waded to a nearby willow tree and secured the boat to the trunk with a sturdy rope. He took the minnow bucket filled with perch from Jonathan's hand, then helped Lillian and Jonathan from the boat.

Robyn watched the smiles Manuel and her father exchanged. She admitted there was something special about the boy and hoped he would be pleased with the summer job she had found for him.

While the men cleaned the fish, she decided to freshen up. Her white denim shorts, stained by the lake water and smelling fishy, had to come off. She pushed the clinging, wet fabric over her hips and spread the shorts over a bush to dry. She was adjusting the leg line of her lavender swimsuit when she felt someone watching her.

Glancing around, she spotted Greg kneeling by the shore, rinsing his hands in the water. He held her gaze for a long, studied moment, then reached into the minnow bucket for another fish to clean.

Robyn did some looking of her own. His chest, tanned a dark bronze tone, glistened with a sheen of perspiration. He dipped his hand in the lake and splashed water over his chest. For a fleeting moment she closed her eyes and remembered how he had looked in his towel the morning of his party. How natural it had felt that night on his porch to lean into his chest, to feel him aroused and pressing into her abdomen.

"Robyn?"

"Hmm?" She opened her eyes and found him standing before her.

"You look a little flushed. Are you okay?"

Now she was the one with a fine mist of perspiration over her chest. She dipped her fingers lightly into her cleavage and smoothed away the moistness that had beaded there on coconut-scented suntan oil. "I'm fine." She squinted at the sun. "It . . . must be the heat."

He pressed the back of his hand to her forehead. "You're hot. Are you sure you didn't get too much sun?"

"I'm sure." She felt like plunging into the water, but she was sure if she did the lake would rise to a rolling boil. "I could use a cold drink."

"A cold drink. Sure." He paused. "You don't mind if I get out of these wet shorts first, do you?"

Without waiting for her answer, he thumbed open the button on the low-riding denim, unzipped the fly and shoved the soaked fabric over his tightly muscled hips. Robyn couldn't help staring at the narrow expanse of sea-green nylon that clung to his loins.

She heard what sounded like a faked cough and glanced up. Lillian was standing behind him, her chest filled with air and two fingers to her pursed lips. If Lillian whistled at Greg now, Robyn would deck her.

Apparently oblivious to their attentions, Greg turned and headed for the van.

Smiling mischievously, Lillian fluttered her fingers as he passed her, then joined Robyn as they watched him walk away. "My word, would you look at those buns."

"He doesn't look bad in his jeans, either."

"So, you've noticed. Good. I was beginning to worry about you, girl."

"Oh, I've noticed. But he's been acting strange lately— pushing me away."

Lillian elbowed her. "I saw you two on the Fourth of July. He wasn't pushing you away then."

"Things have changed since then, I'm afraid."

"Do you know why?"

"I think I know. He found out I don't want to have kids. He wants them. I'm leaving in a couple of months. He doesn't approve. And now his thoughts are filled with helping Manuel. Greg had to cancel our date for last weekend, and he hasn't asked me out again."

"Hmm. That's a peck of reasons. Still, I wouldn't give up on Greg. I've seen the way he looks at you."

Robyn posed the question that had been on her mind lately. "Do you ever regret not having children?"

Lillian shifted her gaze to the lake and waiting a long moment before answering. "I wanted a little girl in the worst way. But—maybe your mother told you—Rob couldn't have kids. Course, we didn't know that when we got married."

"Would you have married him if you'd known?"

"Of course." Lillian leaned over and whispered, "The man made my blood run hot." She straightened herself and added, "Besides, I loved him."

"Did you ever think of adopting?"

"Rob didn't want to. Said he was afraid of what we'd get. His older brother adopted a little boy, then found out he'd inherited some blood disorder from his mama."

Robyn focused instantly on her father, old fears colliding with new ones in her mind.

"I wouldn't have cared, though. I was willing to take my chances. It sure would be nice to have a daughter. The days get lonely. Maybe that's why I bug your father—for something to do." She chuckled. "That and to get his goat."

Lillian twined her arm around Robyn's and patted her hand. "You might give this business of having children another thought, dear."

JONATHAN AND MANUEL wandered off somewhere together. Lillian set out to pick wildflowers. That left Greg alone with Robyn, a predicament he had hoped to avoid.

She lay on her back on a quilt in the afternoon sun, her oiled, willowy body absorbing the rays. He couldn't keep his eyes off her, and he had to busy his hands, thinking as he was about sliding them over her slickened body. He knotted his fists and prayed for restraint.

He never should have invited her on the outing. All day he'd had to ignore the images of things he wanted to do with her . . . for her . . . beside her.

He swore under his breath. Why couldn't he accept the fact that with Robyn there could be no future, only another goodbye he could ill afford to endure?

She stirred slightly, and her dark hair spilled across one cheek, the golden highlights captured by the sun. She was a beautiful woman. Although she appeared to be asleep, her lips pouty, her long, dark lashes resting peacefully against her face, she beckoned him like a seductress. A seductress who would make him want her before she left him. The thought was a sobering one.

She lifted her head, rolled lazily to her side and propped her head on her palm. "Where is everyone?"

"Oh, here and there." His eyes feasted on one breast that threatened to spill from its lavender cup.

She patted the quilt beside her. "Why don't you come over here and sit down? You haven't done anything but work since we got out of that boat."

If he sat there, he'd run his fingers over her satiny skin. "The sun'll set soon. Better build the fire."

She scrambled off the blanket. "I'll help," she said. "Where do you want it?"

He stifled the answer that sprang to his mind and answered instead, "Right there's okay." He turned and braced himself on the bow of the boat. If he had an ounce of sense, he'd put his cutoffs on.

ROBYN HEARD A TWIG SNAP and opened her eyes expectantly. "Oh, hi, Manuel." Trying to hide her disappointment that it wasn't Greg, she sat up on the quilt and smiled into eyes darker, bigger than her own.

"Hello, Robyn."

Where had Greg gone, anyway? After she'd helped him build the fire, he had made some feeble excuse to put distance between them again. "What can I do for you?"

"You want a soda?"

"No, thanks. I just had one."

"Can I talk to you for a minute?"

"Sure. Sit down."

Manuel chose a spot on the far corner of the quilt. "Have you heard anything about my mother and father?"

"No, but I'm working on it. When I hear something, I'll let you know."

"Greg told me you're moving away. Is that true?"

She hesitated before answering, mixed emotions clouding her thinking. "Yes, in about two months."

"I wish you wouldn't go. I'm worried about your father."

Robyn groaned. Now Manuel was laying a guilt trip on her. "I'm thirty-one years old, Manuel. I can't live at home forever."

"But your father needs you."

"My father can learn to live by himself. Lots of deaf people do." Still, she remembered what Lillian had told her earlier that day, about Jonathan's lack of progress with the therapist. Was she only kidding herself that he would be safe without her, with only the dog?

"Is it hard to learn signing?" Manuel asked.

"It's like learning a new language. How long have you studied English?"

"A long time. There was a priest from California who moved to our village. I used to practice my English with him."

"You have a superb command of the language. I'd be willing to bet you'd pick up American Sign Language fairly quickly. I'll be happy to teach you. Would you like that?"

Manuel looked across the clearing to where her father sat dozing beneath a tree, his fishing hat pulled over his face. "Your father is a nice man. I'd like to learn to talk to him."

"Just tell me when you're ready to start lessons. There's also an excellent videotape you can rent to get the general idea."

Manuel shuffled his bare feet in the dirt and feigned a smile. "I need to tell him something tonight. Could you do it for me, Robyn?"

"What is it you need to tell him? Maybe I can teach you to say it yourself."

When Manuel told her his message, Robyn's opinion of him went up several notches. For the next thirty minutes she worked with him, teaching him basic sign language sentence structure and the signs he needed to know. She was amazed how quickly he grasped the concepts. She was also overwhelmed by the boy's sensitivity. He would definitely be an asset at the kennel—if he agreed to the job she had found for him.

"Are you serious about wanting a job?" she asked him.

"I sure am."

Manuel was well developed for sixteen, certainly capable of a good day's work if he applied himself. "Are you willing to work hard? Do you mind getting your hands dirty?"

"I don't mind hard work. In my village in Mexico I worked in the gardens when I was not in school."

"Have you ever worked with animals?"

His eyes lighted up. "No, but I have always wanted to do this."

Robyn liked the eagerness in his expression. "Have you ever had a dog?"

"Yes, but I had to leave her in Mexico."

"I guess Greg told you I work mornings at a kennel."

He nodded. "Someday I would like to visit you there."

"How's Monday sound?"

The boy's face broke into a broad grin. "All right!"

"Kendra, the kennel owner, is looking for help. The work isn't glamorous." She hesitated, wondering just how bad Manuel wanted a job. "You'd be cleaning out kennels and helping dip dogs when they check in for boarding."

Manuel frowned. "Dip dogs? What does this mean?"

Robyn explained about flea baths while Manuel rubbed his hands up and down his thighs, his eyes dancing with enthusiasm.

"I could start tomorrow after church. I could work until dark. I've finished my homework already."

Robyn laughed. "Monday after school's soon enough. Besides, tomorrow I'll be busy with my father. We have a crew coming over to help build our raft."

Manuel snapped his fingers. "I almost forgot. Greg told me we have a meeting tomorrow, also."

"We?"

Manuel grinned. "Greg said if I stay out of trouble and bring up my grades, I can be on his team for the raft race."

"So, you're going to be on his team." She wondered how many other team members Greg had recruited and how her crew would compare against his. Manuel could probably give her the answers. She thought about pumping him for information, but personal ethics won out over curiosity and envy. "I guess that means you'll be going to Tulsa."

"I can hardly wait. I'll do my share of the work building the raft, of course. We have already designed it."

With great effort, Robyn tamped down the loose ends of her curiosity, but two short questions wriggled free. "What's your raft like? Is it big?"

Manuel looked at her guardedly. "Robyn, I don't think I should—"

"I don't want a detailed description, just, well, I'm curious, that's all."

"I don't suppose Greg would mind if I told you that—"

"If you told her what, Manuel?"

Robyn whipped around and felt her cheeks burn. "Oh, nothing. Manuel and I were just passing the time. I told him about the job I found him."

"I'll be working at the kennel," Manuel said excitedly.

Greg sat beside her, hardly suppressing a grin. "You were grilling him about our raft, weren't you?"

"Of course not! I merely asked—"

"You merely asked what it looked like. Admit it. You were engaging in a bit of espionage."

Robyn scrambled to her feet. "My father and I don't need to stoop to spying. We're going to win that race, no matter what kind of raft you have."

"Did it ever occur to you that someone else might win?"

Every time that thought crept into her mind, she swept it away with positive thoughts. They had to win that raft race or her father wouldn't get his hearing dog soon enough. She could never persuade him to stay in Washington with her for three years.

"We'll win. Dad's had lots of experience at this sort of thing." she glanced around. "Where did he get to, anyway?"

NIGHTFALL BROUGHT a welcome breeze off the lake, stirring the trees over Manuel's head. The leaves rustled like the skirts of a dancing *señorita* on Cinco de Mayo.

Slouched against a tree trunk, his eyes almost closed, he peered through the slits at Greg and Robyn. Sitting stiffly at arm's distance from each other by the camp fire, they were trying their best to ignore each other.

He didn't know why they couldn't forget their stupid differences and admit they cared for each other before it was too late. Robyn would be leaving in a couple of months. They might not have another chance.

He scratched his back against the rough bark of the tree and stared through the branches at the half moon. He wondered if his mother and father, wherever they were, could see the same moon. If they came back safely, he would never again let a day pass without telling them he loved them. He wouldn't take the risk Greg and Robyn were taking by hiding their feelings from each other.

He shifted his attention to Mr. Woodson, who sat before the fire, ignoring Mrs. Chatwell. He had a lot to make up to that man. Now that he had a job that paid, he would be able to give Mr. Woodson the money for his hospital bill. He would also find a way to make up for running into him with Lyndon's car.

Mr. Woodson signed something to his daughter with his left hand, lumbered to his feet, then headed down a narrow dirt path in the direction of the cove's far reaches.

With a wave of his hand, Manuel signaled Greg he was going for a walk, and he set out in the dark after Mr. Woodson. After a few jogging steps, he heard the crunch of feet on twigs, then spotted a shock of graying hair. His pulse quickened, and he resisted the impulse to return to the camp fire.

No, he had to do it now. Gathering his courage, he tapped Mr. Woodson on the shoulder. With a start, Robyn's father whipped his head around. When he saw Manuel, his eyes widened in surprise.

Manuel was aware of a stinging lump in his throat. Mr. Woodson reminded him of his own grandfather. *Mi abuelo*. He had died only weeks before Manuel and his parents had loaded up what was left of their possessions and abandoned their village to go north to the States.

Tender thoughts of his grandfather swelled in his heart, thoughts of feelings he had always meant to share with him. Manuel decided he would not put off what he needed to share with Mr. Woodson.

To make sure Mr. Woodson could see his face, Manuel guided him around until the moonlight spilled over his shoulder. Pointing to his own chest with his forefinger, Manuel mouthed the word "I." Then, his shoulders bowed in the language of shame, he drew small, slow circles with his fist in the center of his chest, as Robyn had taught him to do. Lifting his head to meet Mr. Woodson's gaze, he said out loud, in case Mr. Woodson could read his lips in the moonlight, "I'm sorry."

Backlighted by the moon, Mr. Woodson stared at him for a long moment. Manuel couldn't read his expression in the dark. Still, Manuel knew he had seen the gesture of apology. He waited for a sign that Mr. Woodson could find the forgiveness in his heart he so desperately needed.

Perspiration dampened his palms, and a gentle breeze brought the scent of fish off the lake. Still, Mr. Woodson gave no indication he had been able to forgive him.

Manuel's chest ached with the weight of guilt. He slowly turned, then took several steps along the path to the camp fire.

Suddenly, a hand clamped tightly over his shoulder.

Jonathan felt the muscles in Manuel's shoulder knot beneath his hand. The boy turned. His dark eyes glistened with tears, and Jonathan's heart ached for him.

Manuel was a good boy. Jonathan had known that the moment Manuel knelt at his feet, anxious to help him bait his hook. He was ashamed for the way he had treated the boy when he came to the door earlier in the week.

He wished he could tell the boy to forget about the accident, but he knew Manuel did not know sign language. Robyn must have taught him the apology signs.

He thought of his therapy sessions and the sounds he practiced in his workshop when he was sure Robyn couldn't hear him. He was supposed to practice the sounds with Robyn or—he shuddered—with Lillian. But he couldn't. Not yet. He needed more time. He didn't want to sound stupid.

He would never forget the look of horror on his second grade teacher's face when he tried to sing with the other children in the Christmas program. She had tapped her conductor's stick briskly on the podium until everyone had stopped singing—everyone but him. He was concentrating on the rhythmic movements of the metronome. Finally she marched to the back of the room and rapped his knuckles with her stick. That's when he noticed the children around him were laughing and pointing at him.

His teacher had pinched his lips tightly together while she shushed him with a finger to her mouth. Then she had stuck him on the back row behind the Madison twins, who were a head taller than he was.

The lesson was one he would never forget: don't risk looking—or sounding—like a fool.

He gave Manuel's shoulder a roughish man's shake and smiled. The boy smiled back, his dark eyes brimming with feelings. Jonathan pulled him to his chest in a welcome,

manly embrace, feeling tiny fissures in the protective wall
he had built around his heart.

He hoped Manuel would stay at Greg's for more than a
few days. He wanted to get to know the boy. Maybe he
would teach him to use his carpenter's tools—as he had
planned to teach his grandchildren. Grandchildren he
would never have if Robyn didn't clear her head of foolish
ideas.

CHAPTER TEN

AT THE CAMP FIRE, Jonathan sat beside Manuel and roasted marshmallows. Across the flames he observed the narrowing gap between Greg and Robyn. About time.

When Greg scooted behind Robyn and looped his arms around her shoulders, Jonathan pretended not to notice the glow on her face. She caught him watching them, so he winked, then quickly glanced away. If he encouraged her too much, he might scare her away from that nice young man.

Manuel itched with the energy of youth. He pointed to the curve of the cove, where another boy was casting a fishing line. With a smile, Jonathan waved him off.

As soon as Manuel left, Lillian handed him a small bowl containing something dark, shiny and lumpy looking. He regarded it cautiously, then sniffed it. Hmm. Blackberry cobbler, his favorite. At least it smelled like blackberry cobbler.

Remembering how he had insulted Lillian's cooking earlier, he filled his spoon and said a prayer. On the first bit, he gagged on a salt lump. That confounded woman must have gotten the salt mixed up with the flour.

Lillian snatched the bowl from his hands, dumped it into the trash and stalked off into the night. When would she learn she plain couldn't cook?

Across the campfire, Robyn singed him with a look that could have melted an ice block. Now he was in for it.

She sat up straight as a two-by-four, and her hands started flying. "You can't let her run off like that!" she insisted in angry, jerky motions. "There's no telling who might be out there hiding in the bushes."

He was about to tell her the woman could defend herself with her mouth, if nothing else, when Robyn's eyes lighted up like her mother's had when she was beyond reasoning with. "All right," he told her, staying her tirade with an open palm. "I'll go find her."

EVEN THOUGH the night air carried only a hint of a chill, Robyn welcomed Greg's arms around her shoulders. They were alone by the fire, stars glittering in the night sky like so many rhinestones. The dry wood in the fire crackled and popped. The smoke smelling pleasantly of hickory wafted around the clearing.

Robyn snuggled her back to Greg's chest, crossed her arms over her breasts and murmured a sigh of pleasure as she rubbed her chin over the soft hair on his forearm.

"Alone at last," he said, the warmth of his breath tickling her neck.

"Miracle of miracles. I was beginning to think we'd never be alone."

"Because of Manuel?"

"Uh-huh."

"You didn't think I'd let him keep me away from you, did you?"

"Well, it's not easy parenting a teenager, especially a troubled one."

"He's not a bad kid. He just needed a few days to understand I have rules and I mean for them to be obeyed."

"Who would have thought he'd be so good with Dad?"

"You're good with Manuel, Robyn. You have—" he paused, as if searching for the right word "—almost a gift.

I noticed it on the Fourth of July with those little rascals. And today with Manuel, well, he's a different boy when he's around you.''

"Uh-oh. I feel a lecture coming on."

"Naw. You know your strong points. Far be it from me to point out what a wonderful mother you'd make."

"Greg, please—"

He kissed her loudly on the cheek. "I know, little miss career woman. I was just teasing. Don't get your dander up."

It was up all right—and stoking her anger. "And don't you be so patronizing with me." She pushed his arms off her shoulders and turned to glare at him.

With a firm but gentle hand on her jaw, he forced her to listen to him. "I wasn't patronizing you. You're too defensive for your own good."

"I wouldn't have to be so defensive if you'd stop badgering me. As far as I'm concerned, whether or not I choose to have children is none of your business." She slammed her balled-up fists onto her hips. "Once and for all, the subject is closed."

While her resentment boiled over, he smiled into her eyes with maddening composure. "Oh, hell, Robyn, come here, will you?" He grabbed her wrist, peeled open her fingers and kissed her palm. Eyes twinkling, he watched her reaction as he moved on to kiss her wrist.

"Stop that, will you!" She tugged but could not free her wrist from his two-handed grasp.

"Uh-uh. I've been thinking about doing this all week, and I do not intend to stop until I reach at least here." He pointed to the bend of her arm and continued kissing.

With a quick jerk she freed herself from his hold and scrambled to her feet, dodging him as he lunged for her.

"Wait until I get my hands on you!" he said, chuckling.

"You'll have to catch me first!" she taunted as she darted around the camp fire. He chased her, but she was quicker, lighter on her feet.

"What did you major in in college—dodge ball?" He grabbed for her, and she hopped as his fingers grazed her abdomen.

Her heel landed on a large rock, and she felt the ground whooshing up to meet her back. "Uh-oh...."

In a racing dive Greg cushioned her fall with his arm. Rolling over onto his back, he winced at the pain. "Oh, man, that hurt."

Rubbing what she knew would become a nasty bruise on her hip, she sat up and gently probed Greg's arm. "Oh, dear, I hope you didn't break anything."

Suddenly he grabbed her and hauled her atop him. Though she struggled, he managed to pin her arms to her sides. "Aha! Gotcha!"

"You cheated, you rat!" Laughing, she wriggled to free herself, not altogether sure she wanted to escape. Gradually she felt his hold on her loosen. At the same time she watched his smile fade and felt a telltale hardness swelling beneath her abdomen.

"Robyn, if you don't want me to hold you like this, you'd better..." He let go of her arms, letting her decide whether to stay and risk the consequences or move away to safety.

Her reaction was as natural as the night. She slid her hands up his bare torso, feeling the coarseness of the hair that swirled across his abdomen before it became softer over his chest. She felt the thundering beat of his heart and bent to kiss it. He was warm and smelled of hickory.

"Ah, Robyn, I hope you know what you're doing." With his hands on her elbows he pulled her higher until her lips were above his.

"I know what I'm doing," she whispered, then bent to show him she meant what she said. She parted her lips and whimpered into his mouth.

Greg crushed her to his chest and poured himself into a kiss that made her feel like the woman she had not been for many long, lonely months. Like the woman she might never have been.

He broke the kiss, pulled her hands from his chest and rolled her to his side. "It's been a long time, Robyn. A long time since I've . . . been with a woman. I feel like a starved pup."

She smiled, tracing the curve of his shoulder with her fingertips, loving the smooth texture of his skin. A telltale tremor squiggled across her shoulders.

A smile of understanding crossed his face. "You, too, huh?" He drew her close to his chest and kneaded the muscles on either side of her spine. "There, is that better?"

She didn't know about better. She only knew that wherever he touched her, he heightened the need building within her. She opened her mouth to tell him how exquisite his hands felt on her back. When she did, he smothered her words with his lips and dipped into the moistness of her mouth with his tongue. He tasted of blackberries—blackberries warm enough to melt ice cream. Or a woman's heart.

His hand strayed to her breast, but then he rolled onto his back, slung his wrist over his eyes and moaned, "God help me, I don't want to stop."

Supporting her weight with her palms, she leaned over and kissed the inside of his wrist. "Then why stop?"

"I'm not just talking about kisses, Robyn. I'm talking about this." He hooked an arm around her neck, pulled her into a tongue-thrashing kiss, slid his hand over her breast and thumbed her nipple until she moaned.

"I want to touch all of you, and I'm not sure I can stop," he murmured, punctuating his words with kisses. His hand explored the curve of her waist, the fullness of her hip, the silkiness of her thigh. "Do you understand? I want to crawl up inside you and surround myself with you."

Warning signals finally flashed in her head. She couldn't. Not now. She wasn't . . . prepared. And the others could return any minute. Yet, the more he pleasured her with his touch, the more she ached for the completeness only love-making could bring.

Feeling light-headed, she pushed away and sat up. "I—I guess we'd better get ready to go. Dad and Lillian should be back soon. Not to mention Manuel."

Sitting beside her, Greg raked his hair with both hands, then managed a thin smile. "I'm sorry. I almost forgot where we were." He traced her lips with his finger. "Soft. So soft. I'll bet you're soft all over."

His gaze grew hot again, wandering over the places of her body he had touched. But neither of them moved or reached out to each other again.

"Energy is obviously something neither of us is short of," he said with a knowing grin. "Do you like to dance? I know a great place that plays fifties music."

"I love to dance, but I haven't in a long time."

"Want to go Tuesday night?"

"Sure. Tuesday's fine." For what? Dancing?

One corner of his mouth twitched, and he dragged his hand across his face, revealing the emotions he'd been masking with casual talk of a date. "No, Tuesday isn't fine. It's too damned far away. I don't want to wait three days to be with you."

It was the "be with you" that churned up Robyn's insides. "How about Monday, then?"

"No, Monday's out. I have to speak to the Lions Club." He grinned devilishly. "How about later tonight?" He frowned and shook his head. "I'm sorry. Forget I said that. We'll go Tuesday." He stood and pulled her to her feet. "We'd better find something else to talk about. When I think about dancing with you, holding you close, I—"

"Joe taught me to dance when I was in junior high," she improvised, diverting Greg from dangerous territory.

"We're still talking about dancing here," he warned her. He picked up one side of the quilt while she took the other to help fold it. "Joe, you say? Why Joe?"

"Dad asked him to."

"I guess your father doesn't dance, does he? Shame. Women like that sort of thing."

"Mom tried her best to get him to learn. But he wouldn't try. Not that he refused her much. They had a strong marriage. If you believe in that business of finding your soul mate, I guess you'd say that's what happened for them. They were lucky."

"Do you think he'll ever remarry?"

"I don't know. I guess he might someday."

"Would that bother you?"

"Probably at first, but I want him to be happy. If that means remarrying, I'm all for it. I know he'll always love my mother, though."

Greg said nothing, only stood there, holding the folded blanket to his chest. She wondered if he was thinking about his wife, and she felt that maddening twinge of envy. "Was it like that with you and Chelsea?" she asked, then regretted her question. "Forget I asked that. I had no right to—"

"No," he said. "It's okay. Really. It's just that no one's ever put it to me like that."

He stared out over the lake before continuing. "For a while after Chelsea died, I felt guilty. I thought maybe, if I had loved her enough, she wouldn't have died."

"Surely you don't blame yourself for her death."

"I think deep down I feel guilty because I never loved her as much as she loved me. We dated through high school, then college and sort of drifted into marriage. There was a big wedding, we bought a house, Chelsea got pregnant, but . . ."

"But what?"

"I always felt something was missing. Maybe it was that spiritual oneness your parents had. If I ever get married again, I hope I'm as lucky as your father was."

"One thing's for sure," she reminded him, at the same time she reminded herself. "You'll have to find someone who wants children as much as you do."

"Yes," he said, "I will."

She laughed nervously. "It's a sure bet I'll never be on your prospect list."

"Why, Robyn," he said, mischief dancing in his eyes, "I didn't know you wanted to be."

Why hadn't she kept her big mouth shut? "Oh, well, I was just speaking hypothetically, and—"

"I know you won't believe me," he said, now serious, "but I'm all for women having careers. Unfortunately, though, men can't have the babies."

"Some couples never have children. They chose to adopt."

"Wait a minute here," he said. "I thought you were against having children at all, yet you're saying adopting kids is okay. How does that change things?"

"Oh, Greg," she said, squirming under his questioning. "I was just speaking hypothetically again."

"I could be wrong, but I don't think you were. I think you were implying that some couples adopt kids so neither partner has a big interruption in career. But earlier you told me you didn't want kids because you'd have to leave them in day care while you worked. What's really the issue here, Robyn? Or do you know?"

"I merely meant," she said, skirting the issue, "that for you the answer might be adoption."

"Uh-uh. No way."

"Why not?"

"It's ludicrous to stand in line to adopt when you're perfectly capable of having your own kids."

"But there are lots of kids who need good homes. Minority kids, for example."

"I won't argue that point with you, and I'm not opposed to adoption, but for me, well, it isn't the answer. I want to have my own children."

"Do you know why?" She threw the question at him.

"You want reasons?" he said, snatching the picnic basket. "I'll give you reasons. When Christopher died, I told myself, it isn't the end of the world. You're young. You can have another baby. Then Brad died, and I said, okay, Brad's gone, too. You can't do anything about that, either. But when you have that kid you want you can name him Brad, and maybe he'll be all the good things Brad was. Maybe he'll even look like Brad. Be as smart as him. This may sound crazy, and you can argue all you want, but it's the way I feel, period."

Robyn decided she could think for a month straight and not explore all the implications of Greg's disjointed answer. "Okay," she said, giving up on logic, "you have your reasons for wanting kids. I have mine for not wanting them. I'll respect your reasons if you'll respect mine.''

"But not to want kids because of a job? I keep pressing this point for a reason, Robyn. I can't help thinking someday you'll look back and wish you'd taken a few years out to have a family."

Robyn expelled a deeply drawn breath. "Why are you so determined to change my mind about having children?"

"Why, indeed!" he said. He opened the van, tossed the quilt and picnic basket inside and slid the door shut with a bang. Leaning against the door, he folded his arms. "I'll be honest. I feel more for you than I've felt for a woman in a long time. It isn't just that you make my blood race—and you do that to me. Boy, do you ever!" he said. "It's more than that. I keep wondering if there's the tiniest possibility we might have a future together. But I keep getting hung up on our differences on having children."

Whew! He had said a mouthful. The implications staggered her. But she decided to match honesty with honesty. "I'd be lying if I said I didn't care for you. But no matter how I feel about you, I will continue to be a career woman. I decided a long time ago to exercise my right not to have children. I love my work. It fulfills me. I don't need to experience motherhood to be a whole person. So, if you're looking for someone to be the mother of your children, Greg, you'd better look somewhere else."

"I guess I'd better, then, hadn't I!" He brushed past her, icing her with his stare. "Why don't you help me put out the fire," he said, kicking dirt over the embers. "As soon as the others get back, we'll load the boat onto the trailer and get out of here."

"THE INSUFFERABLE FOOL!" Lillian lashed at an imaginary Jonathan with the willow switch she had snapped from a tree. "I don't know why I try to please the man."

She had baked the blackberry cobbler from a recipe Carol Ann had given her only weeks before she died. "It's Jonathan's favorite," she recalled her friend saying as tears streamed down her thin cheeks in the hospital. "Promise me you'll make it for him from time to time."

Lillian had hugged her fragile friend and tearfully promised her the world. She would bake for Jonathan. She would watch after Robyn. She would make sure they weren't lonely. She wouldn't allow her friend's husband to become a hermit in his own house. She would see to it he learned to live again with the special zest he'd shared with Carol Ann.

So many promises she'd been unable to keep for a man impossible to please.

Tears stung her eyes as she followed the path around the cove to the lake. She knew she shouldn't allow Jonathan to get under her skin the way he did. She knew she should ignore his rude gestures and derogatory comments about her cooking. But she wanted so desperately to please him!

Dear friend, she whispered in her heart to Carol Ann, *I may just have to renege on a few of my promises. A woman's only human.*

Maybe if you didn't care so much, it wouldn't hurt when he's rude to you, a little voice said. She slammed the door on the voice and picked her way over a rock pile.

Truth was, Jonathan Woodson made her blood boil!

She stopped dead in her tracks. Weren't those the very words she'd used when she told Robyn how she had felt about Rob?

The saints preserve us! she thought woefully, casting her gaze across the lake.

The lake. She had walked an awfully long way. She couldn't see the camp fire or the boat. Robyn and the others were probably worried about her. The eerie hoot of an owl made her jump, and goose bumps crawled over her bare arms.

Now don't get all jumpy, she scolded herself, shivering in the night air. She crossed her arms and rubbed her shoulders briskly.

She turned and headed for the cove, trying to ignore the feeling that someone was lurking in the shadows that flanked the path. In a few steps she came to a fork in the path. Funny. She didn't remember that fork.

Which direction should she take? Right? She didn't think so. Left, then? She pressed her fingertips to her lips and felt an uneasiness creep over her. She could yell for Robyn and Greg, but what if some deranged person was out there looking for a victim in the night? What if—

A hand shot out of the dark and grabbed her arm from behind, and adrenaline pumped through her like quicksilver.

"Leave me alone!" she screamed. With all the power in her being, she fought off her attacker, who gripped her upper arms tightly. "I know karate. I know Tae Kwon Do. I know—oh...."

She found herself swept from her feet into the arms of a man. But not just any man. Jonathan!

"Let me down, you insufferable fool!" She pummeled his chest with her fists and squirmed against his hold. But even as she struggled, a strange, not altogether unpleasant feeling seeped into her heart. The burly body smelled pleasantly of cedar and smoke from the camp fire.

Jonathan's hold on her gradually loosened, and she slid from his arms. As her feet touched the ground, she was aware his good hand still held her arm firmly in its grasp.

For the briefest of moments she forgot about the gum-drops, she forgot about the blackberry cobbler and she forgot about her promises to Carol Ann. She looked up from her five feet nothing to a face that registered surprise.

Slowly Jonathan released her arm. With un-Jonathan-like tenderness, he signed, "Are you okay?"

In un-Lillian-like fashion, she said nothing, only nodded.

"I thought you were lost."

"Me? Never!"

With one corner of his mouth curling upward, the way he used to smile at Carol Ann, he shook a finger in her face playfully. Playfully! Was this the same Jonathan who had treated her rudely all day?

"Okay, so I was lost," she admitted.

He tapped his watch and signed that it was almost ten.

"Ten? Dear Lord! I'm sorry. I lost track of time."

He gestured down the path ahead and winked at her. Jonathan Woodson winked at her!

And then, as they walked side by side down the narrow path to the cove, Jonathan did the strangest thing. He placed his palm in the center of her back and guided her with a gentlemanly air.

My word, what had come over Jonathan?

CHAPTER ELEVEN

GREG SLAMMED DOWN the phone and cursed the supplier he'd spoken with. Swiveling in his office chair, he stared out the window into the plant parking lot at the stragglers arriving late for work. Ever since Saturday night, his nerves had been shot to hell.

Robyn didn't fool him for a minute. She might stubbornly maintain she didn't want children because of her career, but he knew the real culprit—fear of having deaf children. The problem was, he didn't think she had admitted that reason to herself.

He smiled at the irony. She'd not only inherited her father's genes for deafness, she'd also fallen heir to his maddening stubborn streak. The latter was keeping her from facing the truth about the former. If he didn't find a way to make her face up to her fears, he might damned well lose her—and she might rob herself of all the love and satisfaction having children could bring.

He thought of their date last night, the evening of dancing he'd hoped would set the stage for intimate conversation and an exploration of their feelings. She'd danced with a brittle aloofness and begged off when he'd suggested coffee at his place afterward. She'd had the proverbial headache!

And tonight they were going to see the Oklahoma City 89ers play a doubleheader—not exactly an evening conducive to conversation . . . or whatever!

The phone rang. He snatched it from its cradle. "Hello!" he bellowed into the receiver.

"Greg?"

"Oh, Robyn, it's you."

"If I'm disturbing you, I'll call later."

She was disturbing him, all right. Plenty! "What's your problem?" he asked. He twisted a pen between his fingers, thinking of the way she had responded to his touch.

"This is obviously a bad time for you," she said coolly. "It can wait until this evening. See you then."

"Robyn, wait. I'm sorry." He flipped the pen across the room and scowled as his secretary opened the door, walked in and plunked the morning's mail on his desk.

"Manuel's on line two," she said softly, indicating the blinking light on his phone.

Greg cupped his hand over the mouthpiece. "Tell him I'll get back to him in a minute." Being businessman, parent and lover—change that to *potential lover*, he thought—was wearing on him.

"I thought you'd like to know I have some news about Manuel's parents," Robyn was saying.

Now there was a glimmer of hope for improvement in his situation. "What have you got?"

"It may not be good news, but it's news. The private investigator I hired said he thinks Manuel's parents were in a bus that washed off a road in that hurricane. A rescue team found some of their belongings. So far, though, they haven't found the Garcias. I'm sorry the news isn't better."

"So am I."

"Are you going to tell Manuel?"

"I think I have to."

"I agree. Do you want help?"

With Manuel or with his own frustrations? "I think I can handle it. I'll call you if there's a problem."

"I'll see you tonight, then."

ROBYN FLIPPED THROUGH a magazine, not reading the words on the pages. Greg was late again for a date—the third time since the lake outing two weeks ago. The demands on his time were unbelievable.

She wondered how he thought he'd have time to squeeze being a husband and a father into his schedule. He couldn't even find the time to pick up the phone and tell her he would be late. She frowned. He hadn't called her at all in the past four days.

She heard voices on the driveway but didn't bother to look. She suspected they were some of the mentors—or maybe the students—who had been showing up at seven o'clock three nights a week to help her dad finish his cedar chests and grandfather clocks.

At first Lillian had served as Jonathan's interpreter. By now, however, Lillian had taught the helpers enough sign language that Robyn could walk into the workshop on any evening they were there and find hands flying.

With mixed emotions, Robyn admitted Lillian was good for her father. He still complained occasionally about Lillian's brash manner, but he was using after-shave lotion again—and a formula advertised to turn gray hair its original color. At fifty-five, he was still very much a man.

Robyn heard a faint rap at the door and rose to answer it. Greg stood there, leaning against the door frame, his tie askew and his face grim.

"Well, who do we have here?" she said. "I think I know you from somewhere—" she tapped her lip with her forefinger and squinted one eye "—but it's been so long that—"

"I'm really beat," he said. "Could I come in?"

"Sure."

He looked beleaguered and sorely in need of a cold drink and a warm companion. "How about some lemonade?"

"Sounds great. It must be at least a hundred out there."

"One hundred and one," she flung over her shoulder on the way to the kitchen. "Why don't you take off that tie. Your face is as red as a beet."

She filled a glass with lemonade and garnished it with a sprig of mint. When she turned she found him at the kitchen table studying her father's sketches for the hearing dogs raft.

Greg tapped the front-view drawing of the raft. "Who did these?"

"Dad." Nervously she scooped them up and deposited them on the dining room table. "He's so bad about leaving things lying around."

"I didn't know he could draw like that," he said, taking the lemonade from her.

"He can do better. He did those with his left hand."

"Has he ever taken art lessons?"

"No, but he's sketched as long as I can remember."

"He's very talented, Robyn. Could I see those again?" He sipped the cool drink.

"Now, Greg—"

He slipped his hand under her elbow and grinned as he gave her arm a gentle squeeze. "What's the matter? Afraid I'll steal your father's design?"

"Truthfully?"

"Yes."

"The thought did cross my mind."

"Don't worry. We're satisfied with our own design."

"It's that good?"

"What do you expect when you put a roomful of engineers with those incredibly bright kids? Drop by the plant someday and I'll show it to you."

"I might do that," she said, suddenly feeling insecure about the unsophisticated nature of her father's design.

"Look, I'm sorry I'm late. Are you about ready to go?"

She wanted to say she'd been ready for an hour, but she bit back her retort. "Why don't we forget about going out. We can stay here and watch TV if you like."

"That's okay. I'll be my old chipper self in a few minutes." He took a long draft of the lemonade, then put the glass down.

"If you're sure. By the way, how's Manuel? I haven't seen much of him lately. By the time he arrives at Kendra's, I've usually left."

"He's fine. He's been working like a dog." He snickered. "Pardon the pun."

She rolled her eyes. "Maybe you should put those kids to work on your jokes."

He moved closer, and she didn't try to stop him. He slid his hand around her neck and tangled his fingers in her freshly shampooed hair.

She let her fingers walk a path up his chest and felt a tick in the hard muscles. "My, you are tense tonight." She moved her hands to the curves of his shoulders to massage the tightness from them. "Why so tense?"

He closed his eyes and gave in to the rhythmic movement of her hands. When he opened his eyes, Robyn knew something was terribly wrong. "Are you going to tell me what's bothering you, or do I have to drag it out of you?"

"Can I have a hug first?"

She slid her arms around his waist, pressed her cheek against his chest and waited for him to talk.

"One of the kids at school—one of my kids," he said, "tried to kill himself this afternoon."

She lifted her head. "Oh, Greg, that's awful. Is he okay?"

"He got lucky. His mother found him after he'd taken a handful of sleeping pills. She rushed him to the emergency room. They pumped his stomach. He'll survive, but—"

"But it brought back the memories, didn't it?"

He nodded. "Manuel called me at work, and I went to the hospital to sit with his mother. She and the boy's father went through a divorce six months ago. She thought the boy was taking it well—until now."

"Do you know him personally?"

"Obviously not well enough. He's a freshman. A brilliant boy." He shook his head. "Fifteen years old. If it's all the same with you, I'd rather not talk about it now. I have some free time this weekend. What do you say we spend it together?"

"Well, Manuel and I are supposed to make the rounds of the animal shelters to see if we can come up with potential hearing dogs," she said, taking note of his abrupt change of subject. "You could help us screen the dogs."

"Sounds like a welcome break in routine."

"By the end of the day, you'll be dying for a break. Your body will ache, and you'll swear you'll never lift another dog."

"I'll do it if you'll promise to massage away my aches and pains."

"I'll make you a deal," she said without thinking. "I'll massage yours if you'll massage mine."

His eyes flashed a seductive mixture of delight and promise. "Robyn, I'm going to hold you to that promise."

SLEEP DID NOT COME EASILY for Robyn. At three in the morning, she still lay awake, watching shadows flicker across her ceiling. For the past three hours she had vacillated between sad thoughts and frustrating ones.

She couldn't get out of her mind the look on Greg's face when he spoke of the boy who had tried to kill himself. And there had been a sprinkling of guilt in his comment that he hadn't known the boy well enough. Greg was still troubled about his brother's suicide—that much was certain. Someday he would have to deal with his feelings. She was glad he had sought comfort from her.

But she wanted to give him more than comfort. His teasing remark about massaging away each other's aches triggered visions of him slowly kneading the muscles in her shoulders and in her back as he had at the lake.

A warmth radiated from a point deep inside her, where love and desire and compassion blended into a compelling need to go to him. She hadn't wanted to fall in love with him, but the truth was, she had.

She remembered the sage words of her mother. "When love comes to you, embrace it, my dear. Don't let it pass you by. You may only have one chance to find what your father and I have."

She rolled over and drew the curtains from the open window, feeling the moist night air on her cheeks. Surely her mother would understand why she still planned to leave Bethany. Some differences couldn't be resolved. As much as she loved children, there was no room for them in her life, and Greg couldn't comprehend a future without them.

So, until she left, she would treasure every moment with him as a gift of love. She knew later the pain would be unbearable, but she'd just have to deal with the heartache when it came.

THE NEXT DAY was Saturday, and Robyn took Greg up on his promise to help screen dogs at the animal shelters.

"You look beat," he said as he opened his car door for her. The day would be a scorcher. At eight o'clock, the air trapped inside the car was already oven hot.

"Thanks," she said teasingly. "I get up, wash my hair, put on makeup, and you tell me I look beat."

"Is your father still keeping you up with nightmares?"

"No. Since he and Manuel made up he's been sleeping much better. Where is Manuel, anyway?"

"At the kennel. When he found out I was going to help you today, he said you wouldn't need both of us along and that he needed to go in to work. Lyndon picked him up an hour ago. Manuel said he'd see us there later. But seriously, Robyn—" he lifted her chin and moved her face from side to side "—maybe you should find a way to slow down. Since you took that job at the kennel, you've been looking a bit frazzled."

She didn't want to admit that her fatigue was related more to her feelings for him than to any demands on her time. "I have slowed down. Mrs. Gilliam has practically taken over Mom's business."

"Have you thought about selling it?"

"As a matter of fact, I have. Last week Mrs. Gilliam and her brother told me they were interested in buying. I've thought about it, but when I leave, Dad could use the income, so I've decided not to sell. I'll hire a manager, instead."

Greg's hand hesitated on the keys in the ignition. "You haven't changed your mind about leaving, then?"

"No." She turned away so he couldn't witness her anguish. She would like nothing more than to change her plans so she could be with him. But he would never commit himself to a woman who wouldn't have children. "I

made my flight reservations a couple of days ago. I
leave—"

"If you don't mind, I'd rather not hear your plans," he
said before he backed out of the driveway.

He whipped around a corner. Robyn grabbed the arm-
rest to steady herself. "I've worked out everything with
Dad," she said. "He's agreed to go with me."

"That's strange," Greg countered. "Manuel said Jonathan told him he didn't want to go." He shook his head.
"How can you take him away from his home and his
friends? And in case you haven't noticed, he and Lillian
have been getting awfully cozy lately."

"What my father and I do and where we live is really
none of your business."

"Oh, but it is, Robyn. It is because I care about your father. Because I care about you."

"That doesn't give you any right to—"

He quickly pulled to the side of the road, slammed on his
brakes and put the van in park. He shifted in the seat until
he faced her, draped his arm over the steering wheel and
glared at her. "Don't you know what I'm trying to say?"

"You're trying to tell me I'm a lousy daughter. You're
trying to say—"

He took her face in his hands and kissed her so deeply,
so completely that thoughts of moving to Washington
faded from her mind.

When he broke the kiss he smiled at her sweetly. "Silly
woman, I'm trying to tell you I love you."

FOR ALL ROBYN KNEW, they could have been testing Tas-
manian devils at the animal shelters. Greg's admission of
love colored everything she did with an ethereal glow.

They laughed and joked, as if no problem were big
enough to separate them. After spending most of the day

testing dozens of dogs, they drove to the kennel, weary but pleased to fill out forms on two hearing dog candidates they had found.

In the kennel's reception area, Greg pulled Robyn away from the forms and gave her a lingering kiss. "I love you," he said, his eyes brighter, bluer than ever. He squeezed her hand, and she squeezed his. "While you finish here, I think I'll go find Manuel. He's been wanting to show me what he does around here."

"I'll meet you here," she said. She tried to ignore the swooning antics of Kendra, who stood, hands crossed over her heart, behind him.

Greg disappeared through a doorway, and Kendra pounced on her. "It's happened. You're in love! Don't deny it. I can see it in your eyes." She pulled Robyn into her office. Eyes flashing with excitement, she plopped into her chair. "Tell me all about it. I want to hear everything. And don't leave out the good stuff."

Robyn shrugged and smiled. "What can I say?"

"I envy you! Such a delicious-looking man." Tilting her chair onto its two back legs, she sobered for a moment. "How did you resolve your problem about children?"

"Well, we didn't exactly."

Her friend slammed the front legs of her chair to the floor. "What are you going to do? Stop. Don't answer that. You're going to stay here and blow off that job in D.C. You're going to admit you were crazy. You're going to love the socks off that guy, and you're going to have his kids."

"I haven't changed my mind about having children, Kendra."

"Uh-oh. So long, happy couple. So long, marriage. So long, chance of your lifetime, foolish girl."

"I have a right not to have children," she said, jutting out her chin.

"Of course you do. That's not the point. But do you love him, Robyn—really love him?"

"Yes," she admitted with an aching chest. "I do."

"Then you might have to consider a compromise. If you don't, you may be sorry." She paused and looked away, a wistful expression on her usually vibrant face. "There was a man once, and he loved me, and I loved him, but I was stupid."

"What happened?"

"We were young. We were foolish. We let insignificant differences keep us apart."

"Having children isn't exactly an insignificant issue."

"Someday, if you look back and realize you missed your one chance to be with the man you love for a lifetime, you might have a different perspective. How would you like to run into Greg someday and find him with another woman, a wife who's given him the children he wants? Could you bear that, Robyn? Could you stand to see someone else in the place you should have had? Could you stand to think of another woman . . . in his bed?"

Robyn heaved a deep sigh. "No, I couldn't."

"You may not have a second chance with this guy," Kendra said, continuing to hammer away at Robyn's insecurities. "He's gorgeous. He's hardworking. He's kind, and—" she lowered her voice and grinned "—I'd be willing to bet he's great in bed."

IF SOMEONE HAD TOLD GREG a boy of sixteen would delight in cleaning up dog manure, he would have called him a liar.

But there Manuel was, smiling as he tackled the most odious of his daily chores. While he cleaned the pens on one side of the building, the dogs housed in cages on the other staged an impromptu barking chorus.

The dogs were as fond of Manuel as the kennel staff was. Kendra said he was everyone's favorite young helper, mainly because of his cheerful attitude and his willingness to do more than was expected of him.

Helping people like Manuel filled Greg with a sense of purpose. The smiling, self-confident youth was a different person than the frightened boy he and Robyn had rescued from the police station a few weeks ago. Manuel had found his passion, thanks to this job. Lately he had even talked about studying veterinary medicine in college.

Why, Greg wondered, hadn't he taken the time to help his brother find a passion that would have served as a focus in his life? If he had, Brad might be alive today.

The guilt again—damn! He couldn't let it drain him of his joy of living. All he could do was work to help others like Manuel—and get that school started. *Win that raft race.*

He felt a pang of remorse, knowing that if his team won, Robyn might be denied the fulfillment of her dreams. The more his feelings for her grew, the more he wanted her happiness. It saddened him that he wasn't part of her dreams, but deep down he believed she loved him. She just needed to work through some problems to allow that love to grow as his was growing.

"I have something to ask you," Manuel said, breaking into Greg's thoughts.

Greg leaned against a chain link fence and crossed his arms. "Shoot."

"I'm worried about Lyndon. His mother and father are going to leave him alone again for the weekend. He's planning another party."

Would the boy's parents never learn? "What do you think we should do about it?" he asked, placing some of the responsibility on Manuel's shoulders.

"Lyndon wants to go to Tulsa with us next month. He's strong. He'd make a good crew member." Then he delivered a punch to Greg's soft spot, showing he'd already assumed some responsibility for helping his friend. "He's always talking about you. He looks up to you, almost like an older brother."

Lyndon was a boy without boundaries who was desperately seeking acceptance—a tinderbox, in Greg's estimation. "If he goes through with that party, there's no way I'll take him. But I need one more crewman. If he stays out of trouble—"

"I'll be responsible for him." Manuel grinned, his dark eyes flashing amusement. "Besides, if you don't say yes, you might have to go to the police station in the middle of the night again to sign for him."

Greg laughed. "Good point. Okay, tell Lyndon I'll save a spot for him at the oars if—and I say if—he keeps his nose clean."

"Keeps his what?"

Greg chuckled. "That means he has to stay out of trouble."

"Oh, well, in that case, don't worry."

Over Manuel's shoulder Greg saw Kendra walking a golden Labrador retriever. About nine months old, with feet too big for its body, the pup took the leash in its teeth and tugged on it playfully as they walked.

Kendra's stern look and tone of voice showed she wasn't in a playful mood. "No, Taffy," she said, giving the leash a quick jerk to the side. "Heel."

"What's the matter with Kendra?" Greg said. "I've never seen her with such a scowl on her face."

"I don't know," Manuel said, frowning. "But Taffy never comes over here. Kendra keeps her in the building with the other hearing dogs."

Kendra led the pup into one of the kennels Manuel had just cleaned. She snapped off the black nylon leash, stepped back and shut the gate.

The pup stuck its nose through a gap in the chain link fencing and whined. Kendra knelt before the gate. "I'm sorry, girl." Her voice broke. "You'll have to stay here until we can find you a home."

"What happened?" Manuel said. He reached over the gate and scratched Taffy's ears.

"She won't work. It started a few days ago. Today she acted only mildly interested when the alarm clock went off."

"Maybe she's sick."

"Joe checked her out. I'm afraid she's through, Manuel."

"She was the best one. Something's wrong."

"This happens sometimes. We'll just have to find her a good home."

Manuel turned to Greg, his eyes pleading even before he spoke. "Can we keep her? Please?"

Greg didn't want to remind Manuel he was only staying with him temporarily. He couldn't permit the boy the luxury of owning a dog he might not be able to keep later. "Maybe someone at the school would like Taffy."

"She's a good dog," Manuel pleaded. "Would you take her? Please?"

The idea of a companion did appeal to Greg. A companion who wouldn't argue with him. Taffy whined, and he weakened. "Well, I do have a fenced-in backyard."

"I knew you'd say yes!" Manuel said. "Can she go home with us tonight?"

Kendra looked at Greg. He lifted his shoulders helplessly. How could he deny Manuel this one indulgence?

"DO YOU WANT TO GO on a picnic?" Robyn asked as they left the kennel with Taffy. "It's only five o'clock. We could go home, get Taffy situated, clean up and be at the park by seven."

"Sounds great. Why don't we pick up fried chicken?"

"I have plenty of leftovers at home—that is, if you don't mind leftovers."

"Actually, that sounds great. Do you think your dad and Lillian will want to go?"

"Not a chance. They're working on the raft tonight."

"Hmm. I'm beginning to like the sound of this picnic."

"I owe you a good meal. You put in quite a day."

"Have you forgotten our agreement? You promised to rub away my aches and pains, and I do have them."

"You mean you'd turn down food for a back rub? I thought the way to a man's heart was through his stomach."

"There are all kinds of food, Robyn. Food for the stomach. Food for thought. Food for... let me see, how shall I put it?"

Robyn poked him in the arm and laughed. "You'll probably fall asleep when I massage away your aches."

Greg caught her fingers in his hand and brought it to his lips for a kiss. "Don't count on it, Robyn."

"THIS PLACE is gorgeous!" Robyn said. "How did you find it?"

Sitting cross-legged on a quilt with a paper plate balanced on her knee, she looked out over a broad meadow of wildflowers in lavenders, pinks and purples. Where the wildflowers met the horizon, the early August sun glowed in the evening sky like a giant crimson ball streaked with purple ribbons. She closed her eyes, drew in the floral scent and listened to the birds call their mates in the stand of dogwoods near the stream.

"When I first moved here, I didn't know many people. Sometimes, after I left the plant, I'd go driving in the country. One evening I came over that hill and saw this place."

"Who owns it?"

"I do. I thought it would be a great place to build a house someday."

He took the empty plate from her hands and tossed it into a garbage bag. Then, folding his hands beneath his head, he reclined on the quilt before her. The sky-blue fabric of his knit shirt stretched taut across his chest.

He had a nice chest. No, a fabulous chest, Robyn decided. Her hands itched to linger on the contours where her fingers had only dallied before. But if she let her hands do their bidding, she would not stop at his chest. She made tight fists in her lap and resolved to keep her distance.

He crossed his legs at the ankles. Time-worn jeans hugged his thighs like supple kid leather and adjusted into creases at the juncture of his legs. Robyn tried not to stare, but unsuccessfully. "Lillian showed up at the kennel today, while you were with Manuel," she said, trying to make conversation.

"Oh? What did she want?"

"She wants to be on our team."

"You said yes, of course."

"Of course."

"You have a good heart, Robyn. Lillian's buffed those sharp edges she used to have. I think Jonathan enjoys having her around now."

"I'm sure he does." She plucked a wildflower and twisted its stem. "We'll see if he can put up with her for a weekend."

Greg changed the subject. "Kendra mentioned that she's starting a new program. I believe she said she's calling it Companions for Deaf Children."

"That's right. She's convinced she can train a dog to keep a child in his yard. That way a deaf child could have a more normal life. So could his parents."

Greg rolled to his side and propped his head on his palm, showing interest in the topic. Robyn liked the way the rosy hues of evening glowed in his light hair.

"Furthermore," she continued, "she says she could train a dog to alert a child when her mother or father calls her."

Greg chuckled. "She'd better watch out. Every parent would like to have one of those dogs."

"Kendra will need more funding to set up the program. As you know, we're always short of money."

"But you wouldn't be if your team won the raft race," he said with a pensive look.

"I wish both our teams could win," she said. "But of course, that's impossible."

"I hope there won't be bad feelings if one of us wins."

"There'll be disappointments, maybe, but no bad feelings. I know what you're trying to do is important. I've learned a lot about gifted kids from Manuel. He's told me about some of his friends at school and their problems."

"I don't want you to get the wrong idea. I don't mean all gifted kids have problems. But some of them have a bunch. The public schools do what they can, considering their tight budgets. I'm convinced I could help those kids if I could reach their parents. But," he said, "most of them work. They're tired when they get home. It will be different at our new school. The parents will be involved in a big way.... But enough of that. I didn't come here to talk about the race—or the school."

There was a different emotion flashing in his eyes this evening, as if he had a secret he wanted to share with her, as if he wanted to—

"I won't bite, you know...."

CHAPTER TWELVE

TUGGING HER HAND, Greg coaxed Robyn over until she sat at his side. "There, that's better. Now, how about that back rub?"

"Well," she said, slipping her hand from his and trying to appear nonchalant, "if I'm going to rub your back, you'll have to roll over."

"Nervous?" he said with a grin, glancing at her fidgeting fingers.

"Of course not. Why should I be nervous?"

"We're alone."

"So? We've been alone before." She thought of the night at the lake and felt flutters in her stomach.

"Not this alone. There isn't a soul around for miles, unless you count those birds over there."

"Be that as it may, I still can't rub your back unless you roll over."

"Oh, no?" he said, mischief dancing in his eyes. Chuckling, he pulled her palms to his chest, slid his hands around her waist and massaged the tight muscles on either side of her spine.

"Hmm, that feels so good," she said, letting her head fall back.

"You are tense. Maybe you're the one who needs the massage. Or—" he slid his hands up her back and exerted light pressure "—maybe you need this."

As he urged her forward, she found her hair spilling over her shoulders and falling onto his cheeks. He kissed her once, twice, gently, then crooked his mouth into a lazy smile. "You really must learn to relax, Robyn. If you run around tense like this, you'll miss half the fun in life."

His eyes, warm in an evening that was cooling, drifted shut. He lifted his chin and rolled his head from side to side, letting her hair slide over his face. "Your hair feels like those things that hang from the hats when you graduate. Tassels, aren't they? Yeah. Thick silk tassels, and—" he inhaled deeply "—it smells great."

He opened his eyes. "Like flowers. Honeysuckle. God, how I used to love honeysuckle. When I was a boy I used to pick it and suck the nectar off those little things that stuck out of the middle."

"Stamen," Robyn said. "They're called stamen."

"Whatever. I wonder, Robyn. Do you taste as sweet?"

She laughed nervously, but her skin tingled with the implications of his wondering. Around them the meadow sang with crickets, with the trickle of water in the stream, and she did some wondering of her own. How would it feel to lie beside him and blend the heat of her body with his, to let him discover the taste and texture of her skin?

"You don't look very comfortable hunched over like that. Why don't you relax?" He patted the spot beside him on the quilt.

She lay next to him in the cradle of his arm and nestled her head on his shoulder. Her hand rose and fell on his chest as his breathing grew rapid and shallow along with her own.

"Ah, Robyn," he murmured after a few moments. "Admit it. You belong with me like this."

The ache of longing swelled in her throat. "I know, but—"

"Hmm. No buts. Let's go with 'I know' for now."

"But you said—"

"Forget what I said. Tonight I just want to be with you like this." And he left little doubt what that meant. As the sky darkened, he pulled her full against him, thighs to thighs, breast to chest, and kissed her—really kissed her this time.

Now was the moment she was supposed to press a palm to his chest and talk rationally about using some protection. But he was doing wonderful things to her, things that made her body sing. And it had been so long . . . or had she *ever* made love to a man as she was thinking of making love to Greg now?

But she wasn't protected. She had to stop, no matter what endearments he whispered in her ear.

"I love you," he said.

Not fair! "Dessert," she said. "I'll cut the pie."

"I don't want any pie," he said. "I want you."

He smiled slyly and coaxed her mouth open again, and this time the kiss dizzied her. She whimpered and dug her fingernails into his arms. When their lips finally parted, she pressed her forehead against his. "I want to tell you how I feel."

"Don't tell me. Show me. Like this." He cupped her head in his hands, traced her mouth with flicks of his tongue and slanted his head for a kiss that fired her passion.

But she had more to give than passion. She balled up her fists and pressed them against his chest, putting inches between them. "You've got to listen."

He glanced at her fists and grinned. "If I don't, are you going to punch me with those?"

"I'm trying to be serious."

"Serious I don't mind. But if you have a long speech to make, could it wait?" His lids grew heavy, and he craned his neck to reach her lips. "Mmm, you do taste good."

"You're impossible."

"No, I'm in love."

"And I love you!" she blurted out. "That's what I've been trying to tell you."

He grinned wildly, devilishly and a bit proudly, too. "I knew it. I saw it in your eyes, and I felt it in your touch. Say it again, Robyn."

"I love you," she repeated, enjoying the sound of the words.

"And I love you," he said, rolling her onto her back and slinging a leg over her thighs. He nibbled at her chin and smiled. "And now that I've said the words, I'm going to show you the love."

The husky texture of his voice sent chills dancing up her arms. His lips brought her even more pleasure than his earlier kisses. There was no restraint as there had been in her front yard, as there had been at the lake. She was responding to him as a woman, matching his stroking in kind.

Closing her eyes, she took his head in her hands and moved his lips to the upper curves of her breasts. There in the meadow she knew he was the man who would possess her spirit as well as her body.

He braced himself on his elbows above her and unfastened the tiny lavender buttons of her blouse. The fabric fell back, and he smiled softly while releasing the front clasp of her bra. He caressed her first with an admiring glance, then with his fingers.

"I knew you'd be soft," he said, and he bent to pleasure her breasts with the flicking moistness of his tongue.

Arching to meet him, she found the heat of his skin with her hands. The muscles on his back tensed beneath her fingers. When she dipped inside his denim waistband and felt the hardness of his hips, he shuddered.

"Ah, Robyn, I've wanted to feel you touch me."

She was vaguely aware of him tugging her pants over her hips, of her blouse being eased off her arms, of moist, night air cooling her skin. But a feeling of dread crept over her as he tossed his clothes into a crumpled pile beside hers.

"You're shaking," he said, taking her into his arms. "Are you cold?"

His body was already heating hers. "N-no." She was anything but cold.

"Then what is it?" he said, showing a tenderness that made her want him even more, in spite of what she had to say.

"I—I just can't do this."

"Why not?"

Fear narrowed the opening in her throat, and she found speaking difficult. "I—I'm not . . . protected."

He smiled and kissed her briefly, sweetly. "Don't go away."

While Robyn lay waiting beside him, Greg reached for his jeans and dug into his back pocket. He was not at all surprised by the fear he had seen in Robyn's eyes. But dammit, fear was gnawing at him, too. Once he made love to her, that was it. He would be hers. If she left, she would destroy him. And he couldn't bear another goodbye.

Should he risk it?

Yes. However much the thought of losing her hurt, the thought of never making love to her hurt more.

He turned to her. As he did, she ran her hand over the coarse hair on his thigh. "God, Robyn, your hand feels good—so good.'' He lay beside her and took her in his arms.

Lips to lips, flesh to flesh, they lay on the quilt in the meadow. Night stole over their heated bodies, covering them with a blanket of privacy. There in the country, with the scent of wildflowers in the air, they pleasured each other until Robyn could wait no longer to feel the fullness of him inside her.

She slid her hands up his torso, over his sweat-slickened chest, and conveyed her readiness by parting her thighs.

Greg saw Robyn's heavy-lidded look and felt a surge of heat at her encouragement. He had wanted to excite her for hours before he entered her, but he, too, was ready. Damned ready. He knelt between her parted thighs, abandoned his restraint and eased into the heaven of her.

Robyn drew him to her, loving him with a tremendous energy he had sensed was there all along. Sometime later, minutes, hours perhaps, she cried his name into the night. He answered her with the most intimate of answers—the thrust of his body, the surge of his passion and the whisper of her name on his lips.

WITH AN OPEN PALM Greg caressed Robyn's flat abdomen and marveled at the softness of her nipples. Before their lovemaking, they had been tight and hard. Now they were as soft as her lips.

Lying in the circle of his arms, staring into the star-scattered sky, Robyn ran her fingertips across his chest and felt a muscle tick beneath her caress. She loved the way he felt.

She kissed his chest, flicking his flesh with her tongue. She loved the way he tasted.

She drew in the scent of his body and smiled. She adored the way he smelled, vanilla blended with musky man scent.

"That was one hell of a back rub."

She nipped playfully at his nipple. "That's funny. I don't remember rubbing your back."

"Robyn, dear, you rubbed everything."

Smiling devilishly, she rolled on top of him, her silky thighs pressing over his coarsely haired limbs. "Then you probably wouldn't want to do it again, would you?"

"Oh, no? Try me."

"I fully intend to."

He hooked an arm around her neck and pulled her lips to his. "It's hard work, but someone has to do it."

She punched him in the chest. "Work? Hard work? And I thought you enjoyed making love to me." She feigned rolling away from him, but he held her tightly.

"I'm not sure. Maybe after the second time I'll know for sure."

"I'll show you for sure!" She ran her tongue over his chest, nipple to nipple, then slowly, torturously circled his navel.

Gripping her shoulders with trembling hands, he moaned into the night.

STANDING IN THE DAPPLED moonlight beneath the magnolia tree in her front yard, Robyn leaned into Greg's embrace. Her chin on his chest, she gazed into his eyes and smiled, feeling inextricably linked to him. "Thanks for your help today."

He rubbed her nose playfully. "As the cliché goes, the pleasure was all mine."

"Will I see you tomorrow?"

"You can bet on it." He pressed her head against his chest and ruffled her love-tousled hair. "Do you want me to make the call or will you?"

"What call?"

"The call to your travel agent. You don't have the kind of tickets you can't cancel, do you?"

"I...don't really know. I'll have to check," she hedged. She slipped from his arms and felt the old, panicky feeling eating away at her euphoria. "I've gotta go. It's getting late."

He regarded her cautiously. "Look at yourself."

She glanced down and discovered that she had folded her arms across her breast. She knew as well as Greg did that she was pushing him away from her. She laughed nervously. "I'm a little chilled, that's all."

He took a step forward, and she, one step back.

"That's not really it, is it?" he asked her.

"Please, can't we just enjoy tonight and not try to analyze it?" She backed up another step and felt panic crawl up her throat.

"I'm not trying to analyze tonight. I'm trying to analyze tomorrow."

"I've really gotta go," she said, turning to start for the steps.

He snagged her arm and forced her to look at him. "You're still going, aren't you?"

Not wanting to answer the question directly, she said, "It isn't simple, Greg. We have...problems. I...don't know what I'm going to do."

"You mean after I told you I love you—after you told me you love me, and we made love, that you..." He backed away from her. "How foolish of me to think that would make a difference in your plans."

"I meant what I said. I love you." She reached for his arm. "And what we shared was important to me."

"Apparently not important enough. If it was, you wouldn't even think about getting on that plane. You'd pick up the phone tomorrow and cancel those tickets, and you and I would—''

"Would what, Greg? Get married? Have children? Those are your dreams, not mine."

"Marriage isn't?"

"I didn't say that."

"Then it's the children, isn't it? I should have known."

"You know how I feel about having children."

"I just thought after tonight you'd change your mind. I thought you'd give us a chance, at least."

"The trouble is, you want everything your way," she said, her blood racing so fast she felt dizzy. "You want me to agree to your grand scheme of things, or you won't consider a future with me."

He frowned. "What do you mean?"

"I mean I either agree to have children, or you shut off your love like tap water. You won't even consider a compromise."

"Like what?"

"Like adopting, for instance."

"Robyn, if you'd look deep in your heart, you'd know you want children, too."

"Okay, maybe I might. But if I did—and that's a big if—I'd want to adopt them."

"Well, maybe you'd better ask yourself why you feel that way. I'll tell you something, Robyn. There's a lot about yourself you don't understand!"

"Oh? And I suppose you do?"

"Yes, I think I do."

"Well, understand this. I need no less than the kids you work to help—unconditional love, Greg. I need you to love me, no matter how I feel about having children."

"Maybe, he said, backing across her lawn, "you'd better not cancel those reservations, after all."

ROBYN SAT in her cramped office at Meals for the Heart, rubbing her forehead in frustration. As if she didn't have enough to complicate her life, the day after she and Greg had made love, Mrs. Gilliam had left town unexpectedly. She needed to care for her niece in Arkansas whose baby had arrived prematurely.

In the past two weeks Robyn had been killing herself managing the business and doing her job at the kennel. She'd also had to keep tabs on the investigator in Mexico, who still hadn't located Manuel's parents.

She worked her way through the long summer days mechanically, without her normal zest for living. The evenings were difficult—the nights impossible—for she could draw back the curtains and occasionally see Greg coming and going, mostly with Manuel. That's why she'd chosen to work today, a Saturday. Greg would probably be home. She didn't want to be.

She had to get out of Bethany—out of Oklahoma—put as much distance between herself and Greg as she could. Labor Day weekend was barely three weeks away. Two weeks after that she and her father would leave. She had five more long, lonely weeks to endure. If only she hadn't been foolish enough to fall in love with a next-door neighbor who thought he knew more about her than she did herself.

The phone rang, and a message printed on her TDD. There, at least, was one ray of sunshine. Her father's therapist had trained him to use his computer. "Come home," the typed message read. "The raft to float the river."

Puzzling over the sign language sentence structure, she thought for a moment, then typed her answer. "Wait. I'm on my way."

When Robyn pulled into the driveway, she saw her father, Lillian, Joe and Greg struggling to hook the huge raft and its custom-built trailer to the hitch on the truck Joe used for his large-animal practice. Her gaze darted to Greg. She cursed her pulse for racing at the thought of speaking with him again. Since the night they had made love, he had been distant, uncommunicative, sometimes downright unpleasant.

She scooted out of the car, all too aware that his unsmiling gaze was fixed on her. She tried to ignore him, but her willpower failed her when she rounded the raft and saw him standing, shirtless, a sheen of perspiration making his body glisten in the noonday sun. His snug jeans hugged his body...as she wished she could again.

"What's going on?" she signed to her father.

"Your father, bless his stubborn soul, decided the raft had to be tested before the race," Lillian provided.

"Today? But we don't have enough crew here to handle it."

"I tried to tell him. You know your father. He said we'll pick up a couple of guys at the river."

Robyn turned to Greg. He lifted a forearm and swiped at the perspiration streaming down his face. A lock of sun-streaked hair fell over one eye as it had the night they'd made love. "What are you doing here?" she asked, blotting that memory from her mind.

"Manners. Some people do have them, you know."

"What's that supposed to mean?"

"Your dad and I were having a hard time getting the raft hooked up," Joe provided. "Greg offered us a hand."

"He's going along for the ride," Lillian announced. "Won't that be nice?"

"Terrific," Robyn mumbled under her breath. "Where's Manuel?"

"At the kennel," Greg said. "He insists he has to work."

While the others went into the house to freshen up before leaving, Robyn and Greg stood beside the raft, awkwardly silent until he spoke. "Robyn, look, about what I said after the picnic.... I'm sorry I was so pushy—"

"No, don't apologize. You said what you felt."

"But I still love—"

"No! Whatever you do, don't say that. I don't think I can take it." She turned away. "It won't work for us. It can't work."

"I have an idea," he said. "Something I want to talk to you about."

She wanted to reach out and touch him, to step into his arms and his life and listen to what he had to say. But she knew better. With Greg there was no compromising. "Please, don't make it any harder than it is," she said.

DESPITE ROBYN'S COMPLAINT that there were good places closer to home, Jonathan insisted they test the raft on the Illinois River near his birthplace in northeastern Oklahoma. There was a broad stretch of the Illinois there where he knew every tree, every bend of the river. Besides, he needed to go back home, and he needed to go now.

With Joe driving and Lillian sandwiched between him and Jonathan in the front seat, they headed through the emerald-green hills, then proceeded through the restored town of Wagoner and over the Fort Gibson Reservoir.

Greg and Robyn sat in the back like two ice cubes, hugging the truck's side panels as if they were afraid they might catch the plague if they touched.

Maybe a little touching was what they needed to thaw the chill, Jonathan thought. Robyn was miserable. She hadn't slept well in a couple of weeks, and there was such a sadness in her pretty brown eyes.

They topped a hill and drove into the heavily wooded town of Tahlequah. Near the big Indian center Jonathan saw a band in the park.

He draped his arm over the back of the seat and glanced as casually as he could at Robyn and Greg.

"It's as cold as a meat locker back there," Lillian signed with hushed movements.

Jonathan nodded, but he had hopes for Greg and Robyn. Those two were in love. There was no mistaking that. He was hoping the country air and the river would work its magic on them as it had on him and Carol Ann.

He directed Joe out of Tahlequah and several miles down the highway to a turnoff by the river. As they bumped from the highway onto the dirt road, he straightened in his seat. Images of his youth flooded his mind. This was his country. His river.

To their left, a mountain shot straight up from the road. To the right, not a hundred yards away, coursed the river. Here, near the highway, the river was swift. Jonathan told Joe to drive twenty miles up the road where the river was broad, the current less treacherous, the water four or five feet deep. Jonathan ached to walk the banks, to feel the power of the river through his bare feet.

He looked out the window at the darkening sky and frowned. Winds were a bit brisk. They'd have to hurry if they wanted to get out on the river today.

They'd only float a couple of miles, then pull up to one of the concessions that rented canoes. While the others waited, he would walk back for Joe's truck. He could drive here, where there wasn't much traffic. He didn't mind a little rain, and he wanted to make a stop along the way.

"WELL, SHE FLOATS," Joe announced. "And she handles like a dream."

Standing beside Jonathan on the raft, Lillian squeezed his arm and signed her enthusiastic approval. "You've done good."

He smiled and patted her hand. Although it was a nice smile, it was a proprietary one, and there was a faraway look in his eyes. He fixed his gaze at some distant point downstream, at some distant point in time.

Not one to stand around and let things happen, Lillian steeled herself to help Jonathan wrestle his conscience. No matter that her heart jumped like a frisky frog when he touched her—she had loved Carol Ann, too. She had done battle with a few dragons over her loyalty to Carol Ann and her feelings for Jonathan. A decent person wasn't supposed to have those feelings for a friend's husband, but the rules had become jumbled up lately. Carol Ann was gone, but Lillian still felt her presence.

Lillian tapped Jonathan on the shoulder and signed, "Where was it you found Carol Ann?"

He pointed downstream. Lillian nodded. The current was swifter there. As she recalled Carol Ann telling her, that year there had been heavy spring rains. For years Lillian had enjoyed hearing how Jonathan had rescued Carol Ann, how they had known from the moment their hands touched that there was something special between them.

Now something special was growing between her and Jonathan. She closed her eyes. With the humid river air whispering over her face, she savored the memory of the one time he had kissed her in his workshop. The raft crew had left, and Robyn had been in bed. Afterward he had held Lillian in his arms and softly stroked her hair.

Since then she had been alive with the realization that part of her hadn't died with Rob. She was fifty-five, all right, but just as alive and responsive as she had been thirty years ago. But caring for a man and doing something about it were two different things when mutual fidelity to a fine woman stood between them.

Jonathan would never love a woman as he had loved Carol Ann. Lillian knew that. But she hoped—well, she just plain hoped, that's what.

She wasn't the only one doing some hoping. She noticed that Greg, on one side of the raft, was having a hard time concentrating on pulling the raft through the water with a pole. He kept staring at Robyn, who was standing at the rear. Of course, any man in his right mind would be staring at Robyn today, dressed as she was in that skimpy green swimsuit.

If Lillian didn't miss her bet, that young man was torn between making love to Robyn and walking away from her forever.

She studied Robyn's expression and wished she could do something to chase the sadness from her eyes. Neither one of those young folks would tell her what had happened between them. Heck, if she didn't know, she couldn't help.

A gust of cooling wind blew out of nowhere, and a fat raindrop fell with a splat on Lillian's nose. The wind plastered Jonathan's hair to one side of his head and rippled his shirt like a sail. Frowning, he pointed to the west bank of the river and drew her with him to alert Joe and Greg to his signed instructions.

Where the river had been flowing as smooth as glass, whitecaps now lapped at the raft. Lillian spotted aluminum canoes downstream bobbing in the rough waters. She'd bet many of the canoers were weekend amateurs, and she worried for their safety. She had been in a storm like this before in a riverboat on Lake Granbury in Texas, and it had been downright frightening. Here they were on a little bitty raft.

The wind clawed the ladybug comb from her hair and flung it into the river. Long auburn strands whipped across her face, obscuring her vision. She pushed the hair away and anchored it to the sides of her face with her hands as she heard Greg yell instructions to the two young men they had enlisted for help at the launch site.

Robyn, her head bent to the wind, crossed her arms and moved to stand beside Lillian. Her teeth chattered as she spoke. "How are you doing?"

"Fine, but I'm worried about your father."

"Don't worry about him. You forget he used to live on this river."

"He was younger then, and he could use both arms."

"You're being a worrywart."

Lillian brushed the hair from her eyes again. "That's something your mother would have said."

"I've been thinking about her a lot today."

Lillian slipped her arm around Robyn's waist and gave her a squeeze. "You're not the only one, my dear."

"Looks like we're going to tie up to that old abandoned dock over there."

Lillian glanced at the rotted pilings and boards extending from the riverbank, then turned to look at Jonathan. She saw him standing at the back of the raft, his arm hooked around the flagpole. The hearing dogs flag snapped in the breeze like a whip.

He raised his hand to sign something but grabbed for the pole. A look of horror crossed his face, and he pointed wildly at the shore.

There was a loud crunch as they collided with the dock, a bone-jarring jolt, the sensation of being lifted and thrown, and Lillian lay sprawled on the deck of the raft. A board beneath her split. For a terrifying moment she saw water lap at her through the crack.

"Jonathan, help!" she screamed, forgetting he couldn't hear her. "Jonathan, where are you?"

CHAPTER THIRTEEN

AS THE CRACK in the raft widened, Lillian gripped the boards on either side of her and prayed for strength. Mere inches beneath her, the Illinois raged like a furious animal.

She struggled to her knees. She had to find Jonathan and Robyn and Joe—and—dear Lord, the raft was tearing free from the dock!

Acting instinctively, she sprang for the dock and skidded on her knees and her palms. Flesh tore, and stinging pain sliced through her arms and her legs. Glancing over her shoulder, she shuddered. The half of the raft that had torn free of the dock was being tossed downstream like a child's toy.

Where was Jonathan?

Suddenly, the dock buckled beneath her. "Joe! Jonathan! Somebody!" she screamed, but the wind swallowed her plea.

Her only chance was to make it to the riverbank. She struggled to her feet, but the dock moved beneath her like an undulating wave. She helicoptered her arms, fighting desperately for balance.

"Hang on, Lil," Joe yelled into her ear. "We've got you." Joe and Greg scooped her up by her arms and planted her in the mud on the riverbank beside Robyn, Jonathan and the two men they'd recruited to help.

Robyn pulled her into a tight embrace. "Thank God you're safe. We thought you were right behind us. When we saw you out there on the dock, we were scared to death."

Over Robyn's shoulder Lillian fixed her gaze on Jonathan's face. He lifted a weathered hand to her cheek, relief in his eyes. She turned her face in his hand and kissed his caressing palm. He acknowledged her affection with a thin, weary smile.

Lillian watched his gaze dart to the wreckage of the raft, which was wrapped around a splintered dock piling. As his eyes betrayed his intentions, fear skittered through her veins.

Suddenly he bolted for the dock.

"No!" Lillian screamed instinctively. Oblivious to the danger, she ran onto the dock after him.

Grabbing him by the arm, she jerked him around and signed in desperate, flying gestures. "We can build another raft. We can't build another you!"

Jonathan hesitated for the briefest of moments. Lillian heard a loud crack and felt something slam into the dock behind them. Reeling from the blow, she grabbed his good arm and pulled him to the shore. "Stubborn man. Stubborn fool. Stubborn. Stubborn. Stubborn."

THE RAIN POUNDED the riverbanks, sending the rafters looking for cover. Lillian hugged her shivering body as she and the others followed Jonathan through the sand and the thick underbrush into the woods. Just when she thought she could walk no farther, they wandered onto the ruins of a rustic log cabin.

Jonathan kicked in the door and halted midway into the cabin's only room. Lillian followed his gaze from the pile of decaying leaves that gave off an earthy odor to the empty tin cans and the refuse of four-legged varmints. From the look on his face she knew he had been there before.

The wind gusted through a hole in the cabin's back wall, spraying a fine mist onto the spiderwebs that clung to the ceiling and wall. Daddy longlegs blanketed one corner of the ceiling, while wasps hovered beneath nearby nests.

Seeming to collect himself, Jonathan gestured for Joe and Greg to help him yank loose boards from the rotting floor for a fire. Lillian's suspicions about the cabin's origin grew when Jonathan removed a loose rock in the native stone fireplace and pulled out a battered tin box.

He removed several matches. The fourth sputtered to flame, and the odor of sulphur joined the scents of mold and decay that pervaded the room.

Shivering, she huddled close to Robyn on the floor. "Was this where Jonathan grew up?" she asked.

Robyn nodded. "Dad's father died when I was seven. Mom and Dad sold the cabin and the land shortly after that."

Greg came to sit beside Robyn. "It's a shame your father didn't keep this place. With a little work, it could be a great weekend retreat."

"Dad didn't want to keep it."

"Why not?"

Robyn sighed, and Lillian remembered all the disheartening stories about Jonathan's childhood Carol Ann had shared with her. "This place holds memories that aren't pleasant for him," Robyn said.

"You might as well tell him the rest," Lillian piped in. "Else he'll think worse than it was."

Robyn took a look around and shuddered. "It all started one Saturday when Dad's father—Grandpa Billie—took Dad and Grandma Constance to Tahlequah. You remember I told you she was deaf?"

Greg nodded. "I remember."

"Grandpa Billie was awfully protective. He never would let Dad or Grandma wander off without him. That Saturday Grandma begged Grandpa to let her go around town on her own. She convinced him she had the private errands of a woman to run, and he gave in. The next thing Dad knew his mother was lying dead in the street."

"What happened?"

"Apparently she didn't hear a man honk his horn. She stepped in front of his car. When they found her, she had Dad's birthday present—a baseball and a catcher's mitt—stuck deep in her bag, along with a handkerchief for Grandpa. That was the last time Grandpa took Dad to town."

Greg took a moment to digest what Robyn had just revealed about her father's unusual childhood. "Tough way to grow up, wasn't it?"

Robyn's gaze wandered pensively over the cabin. "He lived a pretty narrow existence until he met Mother. She said after they married and moved away he wasn't anxious to come back."

THE FIRE FELT GOOD on Greg's bare arms. So did the flame that burned in his heart. Robyn, tensed with a chill, sat cross-legged before him, snuggling into his chest. He wasn't glad the raft had been wrecked, but he was grateful for the excuse to hold her in his arms.

Jonathan, having picked his way around the remains of his childhood home with a pensive detachment, came to stand before his daughter.

She looked up, and her hands moved as she spoke. "I'm sorry about the raft, Dad."

One corner of his mouth twitched upward. "I guess we won't be going to Tulsa," he signed, his slow gestures showing the intensity of his disappointment.

"What do you mean? Of course we will."

"But we don't have a raft."

"You can build another one. The race is three weeks away."

"But we'd have to work every night."

"We can do that."

"I don't know." He shuffled his feet and stared at his rain-wet boots. "So much work."

"You can do it, Dad. You can do anything you set your mind to."

Greg palmed over a grin as Jonathan gave in to Robyn's gentle nudging. She could talk her father into anything when she tried. He admired that quality in her, although he guessed that was how she had managed to persuade Jonathan to go with her to Washington.

Joe stood, brushed his palms on the seat of his faded overalls and signed as he spoke. "Count on my help. Right now, I expect I'll go for the truck. The rest of you stick around, and I'll be back in a bit."

"I think there's a tree blocking the road," Greg said.

"Why don't we all walk back, then?" Robyn uncrossed her legs and rocked forward to the balls of her feet.

Greg, determined to take advantage of the isolated spot, pulled her to his chest. "Not yet. We have a few things to talk about first."

Lillian signalled the young recruits to join her, then tapped Jonathan's arm and shot him a knowing glance. Appearing to read her hint, he offered her his hand.

"You all go on ahead," Greg told them. "We'll catch up in a few minutes."

ROBYN WASN'T SO SURE she wanted to be alone with Greg.
All day the others had provided a protective barrier between them. Now that she and Greg were alone in the cabin,
there was nothing to prevent her from listening to her heart
instead of her head. And her heart implored her to forget
everything but her desire to make love to him.

"Thanks for sticking around," Greg said. He took her
chin in his hand and kissed her slowly, sweetly.

He tasted faintly of Lillian's lemonade, and he smelled
of rain-dampened clothes and river water. "You wanted to
talk to me about something?"

He chuckled. "I have lots of wants. Talking is only one
of them." He ran his forefinger over the fullness of her lips,
and the roof of her mouth tingled. "But right now I don't
particularly want to talk."

"Maybe we'd better," she cautioned him, but she could
feel her resistance fading. "They'll be waiting for us."

"If they weren't, would you make love to me, Robyn?
Would you let me make love to you?" With his finger he
drew an imaginary line from her lips over her chin and her
neck to the plunge-point of her V-necked swimsuit. She felt
her nipples harden, and she answered Greg by lifting her
chin until her lips met his.

He kissed her eagerly, and the loneliness of the past two
weeks faded with his touch.

"I can't stay away from you, either, Robyn. It's dumb to
try. When we get home, I'm going to make love to you."

No matter how many nights she had lain awake longing
for his touch, she couldn't allow that to happen again. The
more she made love to him, the more painful the parting
would be when the time came for her to leave. "I don't
want you to make love to me."

"Who are you trying to fool? Your eyes say yes. And
your lips . . ." He lowered his head to prove she was wrong.

She pressed her palms against his chest, but she choked over her words. "Wanting has nothing to do with it."

He puffed his cheeks and blew out a warm breath. "I have a plan," he said. "A plan that might help us. First, you'll need to agree to see a friend of mine."

"What friend?"

"Doug Cranston. You met him at my party."

"The geneticist?"

"Right. I'd like Doug to do a workup of you—blood analysis, family history, the works."

"How could that possibly help us?"

He held her shoulders in a firm manner, but there was a softness in his smile that set her at ease. "I have a theory," he began. "Will you bear with me on this?"

"I'll try. Go on." If a theory would untangle their jumbled-up priorities, she'd go for it.

"First, you have to know I love you and that I want your happiness. Do you believe that?"

"Yes, I do," she said.

"I'm not sure we're meant to be together. I'd like for us to be, but whether we are or not, I think you need some answers about yourself that Doug can give you."

She frowned. "What are you trying to say?"

"Only that I don't think your unwillingness to have children has anything to do with your career. I think deep down you're afraid to have children because you think they'll be deaf like your father—and suffer as he's suffered."

"Well, you're wrong," she said, amazed at his audacity. "Where did you get a stupid idea like that?" She pulled away from him and went to the hole in the cabin's back wall. She stood there, staring out at the rain-washed hillside, refusing to consider that his theory might have any basis in fact.

"My first clue was on the Fourth of July. When I implied you'd gotten many of your traits from your father, you froze up and informed me in no uncertain terms that you took after your mother. That started me wondering. Then, when you said you wouldn't mind adopting children, I put two and two together. And today, when I heard the stories of how your grandmother died and learned how your father grew up, I was almost sure I was right."

He came to her and pulled her into his arms. As he held her, memories flashed in her mind—memories of those two precious deaf children in Mexico. After living with their family for three months, her predominant impression had been how difficult it was for deaf children to do things hearing children did without effort or forethought.

She remembered stories of cruel tricks children had played on her father. She remembered how her mother had been disinherited by her family when she'd married—God forbid—a deaf man. She felt again the force of Phillip's rejection when he told her he couldn't marry her because she might give him defective children.

Defective children. Was that what she feared?

"I figure Doug could give you an update on the chances that any children of yours might be deaf. I phoned him and talked to him about it. He said he could give you fairly accurate odds."

"There's something you've overlooked here," Robyn said, forcing the memories from her mind. "If you're right about the way I feel—and I'm not sure you are—Doug still couldn't guarantee I wouldn't have deaf children. He couldn't guarantee me my children wouldn't have to suffer as my dad suffered . . . as his mother suffered before him."

"But you could deal with the truth instead of uncertainties and fears," Greg said. "And there's something else I want you to think about."

"There's more?" she asked wearily.

"Only that at some point your mom and dad probably dealt with the same fears you have. They obviously decided the rewards of having a child were worth the risks." He squeezed her hand. "Considering how you turned out, I'd say they made a wise decision."

"What a sweet thing to say," she murmured, truly pleased at his compliment. Yet his observation was well taken. She remembered wondering, as a teenager, if she'd been planned or if her mother had gotten pregnant by accident. One summer night she'd gathered her courage and asked. Her mother had smiled, embraced her and told her she was the result of a conscious decision and an abundance of love. Even so, she couldn't bear to play that game of genetic roulette. But maybe that other doctor was wrong. Maybe...

A tiny spring of hope bubbled up through all the bad memories, and a longing rose in her chest.

She thought of her friends' babies she had cared for in her townhouse in Virginia and recalled the longing she had felt when she held them.

She looked at Greg and for the first time really saw the sweetness in him. She allowed herself to think of having his children, of presenting him with the son he needed so he could heal from the loss of his brother, and his infant son before that. "Call Doug," she said. "Make the appointment. I'll go if you'll go."

Greg took her into his arms with such a tenderness that she felt confident about her decision.

"You won't be sorry, Robyn."

"On the contrary, I may be very sorry," she said, thinking of the possible results of the genetic counseling.

"Are you sure you want me to go with you?"

"Are you kidding? Of course I do. I expect you to submit yourself to the same tests I have. If I get a needle stuck in my vein, so do you."

"You drive a hard bargain, but okay, I'll go. What do I have to lose?"

AS LUCK WOULD HAVE IT, Doug Cranston had an opening in his appointment schedule Monday afternoon.

Not quite ready to go through with her promise, Robyn tried to back out of her commitment. But Greg picked her up at the kennel and took her home so she could change for the appointment. She acquiesced.

They waited, along with two married couples, in the reception area of Doug's office in a high-rise medical complex in northwest Oklahoma City. From the gentle swelling of the women's abdomens, she guessed they were expecting their babies in four or five months.

While Greg flipped through a parenting magazine, she let her gaze fall to her own abdomen. For a moment she pictured the miracle of life rounding her flat belly. What kind of a mother would she make?

Greg tossed his magazine onto the table and draped his arm around her shoulders. "I liked the way you handled your father when he was depressed about the raft."

"At the cabin?"

He nodded. "You made him believe he could do what he wanted to do."

"I know he can rebuild the raft. The positive approach usually works best. My mother taught me that."

"It's funny you should mention your mother. Being here, looking at those women over there, I couldn't help thinking what a wonderful mother you would make, Robyn."

"Please, don't start that again. We're here to get the facts. I don't want to think beyond that—not yet."

"I was also thinking how it would be if one of those women over there had a deaf child. With one of those hearing dogs Kendra said she could train for children, a kid could lead a safer life than your father did, and certainly safer than your grandmother's."

"Look, we've gone over all this before."

"And I read somewhere about a program called Visual Phonics," Greg said, "where deaf people can learn to speak."

"Dad's been working on that with his therapist, but so far he hasn't made any sounds, so I'm not sure it will work with him."

"Think how much easier it would have been for your father if he had been able to take advantage of all these new developments when he was a child."

Robyn would have been a fool to miss the point of the conversation. "You've rehearsed this speech, haven't you?"

"I'm just trying to show you that a child who's born deaf today has a better chance of living a fairly normal life."

"It still wouldn't be easy for the child—or the parents."

"No one has it easy, Robyn. There are never any guarantees."

"I guess you're right about that. Still I wouldn't want to have a baby if I were fairly certain the child would be deaf."

"But, as you said yourself, things could have been different for your father if he had gone to a school for the deaf or worked with a therapist early in life."

"Yes, but..." Her protest faded on her lips as the receptionist crossed the room and stopped before them. "Miss Woodson, Mr. Michaels— Dr. Cranston will see you now."

Greg stood and offered Robyn his hand. "Are you ready?"

More nervous since they had discussed what was really at stake with the appointment, she forced a smile. "As ready as I'll ever be."

ROBYN AND GREG FILLED OUT family history questionnaires and spoke individually with Doug. He asked them questions about their relatives, about possible environmental contaminants, about dietary matters, about births and deaths and illnesses—and about the deafness that ran in Robyn's family.

After explaining what he would do with the information, he directed his nurse to draw blood samples and told them he would phone them for an appointment once the samples had been analyzed. The visit lasted almost two hours.

When they stepped outside, Greg asked "Do you have time for a bit to eat before you have to get back to the kennel?"

Robyn glanced at her watch. "I have a few minutes."

"Good, I've got a big tabouli salad waiting for us at home."

The salad was refreshing. Afterward, Greg dished up generous helpings of frozen strawberry yogurt, which they polished off eagerly.

"Where's Manuel?" Robyn asked, setting her dish on the table.

"Still at the kennel."

"And Taffy?"

"With him. Those two are inseparable these days."

"Manuel's put in lots of hours at the kennel lately."

"He says he's working on a special project."

She nodded. "He's training children to raise the puppies Kendra plans to breed for the program."

"I got the impression he was working on something else, too." He took Robyn's dish and stacked it with his in the sink.

Having followed him into the narrow kitchen, Robyn picked up a sponge and wiped the tile counter. "I haven't been there enough lately to know what's going on. But Kendra comes up with new ideas all the time."

Standing behind her, Greg slid his arms around her waist and bent to kiss the sensitive skin below her ear. "I'm glad Manuel's gone today."

She turned in his arms, feeling playful. Since the appointment with Doug, she'd felt a lightness, which she interpreted as hope. Hope for her and Greg as a couple. "So, are you going to tell me why you're glad he's gone?"

He grinned, slipped his thumb under the top button of his dress shirt and flicked it open. "Oh, reasons."

Slowly, teasingly, he unbuttoned the others, then drew the folds of fabric aside. He stuffed his hands into his pants pockets and leaned against the opposite counter.

Robyn let her gaze slide over his chest, then boldly let it dip to the fullness in his pants. She could almost feel the heat radiating from his body.

"Time for dessert," he said.

"We've already had dessert."

"Not this dessert, Robyn."

"Maybe if you'd give me a sample, I could decide if I want any."

"Why, you little rascal...." He reached for her wrist, but she darted sideways, just out of his reach.

"Don't tell me I have to catch you again," he said, but his eyes glittered with the challenge of the chase.

Laughing, she wheeled and found he had planted his palms on the counter on both sides of her, blocking her escape.

"Not a smart move. I've got you now."

In her peripheral vision she spotted a cake with fluffy pink marshmallow frosting. Suddenly inspired, she scooped up a dollop of the sticky substance and, turning around, held it aloft. "Be good to me, or you'll get this."

"Where do you intend to put it?"

"Let me see—your hair, maybe?"

"You wouldn't!"

"Oh, wouldn't I!"

"Robyn, come on now. That's Lillian's marshmallow cream frosting. I'd never get it out of my hair."

He extended his hands, palms out, and backed out of the kitchen. Feeling devilish, she followed him, frosting in hand. She backed him into his bedroom until the curves of his calves hit the mattress and he fell to the bed.

His shirt gaped open, and an idea popped into her mind. Kicking off her shoes, she scooted onto the bed beside him and pretended to lick the frosting off her hand.

"Well, that's more like it. Can I have a lick?"

Grinning, she slapped her hand to his chest, smashing what remained of the dollop of frosting onto his pectorals. She sprang from the bed, unable to contain her laughter.

This time he caught her and, with a hand gripping each of her wrists, pulled her down with him. Bracing her above him, he said, "Okay, smart one, what are you going to do now?"

She knew exactly what she was going to do. She took a swipe at his chest with her tongue, and his hold on her slackened.

"You're going to get that pretty blouse all messed up," he warned her, his voice husky.

"Why don't you take it off, then?" she challenged him. "Dessert's served, darling."

CHAPTER FOURTEEN

ROBYN DISPENSED with the marshmallow frosting while
Greg dispensed with her blouse. They undressed each other
slowly, relishing in the light of day what they had missed in
the darkness at the meadow.

Robyn's skin was satiny smooth, unblemished and
tan...and creamy white in some places Greg pleasured with
his fingers. "Hmm. So it's dessert time?" he said, shifting
on top of her. "Where should I start?"

"Where would you like to start?" she teased him,
squirming beneath him in a manner that made it difficult
for him to maintain his light mood.

"How about here?" He dipped his head and took the
peak of her breast into his mouth.

She arched against his abdomen. As he flicked his tongue
over the tight bud of her nipple, she whimpered and sifted
her fingers through the fullness of his hair, then trailed her
fingertips down his arms.

He drew back, kissed each cheek and smiled at the sparkle in her eyes. She possessed a creative boldness that he
was sure would make their lovemaking unique and memo-
rable each time. "I love you," he said.

Lying still, pressing her hands lightly against his chest,
she returned the endearment but smiled with a hint of reluctance. "And I love you. Lots."

Although her cheeks were still splashed with the flush of
desire, he felt her passion fading and a tenseness taking over

her body. He understood the reluctance—the same fear she'd shown in the meadow. Someday she would overcome it. Until then...

He applied the protection and was rewarded with the return of her boldness. Her gaze steady, encouraging, she pulled his hands to her breasts. Her body trembled to his touch and his to hers as she caressed him with her hands and lips.

The afternoon sun slanted through the blinds at his windows, splashing ribbons of light across their bare bodies. Robyn rolled him onto his back and with her tongue traced the horizontal paths of sunlight across his chest. Lifting her gaze to his face, she whispered, "I want you."

With his hands at her narrow waist, he lifted her astride him. She smiled at him, and the sparkle in her eyes warmed to a glow. With his guiding hands, she lowered herself onto the erect fullness of him. He curled his fingers around the curve of her hips. "Ah, Robyn. You are so sweet. So...ah."

Robyn watched Greg's eyes drift shut and felt a certain satisfaction that she could give him such pleasure. She leaned forward on her knees and braced herself on his chest with her palms while he moved inside her, driving her wild with the need for completion. Their bodies locked together, she rode the waves of his hips until a shimmering swept over her body.

"Oh, Greg, Greg— I love you!" she cried out. Moments later, she collapsed onto his chest and into the security of his arms.

"YOU'RE LATE," Kendra said, sticking her pencil through her ponytail. "You've had a few calls." She handed Robyn three slips of paper and leaned her chair onto its back legs. "I thought you were going to be through at the doctor's by two."

Still feeling like a warm, cuddly kitten, Robyn flipped her hair over her shoulders and allowed the inner glow to show in her smile. She knew she looked a wreck, but she didn't care. "Sorry. I made another stop."

Kendra regarded Robyn with a knowing smile and plunked her glasses down on the kennel's reception desk. "Oh, I see. Things are going well with Greg, I take it?"

"Much better. We've been... working on our problem."

"Working on your problem? Are you serious, or are you just being facetious?"

Robyn laughed. "I'm serious. Greg and I went to see a geneticist today."

"Why a geneticist?"

"It's a long story, actually," Robyn said, adopting a serious stance. "But the heart of it is that Greg's helping me see I haven't been altogether honest with myself about some important matters."

"You can't expect me to understand what you're talking about with that vague answer," Kendra complained. "What are you talking about, and what does it have to do with a geneticist?"

"I guess I've been fooling myself," Robyn admitted. "Lately I've come to realize the real reason I haven't wanted children is because I was afraid they'd be deaf, like Dad. It was Greg's idea to go to the geneticist—to find out whether I have anything to worry about or not."

The receptionist chose that moment to return to her desk. "Maybe we'd better go where we can talk in private," Kendra suggested. She took Robyn's arm and led her down the hallway and into her office. After shutting the door behind them, she waved Robyn into the spare chair while she sat cross-legged on her desk and took the phone off the hook.

"Does this mean Robyn Woodson isn't the high-powered career woman she thought she was?"

Robyn thought about Kendra's question and sighed. "It means I'm not so sure anymore. I do like to work, but I don't think I'd mind taking time out to have children—if I thought they wouldn't be deaf."

"Robyn, you know the statistics. Your father's deafness is genetic, and those are potent genes."

"At least the doctor can tell me my chances."

"What if he says your children would probably be deaf?"

"Greg's been doing some research. He had a speech all rehearsed about how a deaf child these days can lead a fairly normal life."

"Wait a minute," Kendra said, shaking her head. "I'm confused. Are you or are you not willing to have children if there's a strong chance they'd be deaf?"

Robyn's heart felt heavy in her chest. "No, I'm not. I've seen too much. I wouldn't want to do that to a child."

"Well then, unfortunately, it sounds like you still have a problem."

"Maybe. Maybe not," Robyn said. "I'm hoping if the geneticist's news isn't good, Greg will change his mind and consider adoption. I have a feeling he wouldn't want to inflict a hardship on an innocent little baby any more than I would."

ONE CALL ROBYN HAD MISSED was from the investigator working to find Manuel's parents. Eagerly she returned the call. "Alonzo, this is Robyn Woodson."

"Ah, Señorita Woodson. I have news for you."

"Good news, I hope."

"*Sí.* I have found the parents of your young man. They are in a little village near the Gulf of *Méjico*. It was as you suspected. They were in a bus that washed into the river when the hurricane blew over the land. They had been in the water for days when the villagers found them. There were snake bites and broken bones and—"

"Will they make it, Alonzo?"

"I had them moved to a hospital. The doctor there says yes. But it will be many days, maybe weeks."

Robyn couldn't wait to tell Manuel. Although he loved his work at the kennel and enjoyed living with Greg, there were days when he was so depressed about his parents that Robyn worried about him. "Did you tell them not to worry about Manuel?"

"*Sí*. And Señora Garcia gave me a message for her son. It is a short message. She could not talk very well."

Hearing the crinkling of paper, Robyn grabbed a pen and sat poised, ready to copy the message.

"Señor Garcia is in a coma—"

"Oh, no!"

"But the doctor expects that he will be well in time. The *señora* cannot talk. The *señora* wants Manuel to stay in *Los Estados Unidos*. When she is better, she will call him. He can write to her at this address." He gave Robyn the information. "She asked me to thank Señor Michaels for taking care of her son. And she asked me to thank you also, *Señorita*."

"Tell her to call Señor Michaels collect when she's ready to talk. I'll pass the good news and the message along to her son. Send me a bill for your services, and please, stay in touch with Manuel's parents."

"I will, *señorita*, and be careful. The lady who answered your phone said you will be in a race on a river soon."

"Don't worry. This is a very calm river," Robyn said, "and nothing is going to happen. I'd be willing to bank on it."

WITH SUMMER SCHOOL OVER, Manuel was working earlier hours at the kennel. Robyn found he'd already finished his chores and left for the day. Anxious to give him the good news, she dialed Greg's number, but no one answered. She started to phone Greg at work but decided to wait and tell them the good news that evening.

She worked at the kennel until six, then drove to Meals for the Heart to make sure no problems had popped up at the office in her absence. Even though she was excited about the good news she had for Manuel, she couldn't forget the look of disappointment on the face of the eighty-year-old deaf woman who had come to the kennel that afternoon, desperate for a hearing dog. While the poor woman had been asleep in her bed, she had been robbed. Horrified by the experience, she'd barely been able to sleep since.

Robyn hated having to tell her there were more than thirty others in line before her, equally desperate for hearing dogs. By the time Robyn pulled into her driveway, the responsibility of winning the raft race bore down on her. So did a heavy dose of guilt because she hadn't applied herself to the task as fiercely as she could have. She should have talked her father out of that ill-conceived test run on the Illinois River. She should have hired someone to design a raft that could compete with the technological wonder that would give Greg's team the edge.

Berating herself for letting her feelings for him diminish her devotion to the task, she trudged up the steps to Greg's house and rang his doorbell. When no one answered, she turned to leave, wishing for the good feelings she knew would come when she told Manuel the news about his parents. Then she remembered that Greg had offhandedly mentioned something that afternoon about the nightly conditioning exercises he had scheduled for his crew so they would be primed for the race, and she felt even worse.

Weaving her way around the cars that filled her driveway, she admitted there was no way her crew could be adequately conditioned for the race. Instead of exercising, they were busy building another raft.

At that moment she decided to focus her energies on sharpening the hearing dogs team's competitive edge in every conceivable way. That would mean distancing herself from Greg, something she hated to do, considering the closeness they'd achieved lately. But she couldn't let down all those people.

As she approached her father's workshop, the sound of male laughter drifted into the early evening air, along with the buzz of jigsaws and the pound of hammers. From the yard she heard the irritating squeak of knives slicing through the foam that would form the raft's flotation system.

She stepped into the workshop and waved to her father. Smiling, he waved back. She spotted Lillian with a pitcher of lemonade in her hands. Surely her neighbor would know where she could find Manuel.

"I see you worked late, too."

The deep rumble of Greg's voice and the warmth of his breath tickled the fine hair on Robyn's neck. Wheeling, she found him shirtless, wearing only a pair of tight white shorts. With much difficulty, she ignored the thighs she had straddled earlier in the day and remembered her resolve to focus on the race. "What are you doing here?" she asked him.

"Working, of course." He pressed his frosty glass of lemonade to his forehead. "Did you have a rough afternoon or something?"

"You're working on our raft?" she asked him, ignoring his question about her afternoon.

"Yep. So is Manuel. Thought your dad could use a couple extra hands."

"I'm not sure that's a good idea. After all, you're our competition."

"So? We're also your neighbors. Do you see anything wrong with a neighbor helping a neighbor?" He bent to plant a short, salty kiss on her lips. "Especially a neighbor whose daughter I happen to be in love with?"

Hammers stopped hammering, saws stopped buzzing, and Robyn could tell at least a dozen ears were listening in on their conversation. Trying to show some appreciation while she imposed distance between her team and Greg and Manuel, she said stiffly, "I appreciate what you're trying to do, but I think you and Manuel had better go home."

Watching her over the rim of his glass, Greg took a long drink of lemonade, then said, "Your father needs help. I have the time." He narrowed his gaze. "Wait a minute. Are you afraid I'll plant a time bomb around here or something?"

Robyn cringed at the icy edge to his voice. "Please, let's not argue about something else—okay? Just leave."

"You mean as far as you're concerned, there's no such thing as friendly competition?"

"We intend to beat you in that race, if that's what you mean."

"Beat us?" Greg shook his head and lowered his voice. "I don't think so."

His cockiness sparked her resentment. "Are you making fun of my father's design?"

"I'm not making fun of anything." He glanced in her father's direction, turned and lowered his voice. "I'm stating an opinion based on facts. Your raft's going to look great, but it won't be able to measure up to that computerized machine we've put together."

Robyn was glad her father couldn't hear Greg's words. Even so, she knew most of the team members had overheard the conversation. They were excited about the new design—a sleeker raft that would carry a large, papier-mâché hearing dog on its deck. She couldn't let them think they were defeated before the race began. "We've got you beat on experience," Robyn asserted in a clear voice. "We *will* win."

"I guess we'll see in three weeks, won't we?"

"Look, I don't mean to seem unappreciative, but there are a lot of deaf people desperate for their dogs. Some of their relatives are on this team. Everybody here but you and Manuel will be fighting for them in that race. We'll do everything we can to beat you. You'd better think about that before you come over here offering to help."

"Well," Greg said, moving to the doorway, "I know where I'm not wanted. Manuel?" he called, his eyes flashing.

"I need to speak with him. My contact in Mexico found his parents."

Manuel stepped out from behind a pile of wood. "You found my mother and father?"

Trying to appear civilized for the boy's sake, she smiled sweetly at Greg, then told Manuel what she had learned from the investigator.

The boy's eyes filled with tears, and he hugged her so hard he almost knocked the breath out of her. "*Gracias*, Robyn. I'll never forget what you've done for me—for my family. Nothing is as important as family."

Greg leveled a chilling look at Robyn. "You're right, Manuel. Trouble is, I'm not family here. Maybe I'll never be. Get your tools. We're leaving."

JONATHAN WAS PLEASED with the progress on the new raft. If everyone showed up for the next two weeks as they had tonight, it would be ready for the race.

He pictured the hearing dogs raft gliding down the Arkansas. His raft would fare well in the race. With luck, they might win.

He flipped off the light in his workshop and crossed the street to Lillian's house in the moonlight. Before she had left tonight, she'd said something about a package for Robyn. A truck had delivered it to her house earlier that day. He must have been napping and missed the flashing light over the door.

He remembered what Lillian had said about the package. *Too heavy for a woman to carry, but a strong man like you could manage it with one arm.* It was amazing how Lillian's sour mouth had sweetened up lately.

He smiled and rapped lightly on Lillian's storm door. That's when he saw the note taped to the door frame. "Jonathan, I'm busy. Come in. Lillian."

Puzzling over the note, Jonathan tried the door and found it open. He knew Lillian thought nothing of walking into his house unannounced. He didn't feel right doing so. Especially not in a woman's house. Especially not in Lillian's.

Too curious not to do as she had instructed him, he stepped inside and smelled lilacs. He liked lilacs. Lillian wore perfume that smelled like lilacs. But Lillian was nowhere in sight.

He peeked around the corner, went down the hallway, looked into a bedroom and froze. There, seated at a vanity table with her back to him, was Lillian.

Jonathan's heart beat fiercely. Lillian, dressed in a flowing, silky pink gown, was pulling a silver comb through her hair. Her auburn hair tumbled in waves over her shoulders and midway down her back.

Her gaze met his in the mirror. Slowly she pivoted on the vanity seat and smiled. She patted the bed beside her and motioned for him to join her. In her bedroom? He hesitated. No woman but Carol Ann had ever beckoned him into her bedroom.

Tilting her head, she opened her palm and fluttered her fingers for him to come closer. Slowly he inched his way into her bedroom and paused. "I came for the package," he signed.

"The package can wait," she signed, patting the pink tufted bedspread beside her.

He gulped, feeling tinglings he hadn't experienced for months. Finally he found the nerve to perch on the edge of the bed.

Lillian squared her shoulders and pivoted on the seat to face him. His gaze drifted to the creamy white skin of her neck, to her tempting, deep cleavage. Lillian was a beautiful woman.

"Now," she began, leaning forward and placing her hands on his knees. "Tell me if you like what you see."

Jonathan nodded, feeling as he had the first time he'd seen a picture in a magazine of a woman in a clinging nightgown. He had been thirteen, and he had found the magazine beneath his father's pillow. But this woman in a revealing gown was right here in front of him, and she had her hands on his knees.

"I said tell me," Lillian said.

He signed his words carefully, slowly, so Lillian would be sure to understand him. "You are a very pretty woman."

"No, Jonathan." She patted his knees and bent forward to kiss his lips lightly. "I said tell me."

Her lips were as soft as he had remembered them. He wanted to kiss her deeper, longer. Remaining the gentleman, he puzzled over her words and stared at her questioningly.

"I know you can say the words," she signed. "You just won't say them. You've been practicing, haven't you?"

Suddenly the reality of what was happening hit Jonathan like a two-by-four. Still, he couldn't feel anger for Lillian. Hungry for her touch, he covered her hands with his palms and leaned forward for another kiss. Just as he shut his eyes, he felt her fingertips press against his lips.

"Yes, Jonathan. You can kiss me again, but first, I want you to tell me if you like what you see."

Maddeningly he searched for a word he had practiced that would tell Lillian how he felt. He knew the "fuh" sound. Would Lillian appreciate "fine" for what he felt when he saw her?

He placed his upper teeth on the outside of his lower lips and forced the air from his mouth. As his therapist had taught him, he used the hand signal for *F* to reinforce what he was saying. "Fuh—ine," he said out loud.

Smiling like a ray of sunshine, Lillian planted a smacking kiss on his lips and flung her arms around his neck. Before he knew it she was sitting on his lap and laughing and crying at the same time. Then she pulled him from the bed and danced around the room with him, coming to a halt in front of the mirror. "You old fake," she told him. "Why didn't you do that sooner?"

With a boyish shrug he wrapped his arms around her and looked in the mirror. Lillian turned around in his arms and playfully shook a finger in his face. "Oh, no, you don't. Before we play we have more work to do on a computer your therapist loaned me. You can practice the sounds, and the computer will tell you if you're saying them right. Come on, it'll be fun, and—" she pecked him on the cheek "—we can play later."

"GREG, DOUG CRANSTON here."

Seated at his desk at the plant, Greg glanced at his calendar. It had been two weeks since he and Robyn had seen Doug. Two weeks since they had made love. During that time he and Robyn had been civil to each other, nothing more. All because of her stupid insistence of maintaining the rivalry between them for the race. Two weeks wasted before she was supposed to leave for Washington. He couldn't let her get on that plane! "Hi, Doug."

"I have your tests back—and Robyn's, as well."

"You'd better call Robyn about hers."

"I will. But I wanted to talk with you first."

"Why?" Greg asked, alerted by the hint of concern in Doug's voice.

"I've got to ask you a pretty personal question."

"Okay. Shoot."

"Greg, my friend, do you plan to marry Robyn?"

Plan to marry her? *Plan* was an awfully strong word. Every time he thought he was getting close to resolving the differences between him and Robyn, she manufactured a new reason to keep them apart. Still, Doug's question piqued Greg's curiosity. "Why do you want to know?"

"I need to know."

Greg thought of the day he and Robyn had made love on his acreage in the country. He hadn't been there in two weeks. Every time he smelled the wildflowers, he thought of the way they had framed her willowy body as she lay in the field waiting for him to make love to her.

He cleared his throat and forced the image of her from his mind. "I want to marry her, but I'm not sure it's going to work out."

"Do you mind if I ask what the problem is?"

"I guess you could say we have differences of opinion."

"On what?" Doug prodded him.

"Children, for one thing."

"But there's a chance you'll work things out, isn't there?"

"I haven't given up hope, if that's what you mean."

"Then I'd like to see both of you—as soon as possible."

Greg immediately thought of one reason for Doug's mysterious inquiry, and the possibility excited him. "Robyn isn't pregnant, is she, Doug?"

"I wouldn't know about that," his friend answered, "but I definitely need to see you. And the sooner, the better."

PUZZLING OVER Doug's mysterious questions, Greg phoned Robyn and set up the appointment with Doug for the next afternoon. For all the warmth in their conversation, he might have been speaking with an undertaker. She refused his offer to pick her up at the kennel. Instead, she said she would meet him at Doug's office.

The next morning he tried for an hour to analyze a plan his plant systems engineer had recommended, but the sketches swam before his eyes. His thoughts kept drifting to his conversation with Doug. Why had Doug insisted on seeing him and Robyn promptly?

His phone buzzed. His secretary announced that Robyn was on the line. He tried to sound nonchalant, but he could detect the eagerness in his voice. "Robyn?"

"Greg, thank goodness I caught you before you left."

"What's the problem?" he asked, trying to imagine what new one she had manufactured this time.

"I can't make the appointment with Doug today."

"Why not?"

"Mr. Gilliam's having problems. I have to get over to his house right away."

"It can't wait?"

"I'm afraid not. He has a narrow-minded neighbor who's been trying to get rid of him for years. Now the neighbor claims Crackers bit him. He's called the police. Poor Mr. Gilliam is beside himself. He's afraid they'll take Crackers away."

"Call me when you get back. Maybe Doug can work us into his schedule later in the day." He glanced at his own schedule and frowned. Leaving would be close to impossible later, but he was almost crazy with the need to be with Robyn again—really be with her.

"I'm afraid that'll be impossible," Robyn said, dashing his hopes. "I have three client interviews later this afternoon, and I promised Dad I'd help him get ready for the trip to Tulsa this weekend."

"Are you going to camp out at Sand Springs, too?"

"Yes. Maybe we'll see you there."

Maybe? Only maybe? "Robyn, there's no reason we can't all drive up together in a caravan."

She hesitated before answering. "I don't think so, but thanks for the offer."

Damn Robyn and her on-again, off-again attitude. "I'll call Doug and set up another appointment, then," he grumbled.

"Better make it after the race. I hardly have time to think right now."

CHAPTER FIFTEEN

At DAWN on the Friday of Labor Day weekend, the street in front of Greg's and Robyn's houses buzzed with preparations for the trip to Sand Springs.

Lyndon helped Manuel load Greg's van with ice chests and camping gear for the gifted school's team. Then the boys left in Lyndon's red sports car to reserve campsites for both teams at the launch point eight miles upriver from Tulsa.

Lillian, in a fluorescent yellow jumpsuit, plopped a white box in the back seat of Robyn's car. She was humming and, surprisingly, hadn't needled Jonathan all morning. In fact, Robyn decided, there was a definite closeness between Lillian and her father today. A definite closeness, indeed. "What's in the box?" she asked Lillian.

"A cake, of course. Strawberry-peanut butter, and I frosted it with marshmallow cream—your favorite." She winked. "Greg told me." She glanced around and frowned. "Oh, dear. I seem to have forgotten my purse. Don't leave without me. I'll be back in a minute."

While Lillian scurried across the street, Robyn blanched. Exactly what had Greg told Lillian about marshmallow cream? Thinking about the lazy smile that would spread over Greg's face if he saw Lillian's cake, Robyn wanted to crawl into a hole and hide. Fortunately she'd given Manuel orders to find separate campsites for the two teams in

Sand Springs. If she was lucky, Greg wouldn't see the cake at all.

Greg might complain about the instructions she'd given Manuel. Deep down, though, she knew she and Greg were better off maintaining the distance she had imposed almost three weeks ago—for emotional reasons as well as competitive ones.

Robyn had hoped the time apart would strengthen Greg's feelings and that he would miss her so much he'd cut the strings he'd tied to any future relationship they might have. But if his feelings had grown and matured, she'd had no clue.

How she needed that unconditional love! Phillip hadn't been able to cope with the chance she might have what he called defective children. Greg couldn't cope with the idea she might not have children at all. Either way, she hadn't been able to measure up to their expectations.

She thought of her job and felt a rush of satisfaction. She not only met her boss's expectations, she exceeded them.

Still, no matter how much she told herself Greg wasn't right for her, she couldn't convince her body—or her heart—that she didn't love him. During the past three weeks, when the exhausting work was finished and the night was quiet, she had ached for the tenderness of his hands, for the touch of his lips.

Please, she prayed silently, *let the weekend pass quickly.*

ALL BUT THREE MEMBERS of the hearing dogs crew arrived by caravan in the small, friendly town of Sand Springs before noon. The other three crewmen, on duty at the kennel, would drive to Sand Springs early Monday morning in time for the race.

Robyn followed the signs to the beautiful, unspoiled River City Park on the north bank of the Arkansas. Shaded by a canopy of willows and tall sycamores, the park bustled with a festive air.

The campgrounds, adjacent to the river, were crowded with early arrivals. Barbecue pits spiced the air with the scents of hickory and pungent sauce. Near the launch ramp, country-western music blared from carnival rides that would begin that evening. Crew members and curious onlookers milled around the hundred colorful race entries already lined up beside the river.

While the men unloaded the raft from its trailer, Lillian elbowed Robyn and pointed. "Look, there's Greg."

Robyn spotted him in the distance and felt a powerful tug of longing.

Lillian waved both hands high over her head and jumped up and down. "Yoo-hoo, Greg, over here!"

Her shrill voice caught his attention. He sauntered over, bare-chested, wiped his arm across his forehead and stared unsmiling at Robyn. "Hi, there."

"Hi." He had a streak of dirt on his cheek she was tempted to smooth away with her fingertips, but she restrained herself. While she stared at him, watching the emotions flicker in his eyes, she wondered how she could possibly survive the weekend without pulling his arms around her.

Fortunately, Lillian had the good grace to switch her attentions to the broad riverbed that was more sand than water. "How do they expect us to float a raft in that skinny strip of a river?" she complained.

Tearing his gaze from Robyn, Greg said, "My question exactly. Apparently Sunday at midnight the floodgates upriver will be opened. By launch time Monday, the river will be full, bank to bank."

"How deep?" Lillian asked with a frown.

"About to here," Greg said, slanting his palm sideways beneath his navel, "except for a couple of real shallow spots. They'll mark them with buoys."

"Not much like the Illinois, is it?" Robyn said.

"Let's hope not," Lillian piped in. "I've had enough emergencies. Speaking of which, where are those boys?"

"Checking out the young ladies," Greg said, a hint of a smile showing. "If you need help, I'm available."

He was so close Robyn could have pressed a finger to the bead of perspiration zigzagging down his bare chest. She curled her fingers into a fist and told herself she wanted to do no such thing. "They were supposed to save us a campsite. Have any idea where that might be?"

"Sure." He pointed through the trees. "Over there, next to us."

"Next to you?" Dear God, not next to Greg! "But I specifically asked Manuel to find us separate sites."

"If the arrangements don't suit you," he said dryly, "we'll find you another place. I'm afraid it'll probably be over there, though, near that dusty road." He turned on his heel and headed to the campsite as if he couldn't care less what she decided to do.

Robyn grabbed his arm. "I'm sorry. I didn't mean to sound unappreciative. Those arrangements will do nicely."

"I'll say," Lillian said with a sly grin. She reached into the back seat of Robyn's car and pulled out the white box. "I made a cake, and—" she flipped open the box "—ta-da! Marshmallow cream frosting, just for you two!"

On her way to the car, Robyn ducked behind the trunk lid and fanned her face. How was she going to spend a long weekend eating . . . sleeping so close to Greg?

AFTER THEY UNLOADED the cars, Lillian took off to look for Jonathan. Kendra arrived with Miracle and enlisted

Robyn's help in staging hearing dog demonstrations for the camp crowd. Then came the fish fry and a steamboat casino party that evening.

Robyn found herself looking for Greg in the crowds and wishing they could share the weekend. But she had no one to blame but herself for the emptiness she felt in his absence.

Leaning against a tree by the campsite prior to the midnight curfew, she watched her father and Lillian walk hand in hand from the carnival. He had changed so much in the past few weeks. The day she met Greg her father had been reluctant to leave the security of his home and mingle in a crowd of neighbors. Now he was enjoying himself in a crowd of strangers.

She wondered how much of her father's reclusiveness had been her fault and her mother's for not encouraging him to be more sociable. Lillian was working wonders with him.

"Why the frown?" Greg slipped from the shadows and sent Robyn groping for balance.

"Greg! You scared me!"

"I didn't mean to," he said, steadying her with his hand on her elbow.

His touch was warm and welcome. In the moonlight she let her gaze wander over a different Greg. Dressed in a blue plaid western shirt, snug jeans and boots, he looked like the local gents, who, dressed in their Sunday finest, were squiring their lady friends to the weekend's festivities. Beneath this new image, though, was the same Greg. She had missed him so. "I was thinking about Dad—how much he's changed since the accident."

"People do grow and change, Robyn."

"Sometimes they do." *And sometimes they don't,* she thought regretfully about Greg's inflexibility.

"This isn't how I pictured us spending this weekend," he said, withdrawing his hand from her elbow.

She could only nod, a lump swelling in her throat as he voiced her frustrations, too.

"What do you say we call a truce, Robyn? Our crews are mingling in spite of us."

"I don't know, Greg...."

"We'll be friends for the weekend," he offered with a gentle smile.

She grinned. "Just friends?"

He rubbed the back of his neck with an open palm. "That might call for some powerful pretending, but I think I can pull it off if you can."

She didn't mean to touch him, but she found herself reaching out to trace a horizontal line in the plaid where it crossed his chest.

He halted her fingers and, searing her with his gaze, drew her hand to his lips for a gentlemanly kiss. "But you'll have to stop doing that if we're only going to be friends."

She pulled back her hand, forcing a laugh. "Then maybe we'd better call it a night. We've got to get up early for the parade tomorrow, my friend."

AS THE WEEKEND PROGRESSED, pretending to be only friends became difficult, for each day's events threw Robyn and Greg closer together. After parading through the streets of Sand Springs on Saturday on their rafts, they went with their teams en masse to the tractor pull and the celebrity goat-roping contest. That evening they sat side by side at the rodeo, thighs brushing, shoulders bumping, while they laughed at the clowns' antics.

Sunday evening was the true test. The two crews piled into cars and drove downriver to Tulsa. There, on the west bank of the river, they sat on the grassy slopes of the park and watched fireworks synchronized to music on KRMG radio.

The night would have been perfect if Robyn could have experienced it in Greg's arms. Even so, she knew when she was in Washington she would think often about sharing the holiday with him.

The last to return to the crowded campsite, Robyn and Greg found their sleeping bags suspiciously close. Robyn wondered who had made sure she and Greg would sleep within inches of each other. Pretending not to notice, she stretched out on her bag, looked up and watched the stars blink through the leaves overhead. Were the night skies this exquisitely beautiful in Washington,? she wondered.

Greg's voice, a coarse whisper, interrupted her thoughts. "Dirty shame we can't be on a raft together tomorrow."

She rolled onto her side, rested her head on her bent arm and tried to inject a bit of humor into her answer. "If you want me to defect, forget it. The answer's no."

"We should have had one team instead of two—played to our strengths," he went on. "Our raft and your dad's expertise at rafting. Then we could have won for sure and split the pot."

"Now you think of it. Michaels, your timing's off again."

"Robyn, I wish we could—"

She silenced him with her finger, the fullness of his lips soft and tempting. "Don't say it, friend."

"What are you? A mind reader?"

She heard a stirring close by and lowered her voice to a whisper. "It doesn't take a fortune teller to figure out what you were going to say. You were going to say you wished we could have worked out our problems, weren't you?"

SOUND WAVES

"Well, to tell you the truth, I'm not ready to give up on us yet." He took her hand in his and rubbed her fingers along the stubble of his cheek. "Are you sleepy?"

"Not hardly."

"I didn't think so. Want to go for a walk?"

"Sure."

Holding hands, they snuck from the campsite to a secluded spot by the river. The muted lyrics of a plaintive ballad drifted on the breeze from a lone guitarist at the campgrounds.

Greg found a smooth spot on the sand and, leaning against a boulder, spread his legs to make room for Robyn to sit in front of him. He offered her his hand. "Want to sit down?"

She balked. "Friends wouldn't sit like that."

"Come on, Robyn," he said. "Give me a break here."

"Well, just for a few minutes." She joined him on the sand, nestling her back against his chest. She closed her eyes. *Yes,* she thought, *you do belong here like this.*

He pressed his lips to her temple and hugged her close to him. "I need to explain something to you."

"Please," she said, "let's keep it light between us tonight."

"Robyn, I love you."

Before she could protest the direction their walk had taken, he turned her in his arms and filled her with the sweetness she had missed so much. Breaking the kiss, she said, "I love you, too. Love isn't the problem."

"I realize that. But I've had a lot of time to think these past three weeks. Too much time."

Robyn's hopes soared. "So what have you been thinking about?"

"That we were wasting three good weeks, for one thing. That I've been running hot and cold with you, for another. I'm sure I've given you mixed signals."

"Another famous Michaels understatement," she said.

"The truth is, I'm afraid of losing you, Robyn," he said grimly, "like I lost Chelsea and Christopher and Brad—and even my parents. That's what's on my mind when I act cool to you."

Although Greg's explanation cleared up a few things, Robyn was disappointed he hadn't touched on their real problem. Well, if he wouldn't, she would.

"My turn. Okay?"

"Shoot."

"All your talk during the past few weeks about whether or not I'll have children has made me feel like a baby machine—a walking reproductive facility."

Greg's eyes twinkled. "Oh, Robyn, surely you're kidding."

"I am not. And I'll tell you another thing. I got to thinking the other night, what if I *can't* have children? Then I wondered, if you and I managed to resolve all our other problems, would you ask me to take a fertility test?"

"Now I know you're kidding."

"No, I'm not. Think about it. What will you do if I can't have children? Say, 'So sorry, Robyn. You don't measure up'?"

He was quiet for a long moment. Too quiet for Robyn.

"When you first told me you didn't want to have children—on the Fourth of July, remember?—I thought maybe you couldn't," he said, "but it was pretty obvious there were other reasons, so I didn't give that one much thought."

"Wait a minute. Could you or could you not handle it if I were not able to have children? Would I be on your 'forget it' list?"

He looked away for a moment, propelling Robyn's heart right into her shoes. "I . . . well, no," he said, but his hesitation and choice of words told Robyn he wasn't so sure. "But to refuse to have children because you fear they'd be deaf . . . I'm sorry, Robyn. I can't buy that."

"Okay," she said. "Question number two. You mean you honestly wouldn't mind parenting a deaf child?"

"Of course not. I thought you knew that." He flashed a lopsided grin and ran his fingertip lightly, adoringly over the curve of her chin. "I happen to think we'd be great together as parents. You with your optimism and encouraging manner. Me with loads of enthusiasm and my sterling character." He laughed.

Robyn didn't. "You have no idea what you'd be in for. Even in today's world, people can be so narrow-minded. Take Mr. Gilliam's neighbor, for example. He's made it his life's mission to rid the neighborhood of Mr. Gilliam."

"You underestimate your optimism, Robyn. I've seen you work wonders with your father lately. I'll bet you could help a deaf child overcome whatever challenges are out there for him. And you're overlooking real positives here."

She frowned. "What do you mean, 'real positives'?"

"I mean you've been so worried about passing your father's deafness along to your children that you've overlooked the wonderful qualities your kids might gain from him."

"Like his stubbornness, I suppose?" she said, kidding.

"Like his sense of humor, silly, and his capacity for love. And don't forget his artistic talent."

Robyn sat there, thinking over Greg's insightful observations. "He does have a few good points, doesn't he?"

"Plenty."

"Greg, we could talk all night and still not agree on what's at stake here."

"If we talk all night, we'll never win that race," he said lightly, ignoring the serious tone of her complaint. He stood and offered her his hand. "Maybe we'd better hit the sack. Tomorrow morning's going to come awfully early, and I promised to cook breakfast for your bunch as well as mine. But think over what we talked about, will you?"

"I will if you will," she said.

WAY INTO THE MORNING HOURS Robyn kept rolling Greg's words over in her mind. Just the fact he had told her they would be good together as parents implied he was thinking about a commitment. Still, he hadn't asked her to stay in Bethany. Nor had he told her he'd love her forever, baby machine or no baby machine.

She wasn't, as Lillian called it, a spring chicken anymore. The older she got, the greater chance she had of having problems bearing children.

What would he do if they married and she couldn't produce children? Do away with her like some modern-day Henry VIII? Or would he leave her?

Feeling sick at the thought, she rolled onto her side, presenting her back to Greg. She could never marry him unless he loved her with no strings attached.

And that was probably not going to happen.

LABOR DAY DAWNED with a cloudless sky and a forecast of temperatures in the low nineties. Hearing Greg stir, Robyn pulled her pillow over her head and played possum. When the first rays of sun pierced her eyelids, Greg brought her a glass of orange juice with a teasing grin and a gentle kiss.

"Time to get up, sleepyhead. Launch starts at nine."

She slung her wrists over her eyes and squinted at her watch. "But that's almost three hours from now."

"How can you think about sleeping?"

"Easy. I close my eyes and I—"

"Come on. I could use some help feeding the troops."

Wielding giant iron skillets like a wagon train cook, Greg whipped up enough scrambled eggs, bacon and biscuits for both crews. Lillian and Robyn made the rounds, dishing up portions to hungry crew members. Robyn noticed Lillian winking at Jonathan and sneaking him extra biscuits.

Stacking her empty plate for the boys to wash, Robyn asked Greg, "Where did you learn to cook like that?"

"When I took Brad and his buddies camping, I'd cook. I'm famous for my eggs and onions."

Robyn popped the last bite of biscuit into her mouth and considered the detached expression on Greg's face that came with memories of his brother. "I wish Brad could be here today. He'd be proud of you, Greg."

"He's here—in spirit." He plunked a metal spatula into an iron skillet, grabbed a towel and wiped his hands so hard Robyn thought his skin would peel off. "Look, I've got to get a move on," he said.

His exaggerated reaction to her mention of Brad was another clue that Greg needed to unleash a lot of carefully concealed anger about his brother. If Greg ever hoped to make peace with Brad, he'd have to vent that anger—then forgive.

"Good luck," she said. "Be safe. I hope one of us wins."

Greg grabbed his life jacket, then reached for her hand. "You be careful, too."

"I will." She squeezed his hand tightly, wishing she could go with him. "I'll see you at the finish line. After us, of course."

He looped his arms loosely around her and kissed her one last time. "Dream on, Robyn. Dream on. And may the best team win."

CHAPTER SIXTEEN

RED-FACED AND FLUSTERED, Robyn's father signed in
frantic, jerky gestures. "What if they don't get here in
time?"

Trying to appear unconcerned, Robyn glanced at her
watch again. Eight o'clock. The three crew members who
had weekend duty at the kennel and had promised to drive
up that morning hadn't arrived. What could have happened to them? Were they hurt? Would they get there in
time for the race? Robyn knew if they didn't, her team
would be short on manpower. Too short to win.

The other crewmen had lined up with the raft in the six-
tieth slot for the race, six ahead of Greg's. Shifting back in
the lineup wasn't an option. There simply wasn't room back
there to maneuver the big raft. Robyn's team would be in
the water by nine-thirty, with or without a full crew.

"Don't worry," Lillian told Jonathan with calming gestures. "We still have an hour and a half before launch.
Why, I'll bet those fellows stopped to have breakfast along
the way and just got to talking."

Lillian's platitudes did nothing to calm Robyn's father.
He paced the raft while the others sipped coffee and made
friends with the boisterous crew of the Nordic raft behind
them. Dressed in ludicrous horned Viking helmets, the
Nordic crewmen were already into the spirit of the race,
dancing on their raft's deck with boom boxes blaring.

To prevent logistics problems, the race organizers were launching rafts as they had lined up, regardless of category. Time cards punched at the beginning and the end of the eight-mile course would determine the winners. An announcer in the radio station's helicopter updated listeners on the launch.

To avoid fretting about her missing crewmen, Robyn busied herself by sizing up the competition. Although the nonprofit division had drawn more than one hundred entries, only two besides Greg's were within Robyn's view. The Oklahoma League for the Blind's raft sported a giant block of mouse cheese. The Telephone Pioneers of America entry carried a Conestoga wagon. Greg's entry, more of an oversized canoe than a raft, was by far the most sophisticated. And probably as fast as a fish in the water, Robyn thought enviously. Well, even if they did cross the finish line first, that didn't mean they'd automatically win the money.

His crew, in slick blue shorts, matching tank tops and blue ball caps, were spreading fluorescent yellow sunscreen across their faces. With their rock-hard thighs and well-sculpted upper bodies, they looked like a contingent from a health club.

Robyn shifted her attention to Greg and admired the more mature lines of his build. He lifted a finger to his cap visor in a smiling salute and gave her the thumbs-up signal. Trying to appear confident, she mocked his salute and smiled.

Lillian tapped her arm and pointed to a rail-thin man in his mid-fifties who was busy scribbling notes on a clipboard. "That's one of the judges."

"How do you know?"

"Oh, I get around, my dear."

"That you do," Robyn said wryly. "Which reminds me. Have you managed to find out how they're going to pick the money winner? It's some sort of point system . . ."

"I'm not sure." Lillian frowned. "Well, will you look at that? He's talking to that bunch on the League for the Blind's raft again. I don't like the looks of that. Not one bit."

"I'd feel better if he'd at least walk over and say hello," Robyn said, her spirits sagging.

Lillian hopped off the float and smoothed her yellow team shirt over her Bermuda shorts. "If that's what you want, that's what you'll get. Be back in a minute or two."

"Lillian, just forget it. I don't think it's a good idea to bother the judges."

"I do know a thing or two, Robyn," she said with a cocky grin. "Trust me on this one, will you?"

THE RACE OFFICIAL, knee-deep in water at the launch ramp, punched Greg's time card and thrust it into his hands. "Good luck. Keep those life vests on, and watch out for the orange buoys. The river's going to be busy today."

"Will do," Greg responded. From his coxswain's position in the raft, he gave the go-ahead signal, and his team's raft glided into the water.

Feeling a surge of adrenaline, he flipped on the portable stereo and adjusted the volume on the rock music to set the cadence for his twelve youthful rowers. They sat in twos, divided by a center aisle, in the wide, canoe-type raft built of recycled aluminum.

His raft had been the talk of the campgrounds all weekend. The mentors had designed two systems for propelling the raft through the water. In front of each seat were bicycle pedals, connected by chains and gears to alternate oars mounted on the outside of the raft. When Greg's crew tired of rowing manually, they could sit back and pedal their way down the river.

With his computer terminal, Greg kept in touch with the mentor who was monitoring the computerized control board in the raft's bow. The system detected underwater obstacles and gauged each oarsman's pull in the water. Computer screens mounted in front of the oarsmen helped them coordinate their efforts. Rowing smoothly, they quickly passed six rafts and bore down on Robyn's.

Her three missing crewmen had finally contacted her through the race headquarters. They were still stranded somewhere on the highway with a blown water pump in their aging car. In their absence, Robyn and Kendra were manning oars. The raft was making good time under the circumstances, but it couldn't compete with the computerized efficiency of Greg's.

The disappointment on Robyn's face as his raft swept past hers ate at him. The triumph he was sure he would feel at that moment soured in his stomach.

Passing rafts became the order of the morning. So did getting wet. Along the riverbank onlookers jettisoned water balloons at the rafts with slingshots. Some crews goodnaturedly lobbed them back. Greg cringed every time a balloon burst in his raft. The computer system would not take kindly to getting wet. So far the water shields the engineers had installed on the equipment were doing the job.

At the halfway mark, Greg ordered a rest period and opened the ice chest. He had just popped the top on the last drink can when he heard someone call out from the riverbank.

Squinting in the glare of the sun off the water, Greg shaded his eyes with his hand and scanned the shoreline. Then he saw it—a water cannon aimed directly at his raft.

"No! No!" he yelled, waving his hands frantically overhead.

Apparently interpreting Greg's gestures as tacit approval, the cannon's gunner swept the raft with a steady stream of water. The dousing was enough to put out a good-size fire—and a computer system.

"System's down!" the controller yelled.

Greg swore under his breath. "Can you fix it?"

"Maybe. Maybe not."

"Great, just great," Greg grumbled.

He stood to move up front and felt the raft lurch. Stumbling, he grabbed Manuel's seat and fought for balance. With the scream of tearing metal, the flooring split near his feet. Water gushed into the raft.

"Everybody overboard," he yelled. "And jump. Don't dive."

ROBYN BENT her aching shoulders and pulled on the oar with all her strength. Greg had been right about his raft's superb design. What she wouldn't give to rest her shoulders and pedal down the river for a change.

If he'd maintained the speed at which he'd passed them, he would be close to the finish line now. For the first time she pictured him accepting the million-dollar check at the awards ceremony that evening. What would she do if she didn't win?

You haven't lost yet, she chided herself. *Keep rowing. Don't quit.* She concentrated on an image of a money bag containing a million dollars and tightened her blistered hands on the oar. She wouldn't give up.

Miracle, standing over an empty water bowl, whined.

"Okay, girl," Robyn said. "I could use a drink, too." She signaled for a break, pulled her oar from the water and filled Miracle's bowl. The collie had only slurped a few

ounces when her ears perked up and her tail wagged slowly
from side to side. Then came a sharp bark, and Miracle
bolted for the front of the raft, sniffed the air and strained
at her leash.

"What is it, girl? What do you see?"

Lillian pointed in the distance at an official airboat
skimming over the water. "Trouble, that's what. I think
someone's wrecked. And dear Lord, Robyn. I do believe
it's Greg."

Robyn followed Lillian's gaze downstream and felt her
stomach swirl. Wrapped around the branches of a partially submerged tree, Greg's raft looked like crunched-up
aluminum foil. Floating in the vicinity were life jackets, the
faces above them smeared with fluorescent yellow.

Robyn turned to her father, but he had already spotted
the wreckage. He narrowed his gaze and signed fourteen.

"Thank God!" she said, turning to look for Greg.
"That's all of them."

In a moment she saw him and felt a rush of relief. He
raised his hand wearily from the water and waved at them.

"Poor man," Lillian said. "He's going to be devastated."

"He was so sure he'd win," Robyn said. "I wonder what
happened."

Lillian pointed at an orange warning flag in the middle
of the wreckage. "Looks like he missed a buoy."

Robyn grabbed her oar. "Let's go see if he needs help."

Lillian gripped Robyn's shoulders firmly in her hands.
"I'm not one to make good of another man's misfortune,
but with Greg out of the running, we might win this race if
we keep going."

"Yes," Robyn said hesitantly, "we might." She wondered if she had it in her to turn her back on him and leave
his fate to the authorities. Late last night she had accepted

the painful truth. Lying on her sleeping bag, so close to him she could have snuggled into his arms by moving a few inches, she realized she wasn't destined to live her life with him.

For purely personal reasons, she needed to win this race. Others were depending on her to win it for them, too. Since fate had intervened on her behalf, she felt obliged to take advantage of the opportunity. Yet she felt Greg's disappointment as surely as if it were her own. "It's so unfair," she said softly, as much to herself as to Lillian.

"Life isn't always fair, Robyn. Sometimes we have to make the best of a situation. The officials will help Greg. I'm sure if he could yell loud enough, he'd tell us to keep going, to win the race for him, too."

"He'd never leave us like that," Robyn said, realizing she'd already made her decision. "Stick your oar in the water. We're going to see if he needs help."

If ROBYN HAD any lingering doubts about her decision, the look in Greg's eyes banished them. When he saw that Robyn's crew was rowing to his aid, he swam over to her raft and crooked his finger. She knelt at the edge of the raft, and he looped a wet arm around her neck and kissed her.

"What in the world happened?" she asked, brushing his hair from his eyes.

"Long story. But why did you stop? You could have won if you hadn't."

"I'm only doing what you would have done."

The official's airboat, which had plucked several of Greg's crewmen from the water already, buzzed over. A heavyset man extended his hand to Greg and braced himself to pull him into the craft.

Greg hesitated and looked at Robyn. "I've got an idea," he said. "One that might help both of us."

"What is it?" she asked, intrigued by the sparkle in his eyes.

"You're short three men—right?"

"Right. And my arms are killing me."

"And as it stands, you probably don't have much chance of winning."

Robyn shrugged. "So? We knew that when we stopped to help you."

"Then why don't you let three of us join your crew?"

"Now how is that going to help? I'm sure if you did, they'd disqualify us immediately."

"Maybe. Maybe not," Lillian piped up, kneeling on the raft beside Robyn. "I did get awfully friendly with that skinny guy with the clipboard. Besides, our hands will be a bloody mess by the time we get to Tulsa if we don't get some help."

"We might be able to talk the officials into approving the crew change," Greg said. "Then, if we win, we could split the pot. We could both get what we want."

Not really, Robyn thought, but she was beginning to warm to his idea. Realistically she didn't think they could win without the help Greg offered. Half a pot was better than no pot at all. Although Greg needed all the money he could find for his school, Kendra could expand her facilities sufficiently with half a million dollars. Her father could still have his hearing dog within six months. She could go back to her job.

"I guess it's worth a try," she said, waving him on board.

"So are we, Robyn," he said, hoisting himself onto the raft. "When we get home, we're going to give us another try, too."

Smiling, she handed him a towel, drawn by the hope in his eyes. Their fingertips brushed, and they exchanged warm, caring glances. He leaned over to kiss her, but Joe thrust an oar in his hands.

"Time for that later, son. I expect it's time for you to earn your keep."

Greg, Manuel and Lyndon, the additions to Robyn's crew, took their responsibilities to heart. With the added manpower, the raft picked up speed, and Robyn entertained hopes of winning again. When they rounded a bend in the river in Tulsa and saw River West Festival Park, a loud cheer erupted from the crowd.

Robyn knelt beside Greg. "Could they be yelling for us?"

Both hands on the oars, he lifted his chin to point at the helicopter circling overhead. "I think we're celebrities. The word must have gotten around about the accident."

"Think that'll swing any weight with the judges?" Robyn asked, still hoping for a miracle.

"Don't know," he replied with an encouraging grin. "We can only hope."

Enthusiastic onlookers soaked them with water balloons when they crossed the finish line downstream from the park. Robyn thrust her wet time card into the official's hand.

Greg hopped into the river to begin the back-breaking process of lifting the raft from the water. "How fast?" he asked her, his expression one of hope.

"Two hours, two minutes. Is that good?"

"I just heard a guy over there say the best time in the whole race so far is fifty-six minutes. But that was a two-man canoe—not in our division."

"Still, it doesn't sound like we did too well," she said, frowning.

"Well, we'll find out tonight," he said, referring to the awards ceremony. "Any regrets?"

She thought for a moment. "Yeah. I regret like heck you didn't come up with your idea sooner. My shoulders will never be the same."

FOR THE AWARDS CEREMONY at five o'clock, both crews sat in one large, boisterous group halfway up the amphitheater's grassy hill. There they had a good view of the band shell on the floating stage where the trophies were awarded. Behind the stage the late afternoon sun glistened on the river, and a light breeze provided a respite from the heat.

Robyn enjoyed seeing friends they had made that weekend retrieve trophies in the traditional categories. She knew Lillian had spent half the afternoon pleading their case to the race officials to certify the combined team. But the officials had held out little hope a change could be made in the middle of the race, especially with a million dollars at stake.

Before the mayor of Sand Springs awarded the parade trophies, he teased the crowd with a few jokes, then pulled his reading glasses from his shirt pocket, along with a sheet of paper. The award for the most spirited crew went to the Viking float's Nordic oarsmen.

"And now, ladies and gentlemen," the mayor said, "I'm sure it comes as no surprise that we have a tie for most original raft design. I'm sorry one of those rafts doesn't exist anymore, so you won't be able to see it. The crew missed a warning flag in the river. Before it crunched around a tree, however, it was a doozy. Let's hear it for the bunch from Bethany, Oklahoma—they call themselves the Gifted School."

Greg rolled his eyes and covered his face with his hand, but Robyn could tell he was as pleased as he was embarrassed. He and his crew trooped to the stage for the trophy.

Robyn was so proud of him she almost missed the announcement that her team had tied with Greg's for the design award. Her entire team joined Greg's on the stage, and they reveled in their few brief moments of glory.

As they returned to their spot on the grassy hill, Gordon Denison, the wealthy Tulsa benefactor, stepped onto the stage. He carried the white money bag that had appeared on all the literature advertising the million-dollar prize for the nonprofit division.

"It's amazing how much attention a million dollars will get you," he joked. He waved the bag over his head, and the crowd cheered.

"It's been fun keeping you in suspense this weekend. Everyone wanted to know how we planned to pick the winner, but we decided to keep that information confidential."

"Why?" someone yelled from the crowd.

"I'll tell you why—because if we hadn't, you would have fallen all over yourselves to cooperate with your teammates. We were looking for true teamwork—that's what made me my fortune. That's what will win the prize.

"We designed a system of points," Denison went on to explain, "but in the end the winning team distinguished itself three weeks ago. That's when one crew wrecked their raft on a test run, and the members of a competing team pitched in to help them rebuild."

Robyn and Greg exchanged looks, their eyes wide with surprise.

"Then today," Denison continued, "when the other crew wrecked and the first extended a helping hand, we knew without a doubt we had our winner."

Robyn's mouth flew open, and she gripped Greg's hand tightly. She knew she was dreaming.

"I hope they won't mind splitting the prize money between their two causes," Denison said. "That's my only
stipulation. From what we've seen, that's what they'd
probably decide, anyway. I want to see all the crew members for the hearing dogs and the Gifted School's rafts up
here on stage. Folks, let's give them a hand."

CHAPTER SEVENTEEN

GREG GRABBED ROBYN and swung her around, then danced a jig with her all the way down the aisle to the stage. Lillian and Jonathan followed, along with every last crew member on the two teams. Favorites of the crowd, they stayed on stage until the applause stopped, then delayed their personal celebration long enough to accommodate the local news media.

Greg couldn't believe his luck. The weekend had not only brought him closer to Robyn, it had provided him with the money for his school. Now he might be able to open the school next fall—and maybe persuade Robyn to marry him.

Late that evening, she sat beside him in his van as they drove home from Tulsa. Gripping the pale green check between her fingers, she gave it a loud, smacking kiss and turned to him, her eyes glittering. "A million dollars! Can you believe it? A million beautiful dollars and they're all ours—yours and mine."

As she pressed the check to her breast, he smiled at her childlike enthusiasm. They had won that money because of her caring nature and flexibility, just two of the many qualities he admired about her.

The lights of Oklahoma City twinkled ahead. Manuel, riding in Lyndon's car in front of them, pulled over. Greg angled his car to the turnpike shoulder. Lillian, driving Robyn's car behind them, stopped, too.

Manuel hopped out of the sporty car and strode to the driver's side of the van. Greg rolled down his window.

"I need to stop by the kennel," Manuel said. "Why don't we all go?"

"Sure. But why?"

Manuel grinned. "I . . . promised Kendra I'd look in on the new pups. It'll only take a few minutes."

"No problem. Then everyone can come over to our place, and we'll order in pizza." He turned to wink at Robyn. "I don't know about you, but I'm not ready for this party to end yet."

"Me, either," she said. "See you at the kennel, Manuel."

Inside the kennel, Manuel flipped on the light in the reception room, then disappeared into the boarding area with Lyndon while the others took turns holding the check. Manuel returned shortly with an exuberant Taffy in a bright yellow collar and leash Greg hadn't seen before.

He stood to leave. "That didn't take long."

"I'm not finished yet," Manuel said, grinning at Lyndon. "I have an announcement to make."

Robyn seemed puzzled about Manuel's mysterious announcement. They all sat, and Manuel moved to stand in front of Jonathan. He handed Taffy's leash to Robyn's father and told the dog, "It's okay, girl."

Taffy thumped her tail and hooked an oversize paw over Jonathan's leg. Jonathan scratched the dog behind one ear and looked at Manuel questioningly.

"She's your dog now, Mr. Woodson," Manuel signed.

"My dog?"

Manuel knelt beside Taffy. "After the accident, I promised myself I'd make up for hurting you."

Jonathan handed the leash to Manuel and shook his head briskly. "Taffy is your dog."

"Not anymore. Now she's a working dog." He handed the leash to Jonathan again. "She's your hearing dog. See her yellow collar and leash? I finished training her myself."

Jonathan's eyes misted over as his gaze slid from the boy to the dog. Greg knew how much Taffy meant to Manuel. He had never been prouder of the boy than at that moment.

"Wait a minute," Robyn said to Manuel. "I hate to be a killjoy, but Taffy can't be a hearing dog. She got lazy. Washed out of the program. You knew that. The rules say—"

"Kendra gave her another chance," he said, a hint of irritation in his voice. He hugged the dog to his chest and shot Robyn a look that bordered on resentment.

Greg didn't appreciate the way he was talking to Robyn, but before he could correct him, Manuel said more.

"She knew you were leaving for Washington. I told her if your father didn't have a hearing dog, he'd have to go with you. I knew he didn't want to go."

Robyn's eyebrow shot up. Greg waited for her to deny Manuel's accusation, to explain that everything had changed, that she had decided to stay. But she said nothing, not a damned thing. *Hell, she's still going!* he thought.

"Kendra couldn't keep Taffy in the program because of the rules," Lyndon explained, "so Manuel trained her after hours." He puffed out his broad chest. "With help from me, of course."

"She's a good dog," Manuel said, stroking the dog's head affectionately. "She hasn't been lazy with me once."

"Does she have her papers?" Robyn pressed him. "Can she go into restaurants and other public places?"

"She has temporary papers. If Taffy doesn't get lazy again—and I know she won't—Kendra will give her full certification in six months."

No one said anything for a few moments. The only sounds were an occasional bark from a boarding dog and the swish of Taffy's tail on the floor. As far as Greg could tell, Robyn was blatantly ignoring him. He glared at her while she went to Manuel and hugged him, a tear sliding down her sunburned cheek.

"I couldn't be happier," she said. "Thanks for all you've done to help my father—and me."

While the others hugged Manuel, Greg slipped outside and sagged against the building's brick wall. He felt as if a meat cleaver had just hacked through his heart. Now that Robyn could leave without worrying about her father's safety, she was free to return to her job in Washington. And, after all they'd shared during the weekend, damned if she wasn't going to do it!

The pain of too many goodbyes turned his stomach, and he resolved to get some answers. She either loved him, or she didn't. He wouldn't bother her with his questions tonight, not with everyone around. But tomorrow he would confront her—once and for all.

FOR THE LIFE OF HER, Robyn couldn't understand Greg's moodiness. While everyone else was teary-eyed over Manuel's gift to her father, Greg glared at her, then stepped outside. When she sought him out, he said he was tired. All he wanted was to go home, shower and crawl into bed.

When he didn't tease her about crawling into bed beside him, she knew he was exhausted. Reluctantly she postponed giving him the news of her decision. She wanted the mood to be just right, and she wanted them to be alone.

Morning came too soon, along with interviews scheduled at Greg's house with a *Daily Oklahoman* reporter and a local television newsman. The first appointment was at nine and the second at ten-thirty, which would leave time for her to talk with Greg alone before their appointment with Doug Cranston. She could hardly wait to see Greg's face!

On her way to the shower she paused before the full-length mirror in the hallway. Engaging in a little make-believe, she pulled her yellow nightshirt up to her breasts, turned sideways and pooched out her stomach.

"SCOOT IN a little closer, will you?"

"Yeah! A lot closer!"

Seated next to Robyn on his living room couch, Greg shot Kendra a silencing look and obeyed the photographer's instructions. His head throbbed from lack of sleep, and perspiration beaded on his forehead.

The photographer moved his light meter from Robyn's blue dress to Greg's white shirt. "I think we have it now."

Good. As soon as the guy finished, Greg planned to politely ask Kendra, Lillian and Manuel—and yes, even Jonathan and Taffy—to leave. He deserved privacy when he confronted Robyn with his questions.

He wished she didn't look so disgustingly happy. All morning she'd been like a chirpy bird, and that only made his head pound louder. So did watching her tug the hem of her silky dress over her knees. When she did that, he recalled how silky her legs had felt wrapped around his hips.

"I need to talk to you," Robyn whispered in his ear.

"Yeah, me, too." His palms grew clammy as he wondered what she had to say. If she was going to tell him goodbye, he hoped she wasn't going to be so damned happy about it.

"Can we go somewhere quiet after this is over?"

"Sure." That's what he wanted, wasn't it? Still, Robyn wasn't some maiden aunt who made him eat beets. She was the woman he loved, and the thought of her saying good-bye made him want to stick his fist through the wall.

"All right. Look at my hand," the photographer said. "That's good. Now smile like you just won a million bucks."

Flash. Tiny black dots swam before Greg's eyes. They reminded him of the charts on Doug Cranston's office wall. After last night, he'd been tempted to cancel the appointment with Doug. But regardless of Robyn's plans and how he felt about them, he wanted her to have the answers about the genetics of her father's deafness.

Just as the photographer was packing up his equipment, the phone rang, providing a momentary but irritating diversion. The damned thing had been ringing all morning. With the news out that he had a half million bucks to spend, the vultures were circling.

He asked Manuel to see the others out, then went to his bedroom to take the call. He had just hung up from talking with a textbook salesman when the door opened. Robyn, wearing that clingy dress, slithered around the door and shut it behind her.

"What do you want?" he asked, gulping over the mound in his throat.

She sauntered to the bed, the silk dress swishing as she walked. "Isn't that obvious?"

"My, aren't we being aggressive this morning."

"I thought you liked me when I was aggressive. Besides, this is the real me. Happy. Uninhibited."

He thought of the marshmallow cream frosting and felt the color drain from his cheeks. "I've got a call to make and—"

"Can it, Michaels." She slammed her palm against his chest, knocking him to his elbows on the mattress. "What is it with you this morning? You've been acting like I'm the grim reaper."

He opened his mouth to explain that her actions were indeed grim, but she crawled across the mattress, snuggled up to his chest and undid three buttons on his shirt. With superhuman restraint, he resisted falling flat to the mattress and pulling her with him. "What do you want from me, Robyn?"

She swirled her finger in the hair on his chest and pouted. He remembered all the exquisite things she had done with those lips. He knew, if she left him, he would never find such a warm and responsive lover.

"Everything's changed since we won that money," she complained.

Didn't he wish! He pushed away from her and levered himself from the bed. Pacing before her, he concentrated on controlling his anger, but he lost the battle. "The truth is, nothing's changed at all. You're still planning to leave for Washington, aren't you?"

A slow smile of realization brightened her face. "So that's what this is all about!"

"You deny it?"

"I certainly do."

"You what?"

She tapped her red lips with her finger and crossed one stockinged leg tauntingly over the other. "Let me guess. You think now that Dad has his hearing dog, I'll walk off and leave the both of you."

"Isn't that what you plan to do?"

"If you wanted to know my plans, why didn't you ask?"

"I've asked and asked. You always give me the same answer. And last night, at the kennel, you didn't contradict Manuel when he talked about your plans to leave."

"Which explains your rotten mood. Well, if that's what you're worried about, forget it. I'm not going."

What had she said? "You're not going to Washington? Not now? Not ever?"

"I'm not going. *N-o-t g-o-i-n-g*," she spelled out loud. "Not now. Not ever. Unless, of course, for a vacation, in which case—"

Greg grabbed her arms, pulled her from the bed and kissed her. "Is this what you wanted to talk about? You were going to tell me you weren't leaving, after all?"

"Actually, no. I figured you knew that."

"If that isn't it, what is it? Wait a minute. Don't tell me. It might be bad news. I want to enjoy the good news for a while." He hugged her to his chest and delighted in the girlish giggle that bubbled beneath his kiss.

She laced her arms around his neck and tickled a spot on the back of his neck. "I love you, you silly goose."

"That, my dear Robyn, is wonderful to hear, but it isn't exactly news. So, what is your news?"

She smiled softly, then lowered her lashes to her cheeks. When she opened her eyes, her lashes were heavy with the hint of tears.

"Now don't cry," he said, suddenly feeling solicitous. He pulled a tissue from the ceramic holder on his nightstand and dabbed at her tears. "Whatever your news is, I'll be here for you, and we'll deal with it. The important thing is you're not leaving. I can't tell you how relieved I am."

She sniffed into the tissue. "You were right."

"About what?"

"About Dad and kids. I've been so blinded by Dad's deafness I couldn't see the beauty in him."

"Are you saying what I think you're saying?" he said, afraid to believe his ears.

"I'm saying I don't care what Doug says today. I don't care what my chances are of having deaf children. I just know I want to have children."

"Robyn, if this is your idea of a joke..."

She turned to the mirror and patted her stomach. "I want to feel a baby growing inside me, right here. I want to give birth to my very own child." She turned to him. "And, if I'm lucky, my child will have one-tenth of Dad's good qualities."

"And if your child is deaf?"

"I'll deal with it—and help my child deal with it, too."

Greg's hands trembled, and his heart swelled with joy. Right there, in his bedroom, he wanted to hold her in his arms and make beautiful love to her, to give her his child. "I love you. I would have loved you for always, even if you hadn't agreed to have children. But what you said makes me love you even more. You won't be sorry, Robyn. I promise you that. You will not be sorry you made that decision."

"I know I won't be." She took his hand and placed it over her abdomen. "Just think. Someday I'll have a baby growing right here, inside me."

"What changed your mind?" he asked, already imagining his child inside her.

"The way we worked together during the race. I thought, hey, if we can pull this off, we can handle anything."

With incredible restraint, Greg postponed the baby-making, for they were already late for their appointment with Doug.

Grinning like young lovers, they arrived at his office five minutes late. His receptionist immediately ushered them into Doug's consultation room.

Greg couldn't take his eyes off Robyn. She wasn't going to leave him, after all, and she'd as much as said she would have his baby someday. How could he wish for more?

He knew how. Tonight he would pop the question. He'd take her home after the appointment and make some excuse about needing to run an errand. That way he could go buy an appropriate engagement ring.

Doug settled into the chair behind his massive oak desk. "I'm glad to see you could make it today. I have some charts to show you and your blood tests, and—" his gaze shifted to a file folder to the right of his desk "—I have a bit of news to go over with you."

Greg winked at Robyn. She winked back. She would be a knockout bride. A beautiful mother.

"You understand genetics isn't an exact science, but it's getting more precise every day," Doug began. "Through recent genetic mapping, we've been able to identify the markers for certain physical abnormalities. We're making progress with diseases, too."

Greg leaned forward in his chair, uncomfortable with Doug's attitude. "What are you trying to tell us?"

"Two things, actually."

"Two good things or two bad things?"

Doug cleared his throat and shifted in his chair.

Frowning, Robyn came to stand by Greg. "Something tells me the news isn't good."

Unsmiling, Doug folded his hands on his desk. "I'll get to the point. First, the issue of deafness. I wish I had better news, but from all indications that doctor was right, Robyn. Each time you give birth, you will have a fifty-fifty chance of having a deaf child. And the odds will increase if you marry someone with deafness in his genetic background, also."

"If that's all that's wrong, don't worry, Doug. Robyn and I have had some time to talk things over." He winked at her and smiled. "She's decided being deaf isn't the end of the world. Your news won't keep her from having children."

Doug didn't smile. "I'm afraid there's another problem."

Greg narrowed his gaze. "What kind of problem?"

"I'm going to be blunt. You two aren't engaged, but anyone who sees you together has to know you're in love."

Robyn moved behind Greg and draped her arms around his neck. He angled his head and kissed her cheek. "You're right about that," she said, "and we can deal with whatever you tell us."

"Okay, then, here goes." He flipped open the file folder and handed them each a letter on his office stationery. "If you two have children together, there are significant odds that your offspring will have cystic fibrosis."

ROBYN FELT the room spin, the words *cystic fibrosis* echoing in her ears. Greg took her in his arms, and they listened numbly while Doug explained that cystic fibrosis was a disease involving recessive genes. That barring a mutation, the only time the disease occurred in a child was when both parents were carriers of the gene. He gave them one chance in four that a child of theirs would have cystic fibrosis. If either one of them married someone without the gene, the disease would not occur in their children, but those children would be carriers of the disease.

When Doug finished, Robyn buried her face in Greg's chest, asking herself why, after all they had gone through, they had to cope with this horrible genetic curse. It wasn't fair. It just wasn't fair! Tears streamed down her cheeks, wetting his shirt. She felt his arms tighten around her and heard a sob escape his throat.

"Of course," Doug advised her, "you could get pregnant, then have a test. If it turns out your child would have cystic fibrosis, you could have the pregnancy terminated."

"Abortion," Robyn mumbled. "You're talking abortion. I don't think I could handle that." She shook her head, feeling like a product on an assembly line that a factory worker could reject because it was defective. "I'm a real piece of goods, aren't I," she said bitterly.

"We're just beginning to discover the fireworks in our genes. You're not the only one with double problems, Robyn. And there's no telling what wonders medical research will turn up next. Someday we may figure out a way to eliminate this genetic problem."

He stood. "Well, I think I'll leave you alone now. I'm sure you'll want to talk."

Robyn heard the door click shut behind him.

She waited for Greg to say something—to reassure her he loved her, even though they couldn't have children together. Her breast ached with wanting for the baby she could never have—Greg's baby. She wanted to look into the child's chubby little face and say he looked like Greg but acted like her father, that he had her clear skin, Greg's thick blond hair and her dad's creativity.

If the news was painful for her, she knew Greg must be devastated. As if in a trance, she slipped from his arms and sat primly on the edge of a chair. She folded her hands in her lap and marshalled her emotional resources to compose herself and be strong for him. "If we decide to marry, we could adopt."

He glanced away and went to stand by the window. Staring out at the parking lot below, he said, "I'm sorry, Robyn. I don't think so."

His hardened expression reminded her of the time he had told her about Brad's suicide. For all his talk about wanting children, she knew his desire for a son was twisted around his need to recreate his brother. In his mind the only way he could do that was to pass his own genes along to his child. That's why he had ruled out adoption. Naturally, he would also veto them going to a sperm bank.

Even though Greg shared half the problem in his genes, she felt like a spoiler, a tainter. But, considering all his lectures to her, his reaction smacked of hypocrisy. He had to face the fact his genes were defective too.

She twisted her mother's ring around her finger and felt her throat constrict with the effort to refrain from crying. Only yesterday she had finally permitted herself the joy of thinking how it would feel to have Greg's baby growing inside her. To feel his little feet kicking her abdomen. To put Greg's hand over her swollen belly so he could feel the kicking, too. They would never experience that joy together, she thought bitterly.

Hurting, she moved to stand by him, to offer what little comfort she could. She placed her hand on his arm and waited for him to turn to her, but he continued to stare out the window, his face devoid of expression. "Greg?"

"Yes."

"I'm so sorry."

"There's nothing to be sorry about. It isn't your fault."

She took his hand, hoping any minute he would overcome his grief and reach out to her so they could face this together. "It isn't anybody's fault, but it still hurts, doesn't it?"

He gripped her hand for a long moment, and hope rose within her. Then, with a brave tilt to his chin, he turned away from the window, patted her hand and released his hold of it. "I'll take you home. You're tired. I've got to get to the office."

She didn't want to go home. "Please, Greg, we need to talk."

"If you don't mind, I'd like to be alone right now."

She couldn't believe this was the same Greg she'd grown to love. She wanted to feel the real Greg's comforting arms around her and hear his reassuring words. "I love you," she whispered, kissing his cheek tenderly.

"I know."

"'I know'?" she said, her stomach churning with panic. "No 'I love you, too'?"

He moved to the door. "Please, Robyn. Don't pressure me now. I can't even think straight."

Pressure him? The words stung as Doug opened the door. He slipped an arm around her waist and draped the other over Greg's shoulder. "I'm glad you saw me before you made a baby. Too many couples aren't so lucky."

"Funny. I don't feel lucky," Greg said hollowly, shaking his head.

"You and Robyn have your health. If you marry, you could adopt. I'd help you sort through the red tape. Any child would be lucky to have you as parents."

Robyn's lip trembled. "Any child but our own."

HE HAD MADE FUN OF HER cakes, used her homemade candy for fish bait and ignored her invitation to dinner. He had thrown a party and hadn't invited her. Lillian forgave Greg for his lapses in manners, but she would not tolerate what he was doing to Robyn.

Four hours after Robyn had returned from her mysterious doctor's appointment, red faced and teary eyed, Jonathan had gone to Lillian's. The poor man was worried sick. Robyn had locked herself in her bedroom and hadn't come out for dinner. Jonathan had knocked on the door, even banged on the door with his fist, and Robyn hadn't opened it.

She had refused Lillian's offer of lime delight cake with marshmallow frosting. That offer, for Pete's sake, had got her to unlock her bedroom door, but only long enough to run into the bathroom with the dry heaves.

Lillian hadn't wanted to ask, but remembering her promise to Carol Ann, she had posed the question dutifully. If Robyn was pregnant, she would help her deal with it the best way she could. Being pregnant wasn't the end of the world. Even though he had a rude streak, Greg was a decent sort, and he appeared to have a smattering of good parenting skills.

When Lillian had asked the question, Robyn had closed her eyes—and closed her door. Now it was close to midnight, and she and Jonathan were beside themselves with worry. The only other time Robyn had unlocked her door was when she had dragged her big suitcase out of the hall closet.

Lillian was going to find out what Robyn was running away from, and she was going to find out now.

She rapped smartly on Greg's front door and waited for him to answer. He was in there, and he was not going to ignore her. She leaned on the doorbell determinedly.

In a minute, she heard a complaint mumbled in Spanish. Manuel opened the door, his hair in disarray.

"I'd appreciate it if you'd get lost for an hour or so, young man," she said, brushing past him into the house.

Manuel looked at her in sleepy disbelief. "But it's midnight."

"Midnight, Shmidnight. I need to speak with Greg, and I need privacy. Where is the insufferable fool?"

"In bed. Asleep, I think."

"Well, wake him up and get him out here. We don't have time to waste."

Manuel disappeared and soon Greg drifted into the shadows of the room, dressed in rumpled suit pants and a dress shirt. "Manuel said you insisted on seeing me."

Lillian could tell what shape Greg was in when he emerged from the shadows. His red-streaked eyes were sunk in dark sockets, and his face was all puffy looking. After he joined her on the couch, she nailed him. "I demand to know what you've done to Robyn. Jonathan came over this evening, worried sick. From the looks of things, I'm wondering if you've got the poor girl pregnant."

"You didn't ask her that!" he said, gripping the arm of the couch.

"Of course I did. Someone had to help her!"

"It's none of your business, Lillian. This is between Robyn and me."

"Then I suppose you know she's packing a suitcase."

He flinched. She could tell that bit of news hit him with a wallop. His voice broke when he spoke. "Maybe she ought to leave."

Lillian jumped up and screamed like a banshee. "Ought to leave? The way she's hurting? How can you say such a thing! This is the only home she has. Her father and I are all the people in the world who love her."

"That's where you're wrong. I love her, too."

"Well, mister, you have a poor way of showing it."

"You don't know what you're talking about. Go home and leave me alone," he pleaded. "Leave Robyn alone. We've had some bad news today, and it... well, it just changes things, that's all...."

Now that she finally had him talking, Lillian clammed up and listened. He told her about Robyn's fears about having deaf children, about how he had wanted to have his own child rather than adopting, and how he had talked her into going to the geneticist. Then he spilled out the god-awful truth, and she sat there, nailed to her chair. "Cystic fibrosis—dear Lord!"

"So now you know," Greg said. He stood and walked to the window that faced Robyn's house. Lifting one slat of the miniblinds, he looked out.

When Lillian saw tears slide down his cheeks, she choked up herself. "What are you going to do?"

"Until this afternoon, I was planning to ask her to marry me tonight. I was going to go out after the appointment and buy her a ring."

"But you obviously didn't?"

He shook his head, letting the slat click into place.

"Then you're a bigger scum than I thought."

"What did you say?"

"You heard me. But then maybe Robyn's lucky to find out what you're made of before she makes the mistake of marrying you."

"If she marries me, she can't have children."

"Humph!" As I recall, she didn't plan to have kids, anyway. Can't believe that piece of news you got today— awful as it was—would keep her from marrying you."

"You should have heard her talking about having children this morning." He slammed his palm to his forehead. "Dear God, I almost made love to her before we went to the doctor. She could have gotten pregnant, and—"

"Well, she didn't, so you don't have to worry. Listen here, young man. She's a strong woman, that Robyn, and she's got a fierce love for you. She'd give up having kids in a minute if it meant she could spend the rest of her life with you."

He sat beside her on the couch. "You really think so?"

"I know so. Now, I'm not telling you she wouldn't miss going through being pregnant and giving birth. I know I did. And I'm not saying her heart wouldn't ache from time to time. But you could adopt and be happy as jaybirds. Greg Michaels, you'd better look deep into your heart and admit that the real problem is you."

She paused, making sure she had his attention. "You're the one who's not willing to make the sacrifice. You're so all-fired set on having your own baby that you're willing to let that fine woman walk out of your life."

"Lillian, look—"

"No, you look!" She stood, wishing she had a pan of marshmallow cream frosting to push in the man's face. "You've got about twenty hours tops to make up your mind. In that time you'd better do some serious thinking on why you've got to have your own baby. I expect it's wrapped up in the business of your brother's untimely death."

"What does Brad have to do with this?" he asked resentfully.

"I've watched you when you talk about your brother. Do you want to know what I think?"

"Would it matter if I didn't?"

"You'd better listen to me if you don't want to lose Robyn."

Greg braced his arms on his knees and hung his head. "I don't want to lose her. I love her, Lillian."

"Well, that's a start. So here goes... You're a helpful man, Greg. You're always helping somebody. Why, the day I met you, you were helping Jonathan. Now, I expect," she went on, "when you heard your brother had killed himself, you blamed yourself for letting him down. If you'd only helped him a little more, maybe he wouldn't have done what he did. Am I on target here?"

The clock on the mantel ticked while Greg thought over her words. "Yes, I'm afraid you're right."

"But that's hogwash! You can't be responsible for another person's happiness."

"But I was gone when he needed me. I was on a date, and when I got back there was a message from him on my answering machine. It was after one in the morning, so I thought, I'll just wait until morning. He killed himself around one-thirty. How do you suppose that makes me feel?"

"What were you supposed to do? Be available night and day in case he needed you?"

"Well, no—"

"Aren't you angry? Haven't you once wanted to punch the boy out because of what he did?"

A muscle in Greg's cheek twitched something awful. "I don't have any right to be angry with him."

"You sure as heck do! You ought to be madder than a hornet. He hurt you. He hurt your mama and your daddy. He made a terrible, selfish mistake when he took his own life, and he left the rest of you hurting. Get mad at him, for heaven's sake, and then, dear man, maybe you can forgive him! After you work through that, I expect you'll look at this business of having children a bit more clearly."

Greg's shoulders sagged, and he held his head in his hands. Lillian wanted to go to him and hold him in her arms, but he had to work through his agony by himself.

"The real tragedy will be if you let your brother's mistake ruin your chance to spend your life with that pretty, sweet woman next door."

She spun on her heel and marched to the door. "It's up to you, young man. You'd best do some fast thinking. I checked with the airlines. Robyn made a one-way reservation to D.C. on the red-eye tomorrow night."

CHAPTER EIGHTEEN

UNABLE TO SLEEP, Greg sat on the edge of his bed, his shoulders slumped, his arms propped on his thighs, his hands dangling in the space Robyn had once filled with her softness.

Since Lillian had left, her cutting words had bombarded him like angry blue jays.

Terrible, selfish mistake...get mad at him...let your brother's mistake ruin your chance...up to you, young man...do some fast thinking...one-way reservation... red-eye tomorrow night.

He glanced at the clock on his nightstand. Three o'clock. He had to get some sleep. Had to go to work in the morning. Had to pick up the pieces of his life. A life without Robyn.

Bleary-eyed and aching, he pressed his knuckles into the mattress and hoisted himself from the bed. Maybe a glass of milk would help. Brad used to drink milk when he couldn't sleep.

On his way to the kitchen, he paused in front of his walk-in closet, then opened the door and stared into the darkened interior. He knew he had to go in there, but he couldn't make himself do it. That last time he'd done it, the pain was so raw he'd felt as if he were bleeding to death.

But you've got to do it for Robyn. *For Robyn.* Dragging a palm across his face, he recalled Lillian's admonitions and forced himself to take a step nearer the chest. Abruptly he stopped. He was so tired. He'd do it tomorrow, after he'd had some sleep.

Tomorrow might be too late.

Bracing himself for the task, he inched into the long, narrow closet. Once inside, he reached up, clicked on the overhead light and squinted into the far corner as his eyes adjusted to the brightness. There it was, hidden behind his golf clubs, his tennis racquet and his dirty laundry. He brushed past his shirts and came to stand in front of the battered old chest.

There, in the ten drawers, he'd stuffed the mementos and souvenirs he couldn't bear to part with. He ran a finger over the drawers, one by one. Over the drawer that held the records of his civic involvement in Tulsa, over the one where he kept birthday cards that had made him laugh. Finally he hooked his finger under the brass pull on the tenth drawer. His chest constricted painfully at the thought of opening it.

Sucking in a deep breath to bolster his courage, he tugged the drawer open and quickly slipped his hand inside for the two accordion-style envelopes.

Two envelopes: one thin blue one, for Christopher; one bulging red one—Brad's.

He picked up the blue one and slipped off the rubber band. Balancing on the balls of his feet as he hunkered down, he tilted the envelope and poured out its meager contents. Onto the closet floor tumbled a baby footprint on white enamel paper, an infant ID bracelet and a yellowed newspaper clipping from the obituaries.

He fingered each item and savored the bittersweet melancholy as he relived the few minutes of holding Christopher in his arms. Smiling softly, he remembered how he'd joked with the delivery room nurse that his baby boy with long, tapered fingers would probably be an artist, or a surgeon, maybe.

Only minutes later the doctor-had awkwardly assured him someday he could have another child, someday the hurt wouldn't be quite so bad. What the hell had the doctor known, anyway?

He slipped the mementos of Christopher's brief life into the blue envelope, stuffed it in the bottom drawer and glanced at the red envelope on the floor.

With trembling hands he picked it up and emptied its contents onto the floor. Report cards and class pictures. An arrowhead Brad had found when the two brothers had explored a dry riverbed. Brad's emergency identification card the school had made on one of those student ID days designed to help the police find missing kids. *But not kids lost like Brad had been.*

He picked up the arrowhead and tightened his fist around it, feeling the pain as it pricked his palm. But the momentary pain was replaced by a poignant memory of the time Brad, then seven, had come to him, wanting to become his blood brother.

Greg had explained that, as real brothers, they already shared the same blood. In his usual manner, Brad had posed a dozen questions until Greg had explained to him all he knew about genetics. The next day Brad had bugged Greg until he took him to the library to check out a dozen books on the subject.

The following Sunday had been Easter. Greg had bought Brad a duckling at the feed store. Brad had named the duckling Gregor Johann Mendel, after the father of genetics.

Damn it, Brad! You could have been a Gregor Mendel or a Thomas Edison—or you could have . . . still been my little buddy. Why didn't you give me a chance to help you, as I helped Manuel?

Oh, but I did, Greg. You just weren't there!

"The hell I wasn't!" Greg ground out, feeling his anger boil to the surface. "No more, Brad. No more!" He stood, drew back his fist and flung the arrowhead out of the closet and into the mirror on the back of his bedroom door. The stone point nicked the mirror's surface, distorting the image of Greg's face.

Distortion. What does distortion mean, Greg?

How many times when Brad had asked him the meaning of a word had he told his brother, *Look it up. Don't be lazy. The dictionary's over there.* He stared into space, and his mind expanded on the memories. *Now, Brad,* he would have said after his brother looked up the meaning of the word, *give me two sentences using the word.*

Distortion. How's this? I played with the knobs on the television until I made a distortion.

Closing his eyes, Greg could see his brother's face, eyes bright with phenomenal intelligence, as they played the game. *Well, that's close but not quite it. Make up another example,* he would have told Brad.

Distortion. I've got it! I played with your emotions until I made a distortion.

A chill crept over Greg's back and swept down his arms as he replayed the sentence in his mind. He knew his thoughts were coming not from his brother or his brother's spirit, but from the pain he had locked inside himself to cope with Brad's death. *I played with your emotions until I made a distortion.*

Until I made you believe having a son—and naming him Brad—would make the hurt go away.

Lord, Lillian was right. With his neat way of adjusting to Brad's suicide, he almost wound up rejecting the most loving, beautiful person to come into his life.

Robyn. Thoughts of her, feelings for her, flooded his mind. He shuddered as he thought of the way he'd pushed her away. He wanted her so much. Needed her in his life. He couldn't let her slip away from him without a fight.

You can't have children with her, you know.

Maybe I can't, he thought knowing the idea would take some adjusting to. But without Robyn, his life would be empty, anyway.

THE MORNING SUNLIGHT spilled across Robyn's white eyelet comforter and into the suitcase on her bed. She tossed her curling iron and her tennis shoes into the soft-sided damask luggage and zipped it shut.

She pulled the suitcase off the bed and heard her dad's heavy steps on the hardwood floors, followed by the clackety-clack of Taffy's toenails.

He rapped softly on her door, and she went to open it. He glanced at her face, pulled her into his arms and gave her the bear hug she would miss. *Oh, Dad. I'm going to miss you so much. I didn't really want to leave you.*

He pointed at her suitcase with a questioning look.

Why? How could she explain to him that Greg had broken her heart? That his love was conditional, and she couldn't meet his conditions? That her blood was tainted?

She sat on the bed, patted the spot beside her and picked up her mother's picture. "You loved each other a lot," she signed slowly, respectfully.

He took the picture from her hands and ran his fingers lovingly over the image of her mother.

Soon his cast would come off, and he would be able to sign again with both hands. Regretfully she thought of the coming-off party she had planned to give him.

He propped the frame on her nightstand. "I've grown fond of Lillian," he signed. "We have fun together. She makes me laugh. She makes me see things I've never seen.

I may marry her someday. But I'll always love your mother."

"That kind of love is rare, Dad." One corner of her mouth twitched downward, and she pulled a tissue from her pocket.

"You and Greg love each other."

"Yes, but not enough," she signed with movements conveying her sadness. "We had problems."

"What kind of problems?"

"You know—children." Although she thought she was through crying, she felt the familiar burning behind her eyes.

"Are you afraid your children might be deaf like me?" he asked, an injured expression clouding his face.

She was relieved she could answer his question with an honest, "No, Dad. I changed my mind about having children."

His face lighted up. "Then what's the problem? Now you can give Greg the children he wants. You can give me grandchildren!"

Tears spilled over her lower lids and cascaded down her cheeks. "I'm afraid that's out of the question."

"Don't cry. We'll talk about this later."

"No, we have to talk now. I'm taking a ten o'clock flight to Washington tonight."

"I can't be ready that soon," he said, his gaze drifting out the window toward Lillian's house.

"Now that you have Taffy, you don't have to go with me. You stay here with your friends and your workshop—and with Lillian."

"I never really wanted to go," he admitted. "But after all you'd done for me, I figured if you wanted to go back to your job, I shouldn't stand in your way." He grinned sheepishly. "I thought you'd change your mind. I saw how you looked at Greg with love in your eyes. What happened? Why are you leaving so suddenly?"

The languid movement of her hands as she signed the story of the appointment with Doug Cranston conveyed her anguish. "When we heard the news about cystic fibrosis, I thought he would propose anyway and tell me we could adopt." She bit her lip to keep it from trembling. "But he hasn't called. Dad, he's shutting me out of his life, and I love him so much."

"Give him time to adjust to the shock, sweetheart."

"I don't think he'll ever adjust."

"Why not?"

"It's all so complicated. He's eaten up with guilt about his brother's death, for one thing." She explained in detail her interpretation of how Greg's desire for a child dovetailed with his mourning for his brother.

Her father shook his head. "Then, Robyn, Greg needs help, but he needs you more."

"No, Dad. I only make his pain worse. If he marries someone who doesn't have that cystic fibrosis gene, he can have the child he wants. He deserves the chance to become a father. He's a gentle man. He'd make a wonderful father. I have to leave and give him the freedom to find a woman who can give him healthy children."

ROBYN SAID HER TEARFUL farewells to her father and to Lillian and begged them to let her take a cab to the airport. Reluctantly they agreed, exchanging looks of helpless concern.

When the time came for her to leave, she gave each one a lingering hug and bolted for the cab with her luggage. "Airport, please," she told the cabbie. "And hurry. My flight's at ten." With the airport a twenty minute drive away, she had little time to spare.

"Yes, ma'am. Nice weather."

"I suppose."

"Lovely night."

"I guess." Thankfully the driver fell silent. As the cab reached the corner, she twisted in her seat, caught a glimpse of the magnolia tree and choked on the memory of Greg's first kiss.

In a few blocks she realized the cab driver was heading in the wrong direction. She leaned forward and tapped him on the shoulder. "I told you I need to go to the airport."

"I have to pick up another fare, ma'am."

"But we don't have time." She glanced at her watch. "I'm going to miss my flight."

"Don't worry, lady. We'll make it."

He pulled into a service station and sat there, letting the car idle while she drummed her fingers on the seat for a full five minutes. Finally, she gathered up her belongings, determined to phone Lillian for a speedy trip to the airport. Her fingers touched the handle just as the door swung open.

Well-developed male legs dusted with blond hair filled the open doorway. The legs were familiar. "Greg!"

He bent, smiled at her and slid into the seat next to her before closing the door. "Well, hi, Robyn."

"What do you think you're doing?"

"Taking a cab. You don't mind sharing, do you?"

"I have to be at the airport in thirty minutes."

"I know. Jonathan told me."

"I should have known," she muttered under her breath, glancing away.

"But we're going to make a little stop first." He handed the cabbie a piece of paper and told him, "Follow this map, driver."

"Let me out," she insisted. "I'll just call Lillian."

"No. You can't leave without saying goodbye to Manuel and Kendra. They're waiting for you at the kennel. They had to work late. There's a new litter of pups."

"But I'll miss my flight."

"So, there's another one thirty minutes later. What's your hurry, anyway?"

What was her hurry, indeed! The sooner she put miles between them, the sooner she could turn off her feelings for him and throw herself into her work again.

Scooting close to the door, she concentrated on ignoring him. She couldn't look at him without wanting to feel his strong arms around her and his warm breath sift through her hair.

His voice broke the silence between them. "I've thought about what you said."

"Please," she said, "let's not talk about what we said." *Or what we didn't say.*

"I never realized what little progress I'd made in getting over Brad's death," he admitted, ignoring her plea. "Lillian nailed me last night. She said things I didn't want to hear. She made me reexamine my motives...about lots of things. I wanted to call you after she left, but I had a lot of feelings to work through first. Look at me, will you, Robyn? I need you."

He slid his hand beneath her hair and massaged the nape of her neck, and she wanted so much to turn to him. Yet she was afraid to listen to what he had to say. He still wanted children. She couldn't give them to him. Someday another woman would. "I'd appreciate it if you wouldn't do that," she said, brushing his hand away.

"Ah, Robyn, come here and let me love you."

She told herself she was crazy to let him touch her. Still, she couldn't resist the luxury of pretending for one delicious moment that he loved her as she desperately needed to be loved. She moved into his open arms, slid hers around his waist and buried her nose in the hollow of his throat.

He moaned and hugged her closer. "I love you, Robyn. I can't thank you enough for all you've done for me."

She didn't want his appreciation. "Write me about it. Okay?"

"I've been keeping my anger at Brad bottled up inside," he went on. "Thanks to you—and to Lillian—I can deal with it now."

Not believing her ears, she looked up and noticed, for the first time, that he wore a haggard expression. She wondered what Lillian had said to him. She traced the curve of his cheek with her fingertips, her heart filled with love for him—and with sympathy, too. "Oh, Greg."

"I'm sorry for all the grief I've caused you."

"You didn't mean any harm. You're a good man."

He smiled down at her. "Good enough to marry?"

"Please, don't," she said, her chest aching with the knowledge they could never marry. "It hurts too much."

He hitched up his hip, slid his hand into his shorts pocket and pulled out something he held in his fist. "Maybe this will prove I'm not teasing," he said, opening his palm.

In his hand lay a wide band of gold from which a brilliant blue sapphire the color of his eyes glittered in the passing streetlights. "Do you like it?" he asked, lifting her chin so that she met his gaze.

"It's beautiful," she said guardedly, "but—"

"Good." He cleared his throat and held the ring between his thumb and forefinger. "Robyn, will you marry me? Will you spend your life with me and let me make up to you for being so blind about my feelings for you?"

The cab had stopped. Robyn imagined herself at the tail end of a dream. Afraid that if she said anything the dream would end, she touched the ring, sure it wasn't real.

"Say you'll be my wife, Robyn."

"If you marry me, you'll give up what you've always wanted—the chance to have your own children—healthy children."

"Without you, my life would be empty. All the children in the world couldn't fill the void you'd leave if you got on that plane."

"You mean you want to marry me, even though we can't have children together?"

"I sure do. A wise woman once called what I feel for you unconditional love."

Finally convinced his proposal wasn't a dream, she flung her arms around his neck. "Oh, Greg, of course I'll marry you!"

He kissed her so deeply, so completely that she forgot she was in the back seat of a cab. The loud clearing of a throat served as a reminder. "The meter's still running, buddy. Why don't you put the ring on her finger and pay up."

Smiling, Greg slipped the ring on and sealed his promise of their future together with a kiss. Then, while she wiggled her fingers in the moonlight, he pitched a twenty-dollar bill into the front seat, rolled down the window and let out a war whoop.

"My goodness! What was that?" She looked out the window and realized they were at the kennel.

"I wanted the others to know you said yes. They're waiting inside."

"Kendra and Manuel?"

"And Jonathan and Lillian. Probably Joe and Lyndon, too. I'm glad you said yes. If you hadn't, I would have been awfully embarrassed. And terribly disappointed."

Inside a party awaited them, complete with the goopiest cake Robyn had ever seen.

After a round of congratulations, Manuel asked Greg, "Did you tell her?"

Robyn looked at her husband-to-be and kissed him again. "Tell me what?"

"Manuel's parents are coming home next week."

"Tell her the rest," Manuel insisted.

"They told Manuel about some orphaned children in Mexico who need good homes. There'll be some red tape, but I'd like to help them find parents here."

She winked at him. "Maybe someday we can adopt a couple of our own."

"I was hoping you'd say that."

"First we'd better get married."

"Name the date," he said, hugging her close.

"You name the date. I'll choose the place."

"Where would that be?"

"Your meadow. Are the wildflowers still in bloom?"

Grinning, he said, "They sure are."

Lillian clapped her hands and sighed loudly. "I'll bake your wedding cake!" She winked. "With marshmallow cream frosting, of course."

Greg and Robyn shared a knowing smile. Then she dipped her finger in the marshmallow frosting and brought it to his eager lips. "That should set the mood, all right," she said, chuckling. "The right mood, indeed."

HARLEQUIN
American Romance®

November brings you ...

SENTIMENTAL JOURNEY

BARBARA BRETTON

Jitterbugging at the Stage Door Canteen,
singing along with the Andrews Sisters, planting
your Victory Garden—this was life on the home
front during World War II.

Barbara Bretton captures all the glorious
memories of America in the 1940's in
SENTIMENTAL JOURNEY—a nostalgic Century
of American Romance book and a Harlequin
Award of Excellence title.

Available wherever Harlequin® books are sold.

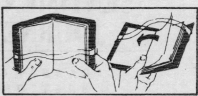

PASSPORT TO ROMANCE VACATION SWEEPSTAKES

OFFICIAL RULES

SWEEPSTAKES RULES AND REGULATIONS. NO PURCHASE NECESSARY.
HOW TO ENTER:

1. To enter, complete this official entry form and return with your invoice in the envelope provided, or print your name, address, telephone number and age on a plain piece of paper and mail to: Passport to Romance, P.O. Box #1397, Buffalo, N.Y. 14269-1397. No mechanically reproduced entries accepted.
2. All entries must be received by the Contest Closing Date, midnight, December 31, 1990 to be eligible.
3. Prizes: There will be ten (10) Grand Prizes awarded, each consisting of a choice of a trip for two people to: i) London, England (approximate retail value $5,050 U.S.); ii) England, Wales and Scotland (approximate retail value $6,400 U.S.); iii) Caribbean Cruise (approximate retail value $7,300 U.S.); iv) Hawaii (approximate retail value $ 9,550 U.S.); v) Greek Island Cruise in the Mediterranean (approximate retail value $12,250 U.S.); vi) France (approximate retail value $7,300 U.S.).
4. Any winner may choose to receive any trip or a cash alternative prize of $5,000.00 U.S. in lieu of the trip.
5. Odds of winning depend on number of entries received.
6. A random draw will be made by Nielsen Promotion Services, an independent judging organization on January 29, 1991, in Buffalo, N.Y., at 11:30 a.m. from all eligible entries received on or before the Contest Closing Date. Any Canadian entrants who are selected must correctly answer a time-limited, mathematical skill-testing question in order to win. Quebec residents may submit any litigation respecting the conduct and awarding of a prize in this contest to the Régie des loteries et courses du Quebec.
7. Full contest rules may be obtained by sending a stamped, self-addressed envelope to: "Passport to Romance Rules Request", P.O. Box 9998, Saint John, New Brunswick, E2L 4N4.
8. Payment of taxes other than air and hotel taxes is the sole responsibility of the winner.
9. Void where prohibited by law.

PASSPORT TO ROMANCE VACATION SWEEPSTAKES

OFFICIAL RULES

SWEEPSTAKES RULES AND REGULATIONS. NO PURCHASE NECESSARY.
HOW TO ENTER:

1. To enter, complete this official entry form and return with your invoice in the envelope provided, or print your name, address, telephone number and age on a plain piece of paper and mail to: Passport to Romance, P.O. Box #1397, Buffalo, N.Y. 14269-1397. No mechanically reproduced entries accepted.
2. All entries must be received by the Contest Closing Date, midnight, December 31, 1990 to be eligible.
3. Prizes: There will be ten (10) Grand Prizes awarded, each consisting of a choice of a trip for two people to: i) London, England (approximate retail value $5,050 U.S.); ii) England, Wales and Scotland (approximate retail value $6,400 U.S.); iii) Caribbean Cruise (approximate retail value $7,300 U.S.); iv) Hawaii (approximate retail value $ 9,550 U.S.); v) Greek Island Cruise in the Mediterranean (approximate retail value $12,250 U.S.); vi) France (approximate retail value $7,300 U.S.).
4. Any winner may choose to receive any trip or a cash alternative prize of $5,000.00 U.S. in lieu of the trip.
5. Odds of winning depend on number of entries received.
6. A random draw will be made by Nielsen Promotion Services, an independent judging organization on January 29, 1991, in Buffalo, N.Y., at 11:30 a.m. from all eligible entries received on or before the Contest Closing Date. Any Canadian entrants who are selected must correctly answer a time-limited, mathematical skill-testing question in order to win. Quebec residents may submit any litigation respecting the conduct and awarding of a prize in this contest to the Régie des loteries et courses du Quebec.
7. Full contest rules may be obtained by sending a stamped, self-addressed envelope to "Passport to Romance Rules Request", P.O. Box 9998, Saint John, New Brunswick, E2L 4N4.
8. Payment of taxes other than air and hotel taxes is the sole responsibility of the winner.
9. Void where prohibited by law.

RLS-DIR

VACATION SWEEPSTAKES

Official Entry Form

MONTH 2 ENTRY

Yes, enter me in the drawing for one of ten Vacations-for-Two! If I'm a winner, I'll get my choice of any of the six different destinations being offered — and I won't have to decide until after I'm notified!

Return entries with invoice in envelope provided along with Daily Travel Allowance Voucher. Each book in your shipment has two entry forms — and the more you enter, the better your chance of winning!

Name _____

Address _____ Apt. _____

City _____ State/Prov. _____ Zip/Postal Code _____

Daytime phone number _____
Area Code

☐ I am enclosing a Daily Travel
Allowance Voucher in the amount of $_____ Write in amount
revealed beneath scratch-off

VACATION SWEEPSTAKES

Official Entry Form

MONTH 2 ENTRY

Yes, enter me in the drawing for one of ten Vacations-for-Two! If I'm a winner, I'll get my choice of any of the six different destinations being offered — and I won't have to decide until after I'm notified!

Return entries with invoice in envelope provided along with Daily Travel Allowance Voucher. Each book in your shipment has two entry forms — and the more you enter, the better your chance of winning!

Name _____

Address _____ Apt. _____

City _____ State/Prov. _____ Zip/Postal Code _____

Daytime phone number _____
Area Code

☐ I am enclosing a Daily Travel
Allowance Voucher in the amount of $_____ Write in amount
revealed beneath scratch-off

CPS-TWO